SATURDAY SHEPHERD AND THE WORLD BEYOND

By Logan Nance

This is a work of fiction. All of the characters, organizations, and events portrayed in this novel are either products of the author's imagination or are used fictitiously.

SATURDAY SHEPHERD AND THE WORLD BEYOND

Copyright © 2021 by Logan Nance

All rights reserved. This book or any portion thereof may not be reproduced or used in any manner whatsoever without the express written permission of the publisher except for the use of brief quotations in a book review or scholarly journal.

ISBN: 9798530276316

First printing: 2021

Second printing: 2023

Cover art credit: mage.space

Dedicated to my wife, Samantha, who has read this book in all its forms and who believes in me even on days when I don't believe in myself. All that I am is yours.

ONE

My name is Saturday Shepherd and I'm a normal kid, as normal as they come. There is absolutely nothing special or unique about me at all, except for my name. Let me address that right out of the gate. I know I have a weird name. I've been told my mom thought it would be fun to name me after the day of the week I was born. Sure, never mind the stack of baby name books, let's go with Saturday. Whatever, it could be worse, I guess. Like my grandfather says, "at least it's not Monday". That joke absolutely kills in the fifty plus demo.

Both of my parents were gone before I was old enough to ask them what they were thinking. My mom died shortly after giving birth to me and as far as I know my father never laid eyes on me, he bounced and went off to do his own thing.

Anyway, the day my life changed forever started off pretty normal, with me on a bus. I was taking the bus from my grandparents' house in the Bronx to Chinatown, and not for the dumplings. I was heading downtown for one reason, to finally land a summer internship. No judgement please. No one wants to spend their summer playing video games and chilling out more than me, but it simply wasn't an option this year. It was the end of my junior year, which meant it was time to start looking at colleges and if I wanted those colleges to seriously look at me, I had to beef up the resume a bit. By this point all my friends had long since locked up their summer plans and I was getting desperate.

I had plans, big plans. I didn't know a lot about my dad, in fact I didn't even have a picture of him, but my grandfather told me my dad had been a lawyer and apparently a good one. "A real bloodsucker" my granddad had said before my grandma swatted him on the back of his head. I wanted to be a lawyer too. I had the grades, and I was a pretty good student, despite having what my guidance counselor referred to as "restless legs and an active mind" which was putting it kindly. Although, I did see her refer to me as a "fidgety little shit" in her notebook, which was not as kind.

Despite my grades, my extracurriculars were less than stellar. My after-school life consisted of playing video games with my friends, reading comics, and trying to binge watch as much programming as possible. Despite my sedentary lifestyle I'm fairly athletic and liked playing sports until my genetic heart condition forced me to stop in middle school.

I spent all year trying to find an internship with one of the high-powered law firms in the city. When that didn't pan out, I lowered my standards a little bit, and started looking at smaller firms and one person operations. Still nothing. Not even an interview. I was getting desperate, really desperate. I knew if I didn't land something fast, I was going to end up flipping burgers all summer which would give me a little cash, but not help at all on the college front.

I was getting hopeless when I received an unusual letter in the mail. As I sat on the bus, I unfolded the letter and read it for what seemed like the hundredth time. It was handwritten in black ink on thick white paper.

>Mr. Saturday Shepherd,
>
>It is with great joviality that we inform you that you have been selected for candidacy for our summer internship program. After a lengthy and competitive search, we have resolved that you would make an ideal candidate. Please deliver yourself to our offices on the 5th of June at 10:00 hours to be interviewed. Please be advised that candidates are required to bring with them an updated resume and a completed family tree.
>
>Faithfully,
>
>Mallory Moran, SSE

Offices of Mallory Moran
601 S. Motte St.

I wasn't sure who Mallory Moran was, and I couldn't remember ever applying to her office, but I was so desperate I wasn't going to question it. In my estimation this interview was all that stood between me and a hairnet this summer. So, there I was wearing my best and only suit, normally reserved for funerals, carrying my grandfather's faded brown briefcase with combination locks, trying to dodge the drool from the guy sleeping next to me on the bus.

This was my first legit job interview. I'd no idea what to expect. I completed the family tree as requested. It seemed odd, but it hadn't been much trouble to do anyway. My family tree was very lopsided. After my mom died her parents, John, and Carol Costa, took me in and raised me. They are two of the nicest and most caring people in the world. I've been told I inherited my dark brown eyes from my mother and almost every day my grandmother says that she sees my mom in my smile. I try to smile often, just for her.

As usual I'm daydreaming when the bus comes to a sudden stop and I lurch forward, face planting awkwardly into the seatback in front of me. My seat buddy doesn't even flinch, his face is still squished against the cold window of the bus, mouth agape, a steady stream of drool puddling just beneath his chin.

Standing up I hefted the large faded brown briefcase with me and began the familiar shuffle down the aisle to debus.

"Excuse me. Sorry." I offered as I awkwardly bumped into knees and shins and almost decapitated a little old lady with my bulky briefcase.

"Watch it." someone said. I knew better than to turn around, I just apologized again as I stepped off the bus and out onto the street. I turned to thank the bus driver as the doors slid close in my face and the bus lurched back into traffic.

In my sixteen years of life, I'd been to Chinatown a handful of times, and I was greeted by the familiar sights and sounds and smells. It was very much like stepping into another world, which is what makes it such a tourist destination in the first place. As I walked down the sidewalk under the colorful awnings and flashing neon signs, I passed countless shops with food and trinkets hanging and waiting to be sold.

I allowed myself to be swept up into the crowd. In one shop a Chinese butcher was exchanging American dollars for fresh meat from an open-air stand. In another store a dealer was peddling jade statues and golden emblems all laid out on colorful rugs. The smell of the roasted duck coming from a nearby shop had my mouth watering, but I knew that if I stopped, I would be late for my interview.

I passed by shops selling traditional Chinese garments, bubble teas, herbal remedies, and just about anything you can imagine. I even walked past a store that exclusively sold a large variety of chopsticks. At one point I was tempted to take one of the side streets and duck down into one of the many tunnels that I'd heard crisscrossed Chinatown to escape the crowd, but ultimately decided against it since it would have almost assuredly ended with me being completely lost. Instead, I decided to grit it out and just enjoy the sights.

Soon the crowd began to slowly thin out around me as I walked deeper into the heart of Chinatown. The buildings began to look more and more drab the longer I walked. The dull stone tenements were spotted with colorful banners and baubles hanging outside of the open windows. Most of the banners were crimson red with yellow lettering, displays of Chinese pride from the inhabitants.

The smells of spices and cooked food were replaced with the sounds of street vendors peddling fakes and knockoffs to anyone they could lure into their shop. There were purses and watches of all different types, as well as DVD copies of movies that hadn't even left theaters yet. From experience I knew often those DVDs were just someone in a theater with a hand camera filming the movie illegally. Piracy is not a victimless crime, people.

When I reached the 600 block of S. Motte Street I crossed the street eagerly, straightening my tie and trying to muster my courage. Butterflies fluttered feverishly in my stomach. I searched around and when my eyes landed on 601 S. Motte Street my heart sank. Hastily I pulled the note back out and double checked the address and then looked back at the building. The yellow sign with the red letters read *Sifu Wok - 601 S. Motte Street*. It certainly did not mention anything about Mallory Moran. I won't lie, I panicked, and the butterflies in my stomach turned acidic. My first instinct was to turn around and leave, but I hadn't come all this way to give up that easily, so I straightened myself up and pulled open the door.

A set of bells hanging from the door hinge let out a loud *pang* as I stepped into the restaurant. The thick hot air and the aroma of fried food hit me in the face. *Sifu Wok* was not a large place as it only had a handful of tables. A cash register sat on a small bar on the opposite end of the room and a colorful beaded curtain was the only divider between the dining area and the kitchen. I was the only soul in the place.

The beaded curtain parted noisily as an elderly Chinese woman poked her head out to see who had dared enter her domain. She gave me the kind of look you give someone for waking you up from a dead sleep, not the look you give someone who steps into your place of business, so I quickly grabbed a seat at a table against the wall. The table backed up to a cooler that hummed loudly. The lady stepped through the curtain and made her way over to my table. The soles of her shoes squeaked noisily against the dingy linoleum floor.

"You eat?" she asked with a thick accent.

"Umm. Sure." I said nervously.

"You order now." she told me, or asked, I can't be sure

which. I had no interest in eating at the *Sifu Wok,* mostly because I had no interest in spending the next few days camped out in my bathroom.

"Actually, I think I'm in the wrong place. Sorry." I told her, which was not a lie.

"You go now." she said curtly and walked back toward the kitchen without giving me another look.

So, I stood and walked toward the door, but in an act of sheer desperation I called back out to her.

"Excuse me. Do you know Mallory Moran? Is her office nearby?"

The lady poked her head back out through the beaded curtain. "You come with me." she said, once again disappearing. I didn't move, instead I just stood staring at the space where her head had been, replaying her words over in my mind. The absolute last thing that I wanted to do was follow the grouchy lady down the greasy rabbit hole that was the back of the *Sifu Wok*. On one hand I imagined that walking into the kitchen would be enough to turn me off Chinese food for the rest of my life. On the other hand, the thought of returning home empty handed and facing my grandfather was less than ideal, so I swallowed hard and pushed aside the beaded curtain.

The other side looked less dramatic than I was expecting. The kitchen itself was small and cramped, little bigger than a hallway, and while the red tile floor was grimy and covered with a significant layer of grease the rest of it was relatively clean. A single stove sat cold, and the large wok was empty. The woman I was supposed to be following was standing next to a large metal door on the other end of the room. She wore a look of utter impatience with her finger crooked beckoning me on.

"So, I'm guessing I don't need a hair net to come through here?" I asked, trying to crack her hard exterior, but she didn't laugh. Up close I could see that her face was devoid of any resemblance of laugh lines, so I shouldn't have been surprised.

"Talk less. Walk more." she said curtly.

"You're taking me to Ms. Moran, right?" I asked, crossing the small kitchen. She said nothing, just pushed open the second door into a small hallway. The door slammed shut behind her. "And not to kill me?" I muttered.

When I stepped through the second door it led into the small dimly lit hallway. The woman stood directly on the other side of the door, which scared the ever-loving hell out of me and caused me to jump back and bump my head hard against the metal door frame. I shook my head, clearing the stars from my vision, and the woman was pointing down the hall to another door at the other end.

"Thanks for your help." I said sarcastically, shuffling down the hallway, rubbing the sore spot on my head vigorously as if that would somehow stop the oncoming headache. The hallway looked like something out of a bad horror movie, which I was super psyched about. One lone light bulb seemed to be working and it lit up the doorway like a gateway to hell. The door itself was plain and ordinary. A small black placard with uniformed white lettering had been placed on the door, it read:

Offices of Mallory Moran
Supernatural Sleuth Extraordinaire

I knocked on the door and when it opened my world was forever changed.

Two

The door to the office swung open with an ominous creak, and the person on the other side was not at all what I expected. A small, almost diminutive, woman peered up at me with large eyes magnified through a pair of oversized glasses with bright orange rims that clashed horribly with her red lipstick. She stood stoically in the doorway as if waiting for me to speak, so I did.

"Hi there." I said sheepishly, but she continued to stare silently. Her glasses magnified her eyes so much that I could almost hear her blinks. "Um. Hi. I'm Saturday Shepherd, and I am supposed to meet with Ms. Moran. I received this letter." I hastily pulled the piece of paper out of my pocket and offered it to her. She took one look at the crumpled letter but didn't take it, instead she turned on the spot and, without even so much as inviting me in, returned to her small desk in the middle of the room.

"Mallory, your 10 o'clock is here." she said in a loud nasally voice. The woman's tiny desk in the center of the room was covered in an assortment of newspapers and coffee-stained magazines. A small placard on her desk read "Ms. V. Poole".

An empty chair sat against the wall, and I thought it best to take a seat while I was waiting. Before I could sit, I noticed a picture on the wall out of the corner of my eye. It was a small picture in a cheap wood frame noticeably missing its glass. There were three people in the photo and none of them were familiar to me, but something about the photo tickled a feeling of a long-forgotten memory in the back of my mind. When I tried focusing on the memory it seemed to flee from me like water through my fingers. I pulled myself away from the photo when I heard the door behind me open. Hastily I straightened my tie, took a deep breath, and turned just in time to see the door swing open so quickly it sent papers flying off Ms. Poole's desk and she glared at the man who stepped into the room.

"Thank you, Vie." the man said as he covered the distance to me in a single step, offering his hand and I shook it. "Saturday Shepherd, I'm Mallory Moran."

"Oh. I'm sorry." I said before I could stop myself.

"Sorry for thinking I was going to be a woman? Don't give it another thought. My parents, like yours, had quite a sense of humor."

"Nice to meet you." I said, making a concerted effort to force the look of surprise from my face.

"Indeed. Indeed. Please, let's step into my office. Violet, hold most of my calls." Mallory said.

I was ushered into his office. Mallory wasn't what I had been expecting, and not just because he was a man. Mallory was tall and lean with a powerful handshake and unexpectedly rough hands. I couldn't quite put an age to him, but if pressed I would have guessed he was in his early fifties. Mallory had his long gray hair pulled back into a ponytail and walked with an apparent stiffness in his right leg. He was wearing black slacks with a button-down shirt of the same color; his sleeves were rolled up to his elbows.

Mallory's office was an absolute disaster. It was not large, but it was covered wall to wall with an assortment of books, many of them losing their bindings and covered in a layer of dust. It had the smell and wistfulness of an old bookstore that my grandparents liked to drag me to on the weekends. Mallory's desk, much like his secretary's, was covered in papers and, oddly enough, fortune cookie wrappers. The single wall not covered by a bookshelf was adorned with numerous photographs held in place by colorful push pins, like something out of a detective movie.

"Please, won't you have a seat?" said Mallory as he lifted a stack of books and papers from a chair. Hesitantly I obliged him and sat down. Mallory pushed a stack of papers back just enough to make room for himself to sit on the edge of his desk.

"There we go." Mallory continued. "Now, Mr. Saturday, why don't you tell me a bit about yourself."

I sat up as straight as possible, trying my best to work some moisture back into my mouth.

"Well, my name is Saturday Shepherd, obviously you know that. I'm a New Yorker, born and raised. I live in the Bronx. I'm a Junior at Stanley Claremont High, and I want to study law and become an attorney just like my dad. I'm looking for an internship that will allow me to get some experience before I go off to college next year." I hesitated for a moment, trying to think of anything else I could say. "I... Um...I like to play video games with my friends, and I guess that's about it."

"I see." said Mallory, seemingly giving me a moment to be sure that I was finished. "You just gave a summation of your entire life in five sentences."

"Sorry. I didn't know what else to say. This is my first interview." I said, immediately regretting adding that last part.

"No need to apologize." Mallory said, holding up his hands to reassure me. "Brevity is sometimes best. And honestly, when you think about it, life really is just a series of sentences. We live, we die, and at the end of it someone is tasked with summing our lives up for us. An unenviable task to be sure. The best we can hope for is that those sentences contain as many verbs as possible. Would you like a fortune cookie?" Mallory reached across his desk and pulled a fortune cookie out of a drawer and offered it to me.

"Um, thanks." I said, caught off guard, taking the cookie from him. I lifted my grandfather's briefcase into my lap and fumbled with the tarnished brass clasps. With a click the briefcase popped open and I reached in and pulled out a stack of documents and handed them over to Mallory. "Here is my resume and the family tree you requested."

"Wonderful." said Mallory, holding the neatly stacked and paper clipped sheets of paper in front of him and glancing over them for a few moments in silence. "Tell me about your parents, Saturday."

"To be honest I don't know much about them really, I was raised by my grandparents, would you like to know about them instead?"

"I see, well that won't be necessary. If you don't mind me asking, what happened to your parents?"

"My mom passed before I was born, and I never knew my dad."

"I am very sorry to hear that. It is never easy to lose a parent, no matter your age." said Mallory, tapping his chin absentmindedly. "An interesting name, Saturday, how did you come by it?"

This was a question I was asked more than any other. "Believe it or not, my mom decided to name me after the day of the week I was born. She thought it would give me character to have an unusual name. I used to try and go by David, my middle name, but it never caught on."

"Your name fits you, wear it proudly." Mallory said. "You haven't opened your cookie yet. Eat up. It's good luck."

"Sorry." I said, opening the cookie and placing the wrapper into my pocket. The cookie snapped in two easily. A small white piece of paper slid free of the cookie, and I held it up to read it, as I did, I could sense Mallory move around to peer over my shoulder.

"Fear foils fortune, fate favors ferocity." Mallory read aloud. "Oh, that is a good one."

"Is it?" I asked. "What does it mean?"

"Well, a fortune can have many meanings, but I believe it to be telling you that fate shines on men of action," said Mallory and then he added under his breath. "I would agree,

14

wouldn't you?"

"Sure, I mean most of my favorite characters are all about action."

Mallory smiled, and it appeared genuine. "Good. That's good." Mallory's posture shifted. "Now Saturday, I need to tell you-." Mallory was interrupted when his office door was thrown open.

"Violet." said Mallory as he stood abruptly. "I'm still meeting with our candidate."

"Sorry, Mallory." the small woman said in her nasally voice. "You have a hysterical client here; she says her daughters been taken."

"Excuse me one moment." Mallory said.

"Of course." I said, rising out of my chair.

"Keep your seat." Mallory said, patting my shoulder as he passed by and stepped out into the foyer.

I sank back into the chair. It was impossible for me to not hear bits and pieces of the conversation coming from the other room. A woman was talking rapidly in Spanish. I couldn't understand a word.

I was too nervous to just sit there, and my legs were starting to shake a bit, so I started pacing around the small office trying to find something to distract me. I couldn't help but wonder why someone would come to a lawyer instead of the police if their daughter had been kidnapped. I've seen my fair share of Law & Order, but I'm pretty sure that's not how it works in the real world.

Beads of sweat trickled down my face and I could feel my heart beating more rapidly in my chest, a common occurrence when I became overly restless, so I forced myself to stop pacing. I focused on a collage of pictures adorning the walls. The pictures were of Mallory with an assortment of other people. In the center of all the photos was the torn-out page of a book that had been stuck to the wall with a single black push pin. It was a quote from Dylan Thomas.

"I hold a beast, an angel, and a madman in me."

"Saturday, would you join us?" Mallory asked from the other room, causing me to jump in surprise, as if I had been caught doing something I shouldn't have. Before walking into the other room, I thoughtlessly stuffed the other half of the fortune cookie into my mouth.

"Yes, sir?" I asked nervously, my mouth now awkwardly full of cookie crumbs. A small Hispanic woman, only slightly taller than Violet, was speaking to Mallory, her eyes were red and bloodshot, her face was pale and strained.

"Ms. Álvarez was just filling me in on the circumstance of her situation. She was given my information by a former client and needs our services. I would very much like you to accompany me. It would be a trial run of sorts, what do you say?"

"Come with you to find her daughter? I mean… I wouldn't want to get in the way." I said, feeling overdressed for a rescue mission, and hopelessly unprepared.

"Nonsense." said Mallory. Meanwhile I was struggling to even process the request, so I hesitated for a moment, which Mallory took for acquiescence. "Wonderful, it's settled then. We can finalize your paperwork on the way. While I am certain I know exactly where to find her daughter, we should act promptly."

"Paperwork?" I asked, which seems like a silly question, when I should have asked if he was out of his mind.

"Onboarding paperwork." Violet answered. "Liability waiver in event of maiming or death, et cetera."

"I'm sorry? Did you say maiming or death?" I asked, my voice squeaking out a high note that caught even me by surprise.

"And et cetera." Violet corrected.

"Misses Álvarez, worry yourself not. Your daughter shall be returned safely post-haste." Mallory interjected, putting his hand around my shoulder, and shuffling me out through the door. "Tu hija te será devuelta."

Mallory grabbed his jacket off a hanger beside the door and slid his arms into it as he walked out into the hallway and back into the restaurant. The kitchen was busier than it had been earlier. A heavy-set Chinese man wearing a dirty white apron stood over a piping hot wok cooking greasy noodles. Mallory reached into a small plastic bucket and pulled out a pair of chopsticks. He deftly used the sticks to pick up a steaming hot dumpling out of a metal bowl, which he ate as he walked into the dining area, offering a friendly pat on the back to the cook and a half smile to the woman I had met earlier. Back out onto the street Mallory led us to a black sports car that was parked nearby, its windows fully tinted.

"I realize owning your own car in the city is completely impractical." Mallory explained. "But carrying some of my equipment on mass transit is frowned upon." I did my best to swallow down the bubble of fear that I was making a terrible mistake and got into the passenger seat of the car. Mallory started the ignition and peeled out onto the street. The interior of the car was immaculate, which was surprising given the state of Mallory's office, and it still held some of that new car smell. Riding in the clean car was pleasant considering I was used to the smells of the bus which often had a certain urine-like quality to them.

We drove along in silence for a few moments before I mustered the courage to speak up. "Can I ask you a question about the job?"

Mallory kept his eyes on the road but reached back into the seat with his right hand. "I would say that this is an appropriate time for that." When he pulled his hand back it held a clipboard with some papers and a pen attached. "If you would be inclined, I would appreciate it if you filled these out while we talk."

I scanned over the paperwork. It was a lot of legal jargon that I couldn't really comprehend. The areas where I needed to sign, and initial were clearly marked with neon tape.

"Ms. Poole mentioned something about maiming and death. Is that likely?" I asked, half joking and half terrified.

"Today? No, probably not." Mallory answered simply.

"What kind of lawyer are you, Mr. Moran?" I asked.

Mallory reached up and absentmindedly adjusted his rearview mirror. "I am no kind of lawyer, Saturday. I am a special investigator of sorts." said Mallory. "I work on a referral basis only. I don't do billboards or ads. In fact, it is only when my clients need me that they know anything about me."

Everything now made much more sense, and I would be lying if I said I wasn't a little relieved. I could now turn the job down with no regrets. It's not that I wasn't grateful, of course, it's just that this dude Mallory Moran was a little eccentric for my tastes.

"So, you investigate kidnappings?" I asked.

"Among other things." answered Mallory.

"Mr. Moran." I started and then after a look from Mallory corrected myself. "Sorry, I mean, Mallory, I really appreciate the opportunity, but I think there has been a mistake. This isn't the kind of job I'm looking for. If you could just let me out here, I can take the bus back home."

Mallory hit the brakes and the car squealed to an abrupt stop. Tires screeched and horns blared from cars sliding to a stop behind us as we blocked the road. I turned my head slowly toward Mallory, expecting to find him furious, but instead he was smiling.

"How about this? If you accompany me on this one thing, I promise you will want this job. If you don't, I will drive you back to your grandparents no worse for the wear, and I'll even pay you for the day. Deal?"

For a few seconds I contemplated his offer. My deliberation was brief as I was spurred on by the blaring horns from the other drivers behind them. I agreed, and as soon as I did Mallory hit the gas pedal and the car sped off toward our destination, with me gripping the door handle and really hoping I at least lived to regret my decision. I was smart enough to know better than to ask, 'what's the worst that can happen', because I was terrified of the answer.

Mallory drove to the FDR and took it north towards Harlem, weaving the car in and out of traffic. It wasn't erratic, not exactly, but I couldn't help but read a little more concern on Mallory's face than had been there earlier. "Do you think you can find her?" I asked if for no other reason than to break the silence.

Mallory glanced at me and then back onto the road before swerving into the left lane and quickly speeding around a truck and then back into the right lane without even looking to see if the way was clear. My foot unconsciously stamped down on the nonexistent brake on my side of the car, and I pressed myself back into the warm leather seat.

"The only predictable behavior of the people that we are dealing with is that they are unpredictable. The girl should be fine, but best not to dawdle." Mallory said.

Before long we exited the FDR and found ourselves on some side street in a part of Harlem that I, with good reason, had never visited. Mallory pulled the car off onto an overgrown slab of concrete next to what looked to be an abandoned warehouse of some sort. The building appeared to have served as a canvas for some of the city's street artists as nearly every inch of it had been tagged and many of the once vibrant colors had now faded. Windows on all levels were broken, the only remnants of the glass were like jagged teeth. This part of town was one of the last remaining holdouts in gentrified New York, a New York of old that I had missed out on.

Across from the building was an overpass with steel construction fencing that looked to have been in place for years, and beyond that was the Harlem River. Trash littered the streets and the broken-up sidewalks.

"From here on, Saturday, it's best if you stay close and let me do all the talking. Do as I say, and this will be nothing more than a great learning experience for you." Mallory said, exiting the car. I followed him, but with great apprehension.

Mallory stepped to the back of the car and popped the trunk. Inside was a large black duffle bag with numerous straps and zippers. He hefted it up out of the trunk and handed it to me. The bag was heavy and solid, so I placed the strap across my shoulder to support its weight.

"You are the guardian of my duffle bag." said Mallory "And one more piece of advice before we go in. If things take a turn for the worse, do not run. You couldn't outrun them anyway. It is better to stand and fight, perhaps they would respect that enough to let you live. It is difficult to say with them, but either way, don't run. Let's go."

A sense of foreboding hit my stomach like a brick as we crossed the street toward the fenced-off overpass.

THREE

When we reached the fence, Mallory pulled open the gate, which was not locked, and moved it out of the way. The area underneath the overpass was cavernous with mounds of dirt piled high like makeshift walls. The dirt was piled so high that it prevented any natural light from getting in, but I could see faint shadows dancing on the ceiling, and I could hear voices talking excitedly up ahead.

As we stepped into the underpass labyrinth, I noticed that the cold damp earthen walls had deep gouges that ran their entire length as if someone had dug their fingers into them and drug them along as they walked. There were also what appeared to be glyphs and runes etched into the walls. If it hadn't been for the rumbling of traffic overhead or the distant honking of horns, we might have been explorers investigating some distant cave that once housed a long-forgotten people. I felt a sense of dread deep within me as if my body knew I shouldn't be there. Each step forward took conscious effort and if it hadn't been for Mallory pushing me forward, I don't think I could have mustered the courage.

The smell of that place was overwhelming. At first all I could smell was earth and a thick musk that turned my stomach. Every sense in my body told me to run, to get the hell out of there, but one look at Mallory steeled my resolve and I stayed by his side. As we got further in, something delicious hit my nostrils. It was unexpected and out of place.

By the time we reached the far end of the tunnel the voices got much louder, in fact they sounded quite raucous. Mallory reached out an arm to pull me back and positioned himself in front as we rounded a corner. The tunnel opened into a large open space which was lit up by fires blazing in three rusty metal barrels.

A dozen people stood around the room talking noisily, and sure enough a small ragged looking man was tending a large, skewered roast that was rotating over one of the flames. To be quite honest they all looked ragged, but I guess that was to be expected of people who hung out under overpasses.

There was a large man sitting near the back who seemed to notice us first. He stood up and pushed his way past two of the others who seemed on the brink of fighting each other. The large man was wearing a tattered and stained off-white long sleeve insulated shirt under a blue jean jacket with cut off sleeves. Long greasy blonde hair fell down his unkempt face giving him a menacing look. *Lord, he is massive, I* thought to myself as the man approached. Everyone else in the room immediately stopped what they were doing when they saw him stand. Silence fell and every single pair of eyes in the room turned to us.

"Mallory Moran, supernatural dick. You better have a good reason for coming to my den." the man said, his voice rumbled like thunder. A shiver ran up my spine.

"Easy, Osvald, I come in peace." Mallory said, holding his hands up in the air in a gesture of goodwill. Mallory started towards the center of the cavernous room, and I'm not embarrassed to say that I pressed myself against the back wall hoping to avoid notice. There were six men and five women that I could see spread out around the room watching what was taking place. All but a few of the onlookers were abnormally large and muscular. *What kind of homeless bodybuilder convention have I stumbled onto here*? I couldn't help but wonder.

The man called Osvald stepped forward until he was right in front of Mallory. The top of Mallory's head just barely reached the man's chin. Osvald was well over six and a half feet tall. Everyone in the room seemed to hold their breath as the two men stood chest to chest. I could feel the tension which hung thick over the room and just when I was sure

Osvald was about to swing on Mallory the large man's head cocked curiously to the side and his eyes landed right on me.

"Who's the pup?" Osvald asked and the tension in the room seemed to lessen for everyone, everyone except me. My heart tried to pound its way out of my chest.

Mallory turned his head to look back at me and a smirk crept across his face.

"That shy individual is my new assistant, Saturday Shepherd. Saturday, meet Osvald Steel, Alpha of The Strays."

Osvald swept his gaze back toward Mallory, who stepped back to put a little more space between them. Some of the others in the room stepped closer to the two men, forming almost a half-circle between them and the fire pits.

"I know you didn't come all this way for introductions, so what the hell do you want?" Osvald said.

"I'm here for the girl," said Mallory, his voice steady and confident.

Osvald looked around the room. "You'll have to be more specific. We have a lot of girls." Laughter erupted from around the room and one of the bigger guys, a dark-skinned man with a face full of scars chimed in with "Yeah we do."

"Specifically, I am looking for this girl." Mallory held out his phone and showed a picture to Osvald. "Her name is Maria Álvarez."

There was the sound of the scraping of boots and I saw someone stand up among the shadows in the far corner of the room. Osvald glanced at the phone ever so briefly and looked back down at Mallory. "Waco, you ever seen this girl?"

The black man with the scarred face stepped over to Osvald and peered into the phone. The light from the phone reflecting on his face made it look even more unnatural. "Oh yeah. That's Mannie's girl. What you want with her?"

"I am here in representation of her mother, who has asked me to bring her home, and I intend to do so," said Mallory.

"Like hell you are." said a voice from the farthest and

darkest corner of the room. Another powerfully built man stepped into the firelight. This guy looked much younger than the rest, probably only a couple of years older than me, and he did not have nearly as many scars as the others. The newcomer was wearing tight black sweatpants and he was shirtless, and he was also completely shredded, I mean he made the jocks from school look tiny in comparison. Trailing close behind him was Maria Álvarez. She was not as small in stature as her mother, but she appeared doubly so standing among this crowd. She was wearing short denim shorts and a navy-blue sweater. Her long black hair was pulled tight in a bun on the top of her head. "No one can have what is mine, especially some creepy old man." Mannie spat.

Mallory looked completely offended. "You must be Mannie?" he said, and Mannie grunted an acknowledgement. "Well, I must admit that I don't appreciate the 'old man' jab. Another day and time I would have to teach you a lesson, but alas there is a worried mother out there waiting for us. Maria, if you would be so kind as to join me, I would like to get you back as soon as possible, as promised."

Maria stepped around Mannie. "I like it here." she said, but Mannie pulled her back behind him and told her to be quiet. Maria rolled her eyes at being ignored, and swatted Mannie's hand away.

"Oz, you gonna let this outsider come in here and walk all over us?" Mannie asked the alpha.

Mallory also turned to Osvald. "The girl is only seventeen and her mother wants her home. I am taking her home."

I cringed. Osvald did not seem the kind of guy who liked people giving him orders, but he stood there silently, a breath away from violence. After a few long moments, a devious smile cracked Osvald's hard face giving it an eerily unnatural look. He started to laugh, and it was as if someone ran an ice cube down my back.

"Well boys, it looks like we will have some

entertainment tonight after all. You know how we do things, Moran. Now, someone bring me a drink." Osvald snatched a slab of nearly raw meat from off one of the skewers and leaned against the wall, tearing chunks off it with his teeth. I wasn't sure what had just happened, but I could feel the energy in the room shift. Everyone jumped up and down in anticipation.

Mallory walked over to where I was standing, but I was so enthralled by what was taking place I barely even noticed. Mannie stepped forward while everyone else backed up, forming a tight ring around the room. Mannie strolled around the circle flexing his muscles. As the firelight illuminated his body, I could make out jagged scars running across his abdomen, the white lines stood out like tattoos on his otherwise tanned skin. Shouts and howls erupted from the bystanders as they pushed and jostled each other as if in some sort of tribal celebration. It was overwhelmingly raw and primal.

"Saturday." Mallory said, raising his voice and it snapped me back to reality. "I need my bag." Shaking my head to clear it as if I had been in a trance, I dropped Mallory's bag onto the dirt floor. Mallory bent down and began to search through it. I noticed him pull something small and shiny out of it and put it into his pocket.

Mallory took off his jacket and folded it, before placing it inside of the bag. "Listen to me closely Saturday." he said as he stood up, placing his hands on my shoulders, and looking me right in the eyes. "Your eyes have been lying to you for years now. Your eyes and your mind have colluded against you, to protect you, but they can't protect you anymore. You must learn to protect yourself."

I didn't comprehend what Mallory was trying to tell me. He sounded like a madman, but he looked deadly serious. There was something in Mallory's eyes that spoke to me and would not allow me to simply dismiss his words.

"What are you talking about?" I asked nervously.

Mallory's grip on my shoulders tightened and he leaned in even closer, so close I could feel his breath. "I need you to See." He smiled reassuringly and let go of my shoulders. "I believe in you, Saturday Shepherd. Believe in me." He patted my cheek and stepped around to face the crowd.

Mallory walked slowly toward Mannie, who stood in the center of the room, surrounded by a dozen or so onlookers. As he got closer, I really began to appreciate how much bigger Mannie was than Mallory. I had no desire to watch what was about to happen, but Mallory had told me he wanted me to see it, to see something. When Mallory and Mannie were within an arm's reach of each other the man called Waco stepped forward.

"Say the words." Waco said.

Mallory stopped walking and finished rolling up his sleeves. He looked up at the powerfully built man standing before him. "Challenge." is all Mallory said before it began. The words had barely left Mallory's lips when Mannie's fist crashed into his face with a sickening crack.

My eyes closed reactively, and I was certain that when they opened, I would see Mallory's lifeless body lying there. However, when I opened them a heartbeat later Mallory was already picking himself up off the dirt, blood dripping from his mouth, and Mannie circling him cockily. Mallory pushed himself up to his knees, wiping the blood from his mouth with his left hand, his right hand was in his pocket.

"That's it? You done already?" Mannie spat. "Old man." he added with a laugh and turned to show off to the gathered crowd.

Mallory reached his feet with surprising strength. Mannie turned to face him; a bloodthirsty smile etched across his face. He lunged for Mallory with an unbridled ferocity and a speed which should be impossible for someone of his size. Surprisingly, Mallory moved just an instant quicker. Mallory moved his head just enough to cause Mannie's blow to careen off to his left. Mallory brought his own fist up in a blur. When he did, I could just make out a glint as the firelight reflected off a ring that he was wearing. When Mallory's fist connected with Mannie's chin a deafening sound like metal hitting metal, a sledgehammer against an anvil, filled the room. Mannie dropped to the ground, lifeless for an instant.

The room went completely silent as everyone drew in a breath. Mallory stepped back defensively, and I was able to see his hand clearly. Mallory wasn't wearing a ring, but instead it was what looked to be a shiny pair of brass knuckles, except they didn't appear to be made of brass, they looked more like silver.

Something shifted in the room. The chanting stopped. Everything felt more serious now and it seemed to me as if the temperature had risen substantially. I had done nothing but hold up a wall and beads of sweat were dripping down my back. Unbelievably, Mannie rose to his feet.

His back was to me so I couldn't see what damage had been done to his face. What I did see was horrifying enough. Mannie was emitting a low guttural growl as he stood, and his body began to shift and contort as his powerful figure seemed to become even larger, impossibly large. Mannie's spine seemed to pop and crack as a large ridge erupted up his back, which was now covered in thick dark hair. As Mannie turned back to face Mallory, I felt a fear rise in me that froze me in place. I tried to scream but couldn't. Everything within me begged for me to run, but I couldn't.

Mannie's face contorted into a twisted visage, his eyes were glowing a deep gold and crimson blood poured from his open maw, which was elongated with a row of dagger-like fangs protruding out of it. A deep open gash along his chin smoked and hissed. Mannie bared his fangs at Mallory, who bravely stood his ground.

"You dare use silver?" said Mannie in a voice so ragged and low that it was inhuman, the words coming out thick and barely recognizable. He raked his hands out toward Mallory, hands that had doubled in size with razor sharp claws protruding from his long thick fingers. Thankfully, Mallory jumped back, and the claws cut harmlessly through the air.

Werewolf. That's the only word that came into my mind and I would have felt like a fool if I hadn't been so afraid. The word played over and over in my mind on repeat. I kept telling myself that it was impossible, but everything happening right now was impossible, yet it was happening. Only one thing made sense, and that was for me to flee, so I ran straight for the exit. Mallory had told me not to run, but I didn't care, and I didn't even think about it, I just ran. I stayed close to the wall, hoping everyone would be too distracted to see me leave. When I turned to give the room one last glance, hoping even to see Mallory running away as well, I crashed into something solid and fell back hard onto the dirt.

My head bounced violently off compacted earth and my vision swam. The blurry form of a woman picked me up off the ground by my collar and dragged me back into the room. As my vision slowly corrected itself, I could see Mallory and Mannie circling one another. Mallory's shirt was in tatters, nearly completely shredded, but he was alive. It seemed as if Mallory was just fast enough to stay out of the range of Mannie's claws, but I wondered how long that could last. It was obvious that if Mallory slowed at all it would only take one swipe from those vicious claws to do some serious life-ending damage. It seemed like Mannie knew this as well, as it appeared that he was not fully committing to his attacks, just harassing Mallory, and forcing him to use up his energy to evade the attacks and wear himself out.

Mallory ripped away the fragments of his remaining dress shirt revealing his own fair share of scars, both old and new. Mannie in his twisted form was hunched over, his claws dug into the ground, and he looked ready to pounce. Hot saliva and blood dripped from Mannie's teeth and the crimson droplets steamed as they hit the ground. Mallory, unbelievably, removed the silver knuckles from his hand and pocketed them. Mannie looked shocked, as much as it was possible for a monster to look shocked. After a heartbeat, the shock wore off and he started to laugh. There was no humor in the laugh, no remorse or pity. It was the laugh of a jackal, the laugh of a predator amused by the frailty of its prey.

Mallory clasped his hands together and closed his eyes, as if to embrace the blow that was to come. Whether it was fear or curiosity that kept my eyes open I was not sure, but I watched. Mannie attacked, lunging for Mallory who rolled out of the way just in time. Mallory reached his feet with a bound and he held his right hand off to the side and spoke a command that sounded like a different language. At once a brilliant beam of light sprang to life in his hand. The glow of the light lessened, and in its place was a hardened silver blade, about three feet long. The firelight reflected off the blade's razor-sharp feet.

There was a loud collective intake of breath from around the room. Osvald, whose feet I had been laid at, made no sound at all. Mannie charged. Mallory rolled under his attack, bringing his sword up to slice across Mannie's abdomen as he did. Mannie came up clutching the new gash that popped and sizzled where the silver had touched him. I could feel hackles rising around the room. Maria, who stood next to me, looked bored by the whole thing. She didn't seem heartbroken to see her boyfriend getting cut or horrified to see him become a monster straight out of a nightmare. It was safe to say this wasn't the first time she had seen this kind of thing.

Mannie let out a horrific howl that sent a tremor of terror through me. Mannie seemed to have completely lost control now, he lashed out wildly with great ferocity, but not much accuracy. Mallory was moving in and out of Mannie's reach, using his silver blade to cause shallow cuts to blossom up across whichever parts of Mannie he could connect. Blood flowed from the cuts and dripped down onto the floor creating a clay-colored mud in which they battled. Their fighting styles could not have been more different. Mallory had thus far managed to avoid maiming, somehow, and Mannie seemed to be slowing from all his wounds.

Mannie made one last ditch effort to bring Mallory down. He charged and when Mallory spun to move out of the way his foot slipped in the muck and mud. Mallory went down to one knee with a painful gasp. Mannie connected. The beast hit Mallory hard and both men went tumbling backward, each fighting desperately to end up on top. They broke loose from each other, and Mallory sprang up to his feet but not fast enough. Mannie grabbed him roughly by the shoulders and threw him into the wall. Mallory hit the wall with a sickening thud and Mannie was on him immediately. Mannie drew his claws back, ready to bring them down with a killing blow.

I was sure this was the end of Mallory Moran, but Mannie's hands never came down. They stayed up in the air, long claws dripping crimson red blood. When Mannie backed up slowly, I could see why. Mallory held his blade with the edge pressed right against Mannie's throat. The area where the silver touched his skin smoked and hissed.

"Relent." ordered Mallory.

The room went silent. The only sound that could be heard were the heaving breaths being taken by the two combatants. As Mannie stepped back trying to edge away from the silver blade he seemed to shrink and slowly return to his normal size which, while still massive, was not nearly as imposing by comparison.

"Relent!" Mallory again ordered.

Mannie twisted in pain, unable to pull himself away from the lethal metal of Mallory's blade.

"Fine. I relent." he said, his voice agony. Mallory withdrew the blade. Mannie clutched at the spot where it had been, rubbing it and trying to stave off the pain. Mannie's body was a bloody mess, he bled from dozens of cuts. A normal man would not have been able to survive that much blood loss, but I now knew these were anything but normal men. "You can have her; I was done with her anyway."

Mannie spat.

Mallory looked at him and shook his head somberly. "You know when you are beaten, that's good." Mallory said. "But you do not know when to shut up. Another lesson for another day perhaps. Come along Maria if you would. You too, Saturday."

I pushed myself up off the ground, dusting myself off before joining Mallory. There was a stunned silence around the room. A few of the younger men looked murderous. The man called Waco stepped forward ushering Maria to join Mallory. "Go on girl. You are not to return. Got it?" Waco said.

Maria shuffled her feet somberly but didn't protest. Mannie didn't so much as look in her direction. Mallory, his blade having been returned to his bag, picked his jacket up off the ground and put it around her shoulders.

"Let's get you home. Saturday, my bag please." Mallory said.

I bent down to pick up the duffel bag and followed closely after them. We had only taken a few steps towards the door when a low visceral growl caused me to turn in time to see Mannie's powerful form flash past me toward Mallory. My voice caught in my throat as I tried to call out, and it would not have been fast enough to alert Mallory anyway. Mannie pounced and Mallory turned too late, far too late. The moment seemed to hang in the air.

Mannie was jerked back mid-air, inches away from Mallory as Osvald gripped him tightly by the throat. Osvald slammed Mannie up against the dirt wall and pressed his face right up against Mannie's, eyes locked.

"You will honor the challenge." Osvald ordered, his voice ragged and dangerous. Mannie whimpered and struggled futilely to escape his alpha's vice-like grip. "You will learn, little wolf. Or you will be culled." Osvald stared silently into Mannie's eyes. Mallory grabbed me by the arm and pulled me along, and with Maria in tow, we all left the den of The Strays.

Outside the sun had given way to the moon and what few stars you can see in the city were visible overhead. Mallory's car sat right where we had left it, no worse for the wear, which by the look of this neighborhood was a miracle. Mallory held the door open for Maria who slid into the backseat while I deposited the duffel bag back into the trunk. Before shutting it, Mallory dug around and pulled out a spare t-shirt and put it on. Mallory also placed his silver knuckles back into the bag.

At this point I was barely holding it together with a mixture of shock and adrenaline and finally found myself alone with my thoughts in the silence of the car. Images of what I had just witnessed flooded my mind. Everything I thought possible and impossible had suddenly become a lie. The images flashed over and over in fast repetition. I could feel my hands start to sweat, and my chest tightened as if someone were squeezing it. I struggled to breathe. My vision began to blur. I placed my hands against the dashboard for support.

"Is he ok?" The voice was Maria's, but it was muffled and distant. I turned my head to face her, and everything blurred. Mallory said something, but it sounded like an echo of an echo. The world went black.

FOUR

The next thing I remember was waking up on the couch in my grandparents' house. I tried to lift my head up off the pillow, but everything hurt. There was a dull ache right behind my eyes that pulsed painfully with every sudden movement. Out of the corner of my vision I could see that the television was on and airing C-Span, so it was possible that I had died, and this was hell.

It took every ounce of energy I could muster to force myself up. My phone was lying next to me and when I picked it up the time flashed across the screen. 9:30 PM. *Was it possible that I had dreamt the entire day?* I couldn't help but wonder. In fact, based on what I had witnessed, it was much more probable that I had fallen asleep and just dreamt every bit of it. Surprisingly, the thought of it all having been a dream was disappointing. The experience in that den terrified the hell out of me, but at the same time I'd never felt more alive in my entire life. The raw power and possibility in that room was exciting, in hindsight. Something about it felt right.

The only explanation that made sense was that I was somehow exposed to a powerful hallucinogen, or that I had been drugged. The crazy lady from the *Sifu Wok* seemed like a likely culprit. Although that didn't explain how I ended up back here. No, I could feel my mind working overtime trying to explain away what I had seen with my eyes. I saw a werewolf, and not just one of them. I watched a man turn into a hulking wolf beast that was harmed by silver, and I've seen enough movies to know that means "werewolf". There was no other explanation that made sense, not that any of it made sense.

Finally, I forced myself to stand up, fully intent on going to the bathroom to splash water on my face to see if that helped with the early onset insanity I was experiencing. I could hear voices coming from the kitchen. As I stepped around the corner, I saw the kitchen was awash in incandescent light, and both of my grandparents were sitting at the table. It was an old faded brown wood table they purchased back even before mom was born.

They were not alone at the table. Sitting next to them, sipping coffee out of one of their ancient coffee mugs was Mallory Moran. Mallory smiled upon seeing me, and lifted the coffee to his lips, taking a long drink.

"Look who's back among the living." grandpa said. "You alright boy?"

I walked over to the sink and poured a glass of water from the faucet.

"Yeah, I think I will make it."

"Mr. Moran here was just telling us that he offered you a job with his firm. It sounds like a great opportunity." grandma said with enthusiasm only a grandmother can have. "And he seems like he would be a wonderful person to work for, Saturday."

"Why thank you, Carol, you are dangerously close to making me blush," said Mallory. "The fact is that I have not had much opportunity to talk with Saturday about the job. After offering him the position he had his dizzy spell. Too much time out in the heat I imagine. After I brought you home, Saturday, your grandparents were kind enough to invite me in for a cup of coffee."

"Well of course he wants the job. Don't you, boy?" grandpa said.

"Um. Well." I desperately racked my brain for a way out of this awkward situation. There were a million questions running through my mind, but none of them were ones I wanted to ask in front of my grandparents. Mostly out of fear they would have me committed.

", Saturday has not even heard about our compensation package yet. I would not want him to make such a decision without having all the information. Saturday, if you come on board, I will supplement your entire first year of college tuition to cover whatever your scholarships will not."

"Oh, that's so wonderful!" grandma exclaimed.

"On top of that, I will pay you a competitive wage and if you stick it out through the length of the internship, I can promise that an offer for a full-time position will be extended to you. Upon completion of your schooling, of course." said Mallory.

"Well, how about that!" grandpa said with a bellowing laugh. He stood and walked over to me, giving me a heavy-handed pat on the back, and pulling me into a half hug. "I told you, boy, stick it out, keep applying, and something good will come out of it."

"Fate favors ferocity," said Mallory. "So, what do you think?" He stood and offered his hand to me.

"Well of course he accepts!" grandpa boomed, grabbing me tighter in excitement.

"If it is okay with you John, I would like to hear Saturday's response," said Mallory.

"Of course." grandpa said. "Go on, boy. Your decision."

The moment hung like an eternity. Mallory stood with his hand outstretched. Grandma was beaming up at me, while grandpa stared at me with a look of encouragement, but I knew he was trying to mentally compel me to accept. On the one hand, the offer was incredibly generous, not having to worry about paying for at least one year of college would be awesome. That would be a huge weight off my shoulders, and the shoulders of my grandparents who did so much to provide for me. On the other hand, I could not ignore the horrors I had encountered under the overpass. I couldn't imagine what a normal day working with Mallory Moran would look like. It terrified me to my core, but deep down inside, somewhere near the pit of my stomach, it also excited me. Desperately I wanted to know more about this world that I stumbled into, and there was only one way to do that.

"I accept." I said, reaching out to shake Mallory's hand.

It was as if I had pushed the play button on my life and everything started back up. Mallory shook my hand vigorously and stepped back to allow my grandparents to swallow me up in a hug. I noticed the warning signs of oncoming tears from my grandmother, and I could see the pure joy written on grandpa's face, and I was at peace with his decision. It was impossible to be apprehensive when I knew how proud it made them.

After a few moments of celebration, Mallory excused himself and I walked him out to his car.

"It is good to have you on the team, Saturday. Tell me, what does your schedule look like this week?" Mallory asked.

"My last day of school is Friday. After that I'm on summer break until the end of August."

"Perfect. We will start work on Friday. Enjoy your last few days of school and I will message you with the details on where we will be meeting Friday evening." Mallory opened his car door and sat down inside, and I was reminded of something.

"Oh, I almost forgot." I said. "What happened to Maria?"

"Maria was dropped off safe and sound with her mother back at my office."

"I can't believe I passed out in front of her." I said, brushing my hand through my hair absentmindedly.

"She seemed concerned about you. I will get a message back to her that you are ok."

"She did?" I asked with a little too much excitement in my voice.

Mallory smiled. "Good night, Saturday. See you on Friday." He backed his car out of the small driveway and out into the night. When I had gone back inside, I found my grandparents had already gone to bed. I went back to my own room and as soon as my head hit the pillow I was out.

FIVE

On Monday morning I was a zombie. I could barely keep my eyes open at school. I was especially exhausted during first period calculus class with Mr. Tubbs. Tubbs had the incredible ability to take a mind-numbing subject and make it even more mind-numbing and dull than it needed to be. Tubbs was one of my least favorite teachers at Stanley Claremont High School. On a good day I struggled to stay awake in this class, but today it was a near impossibility. The equations Tubbs was writing on the dry erase board were all jumbled together and while I was usually aggressively average at calculus, today I was hopelessly lost. What kind of monster teaches new material in the last week of school?

Mercifully, the bell rang to end class, so I gathered my stuff and started shoving everything into my backpack. I filed out with everyone else and was milling along mindlessly with the crowd toward my locker, lost in a daze, when someone shoved me. I was knocked into a group of girls who were caught by surprise just as much as I was. I caught myself just in time to keep from falling, but just barely.

"I'm sorry. I'm sorry!" I said to the girls, bending down to help one of them pick up her phone. They just glared at me and continued. When I spun around, I saw the person who had run into me still standing there with a stupid grin spread across his stupid face.

"What the hell, Wes?" I said.

"Sorry, bro, didn't see you there." said Wes.

Wes Ford was one of my best and only friends. Wes loved to joke around, and he was always smiling so it was impossible to ever take him seriously. He was average height for a junior, lanky, and he had shaggy brown hair that he often had to brush back out of his face. Twin dimples on both sides of Wes' cheeks made his boyish face even more youthful.

"Could you for once just say 'good morning' like a normal person?"

"Not my style, man." said Wes. "Besides, I think that one girl was into you. I was just setting you up for a meet-cute, you should be thanking me."

"Yeah, bro, I'm sure she loved me knocking her over. Like the start of all good romances." I said sarcastically. "I gotta get to Lit class, I don't have time for your nonsense."

"Let's walk and talk." Wes said. "What happened to you last night? We were waiting for you to log in and you never showed."

"Ah damn, my bad man, I forgot we were running the flash point last night. It completely slipped my mind."

My friends and I pumped way too much of our time into video games. We were currently obsessed with an MMO and last night we were supposed to have teamed up to tackle a particularly nasty quest.

"Good luck explaining that to Liz, she was pissed. We had to pick a random to fill out our 4-person team, and dude was garbage. Where were you?"

"I had that job interview, and it ran late. Really late actually."

"That's a good sign, right? You get it?" Wes asked.

"Yeah, I did."

"That's tight man. You think you will like it?"

"I think I'm in for a hell of a summer." I answered honestly.

We arrived outside the classroom that housed third-year literature with Ms. Kline. "You've got this class with Liz and Liam, don't you?" Wes asked, knowing the answer to his own question. I leaned in the doorway to peer into the room, there sat Liz already glaring at me.

"Good luck," said Wes as he walked off to his class,

38

sure to be late as always.

Slowly I walked to my seat, which I now regretted was right next to Liz, who I'm pretty sure was trying to set me on fire with her mind. If anyone could have done that, it would have been Liz. The Arya Stark of our group, she was fierce as hell. With her pale skin, shoulder length black hair, and love for pop culture, she had perfected gamer girl chic.

"Good morning, Lizzy." I said with a smile.

"Oh, good morning, Saturday." she said sarcastically, "And how are we today? Did we get some good sleep last night?"

"I actually did, thanks for asking." I said, taking my seat and immediately felt her open hand slap the back of my head. It had been done out of love, but the sting was real.

"Did you at least get your job?" she asked, her tone much more friendly now.

"Believe it or not, I did."

"Congrats man." said Liam, who was sitting directly behind Liz. Liam was the reserved one in our group, but also probably the funniest once you got him going, and his geek knowledge was second to none.

"Thanks, dude."

"Some Jedi you are putting your own life above the fun of your friends." Liz said.

"You can bring it up at the next guild meeting." I said and Liam stifled a laugh to avoid Liz's ire. Liz was also our group's enforcer. She had an incredible ability to emasculate anyone with a simple stare. She was protective of her guys, and we were protective of her. No one ever approached her to ask her out or anything, and it wasn't because she was always surrounded by our group, it was because she had what she called a "serious case of resting bitch face".

The rest of the day went by in a blur, and I managed to survive. Thankfully, most of my teachers seemed to understand that trying to teach new material with only a couple of days of school left was a fool's errand.

This was no small thing, because as difficult as I normally found it to pay attention in class, after yesterday it was even worse. On multiple occasions my friends had to snap me out of episodes of zoning out and staring off into nothingness. Every single time this happened I found myself thinking about that den and what had happened in there.

Shortly after lunch, my day shifted dramatically. After scarfing down some pizza and fries I joined Wes by our lockers to talk shop. He was giving me a rundown of what I'd missed the previous night in the flash point. I was trying to keep up, but could feel my eyes drifting down the hallway, and it was then that I saw her. Maria Álvarez was walking down the hallway of my school. I couldn't believe it. She was wearing dark blue skinny jeans, a loose white T-shirt, and sneakers. She was chatting with a couple of friends, oblivious to my existence.

"Hey, Maria." I said, before my nerves could stop me. Her friends snapped their heads in my direction, and I wanted to hide, or die, until Maria smiled at me.

"Hey, it's Saturday, right?" she asked, and Wes' jaw dropped.

"Yeah, that's right." I said, not really truly believing this was happening "You go to school here too?"

"For a couple more days." Maria said, "Are you feeling better?"

"Oh yeah, I'm good." I said, feeling my cheeks burn with embarrassment. I was very aware of every one of her friends and Wes staring at me and I wished this conversation were taking place somewhere more secluded, like another planet. It was super awkward to be the center of attention in an already awkward conversation.

"You guys go ahead, I'll catch up." Maria told her friends, seeming to read my mind. They walked away and we were alone, except for Wes who just stood there with a dumb grin on his face. Maria gave me a look that I interpreted as her wanting to speak alone.

"Hey bro, you mind giving us a second?" I said to Wes, snapping him out of his daze.

"Oh yeah, sure. I'm Wes by the way, Saturday's more handsome and intelligent best friend." He said to Maria before jogging off down the hallway, turning around just long enough to give me a thumbs up, and a middle finger. Such a good friend.

"He seems...fun." Maria said, setting her bookbag down onto the floor.

"Yeah, Wes, he's... great." I said, very much aware that I didn't know what to do with my hands at that moment. Being this close to Maria I could really appreciate just how gorgeous she was.

"I didn't get a chance to thank you." she said.

"Oh hey, I mean, I didn't really do anything." I said, finally deciding to just put my hands in my pockets. "Besides, you didn't want to leave anyway, so…"

She smiled at me, and I tried to play it cool, but that smile just did something to me.

"It's not that I didn't want to leave, it's just when I am around him, I get so caught up in everything. It's all so exciting. Well, I don't have to tell you that, right? I lose track of time, and myself, and everything when I'm with Mannie."

"Yeah… I get it, I mean, he seems great. Really, really, great. A little hairy for my taste, and the whole turning into a monster thing doesn't do it for me… but other than that…"

"Shut up." she said, pushing me playfully back against my locker. "You know, he would probably kill you if he knew I was talking to you."

"I'm not afraid of him." I said, and it was a complete lie, but something about her made me want to be brave.

"Well, you should be." She said "He's dangerous. Seriously."

"You can do better than him, you know that?"

"You think so?" she asked, coyly. I sensed an opening, but my tongue felt thick, and I couldn't force the question out of my mouth. Then the moment was gone. "I gotta go to class, maybe I'll see you around, Saturday."

She picked up her bag and started off down the hallway, when a last second flash of bravery struck me.

"Hey, you wanna hang out this weekend?" I asked. She stopped walking and turned back toward me. "Just the two of us, no werewolf ex-boyfriends."

She reached out and took my hand in hers. The feel of her fingers against my skin was electric. She proceeded to write her number down on the back of my hand in blue ink.

"You have no idea what you've gotten yourself into." she said, looking deep into my eyes. "But you're cute, so text me."

I looked around at the empty hallway around me and I've never been so thankful to be late for class in my life.

After school, my friends and I went to Miguel's, our favorite pizza joint. Miguel's was a small place in Queens, not far from their school. It only had a few tables out front, and they were all covered in faded white and red checkered plastic tablecloths. The chairs were wooden and rickety. Miguel and one of his sons were behind the counter making pizza dough from scratch, their aprons stained with years of flour. In the back of Miguel's was a small room with a few classic stand-up arcade machines. When you walked into Miguel's your senses were hit with a wave of the scent of pizza and the beeps and noises coming from the arcade games. It was a little slice of heaven for us.

After Wes regaled everyone with the story of the encounter with Maria in the hallway a dozen times, they all wanted to hear about my new job. Wes, Liz, and Liam had already booked their internships several months back and they spent so much time ragging me about my list of prospects that I felt obligated to give them something.

"Are you going to be like a file clerk or something?" Liam asked.

"Maybe." I answered. "Essentially I just do whatever

they ask me too."

"What kind of law do they practice?" Liz asked. I hesitated. I wanted to be honest with my friends, but at the same time I didn't want them to have me committed to an asylum. Thankfully, I was saved from having to lie to her by Wes interrupting us loudly as he plopped back down into his seat.

"Listen up, losers. Friday night, my place, celebratory end of the school year gaming marathon. You guys in?"

"Hell yeah." Liam said. "Sounds fun."

"I'm in." Lizzy said. Everyone looked at me, and I had just shoved a slice of pizza into my mouth.

"How about you, law man? Can you make time in your busy schedule for your friends?" Wes asked.

"I think I can be there." I said.

"You think?" Liam asked.

"I mean, yeah. I told my boss I could start work after school on Friday." I told them.

"I'm talking about that night, dude." Wes explained.

"Yeah, you're right. No problem. I'll be there." I said, figuring that the first couple of days would just be for paperwork and instructional videos and all of that anyway. I would finish up with Mallory, head home to grab my stuff, and then go directly to Wes' house to hang out.

"Glad that's settled. Now let's go pump some quarters into that Turtles in Time machine, ladies." Wes suggested.

"OK, but I'm Donatello this time. You really suck with the bo staff." Liam said.

"That's fine. I'm the Leo of this group anyway." Wes said.

"Dude, Leo sucks." Liz added.

"Shut your dirty mouth, Liz." Wes said.

I couldn't help but laugh at the playful banter between my friends. For the first time in a while, I was truly happy. The school year was ending, summer was fast approaching, my mind was completely free of the burdens that troubled me all night and most of the day. There was something peaceful in this moment. All was right in my world, but it wouldn't last. My world was about to get a whole lot bigger and a whole lot darker. You see, if I hadn't been so distracted, I might have noticed the quote Ms. Klein had written on her dry erase board in class today. It was a quote by the English writer, Virginia Woolf.

"...*There is no gate, no lock, no bolt that you can set upon the freedom of my mind.*"

If I had noticed that quote, I might have appreciated it. I might have written it down. Maybe I would have even posted it online with a clever hashtag. One thing is for certain, I would eventually realize it was utter and complete garbage. The mind can absolutely be locked, in fact many of them are bolted shut, and my lock had just been removed.

SIX

Friday arrived with little fanfare. The last day of school was always a celebration of sorts. Seniors cried tears as they prepared to leave a place that they had spent the past four years complaining about, and they didn't seem to appreciate the irony. As far as I was concerned, as a junior, it was not much different than any other day, just the countdown to the freedom of summer. Today I also had a little nervous apprehension for what my afternoon with Mallory Moran was going to look like.

Right after lunch was my fourth period pre-law elective class, which meant that most of my classmates were seniors. Today Mr. Patterson was taking the time to meet with each student individually to go over our end of year briefs we submitted a few weeks prior. As always, my name fell towards the end of the alphabet, so it would be closer to the end of class before it was my turn. A movie was playing on the small, wheeled television cart for everyone to watch until it was their turn to come forward. Mr. Patterson, ever the cliche, had decided to put *To Kill a Mockingbird* on the TV. Respect to Atticus Finch, but I couldn't sit through this movie for the thousandth time.

My mind started to drift to Maria. We texted some last night and made plans to grab some pizza this weekend. I really hoped she was done with Mannie for good, and not just because I liked her. Mannie just seemed like bad news, and not to mention his ability to shift into a horrific murder beast, dude took toxic masculinity to a whole other level.

"Saturday. Saturday. Earth to Saturday." said Mr. Patterson. It took me a moment to realize that I was being addressed. Mr. Patterson was hanging up the phone on his desk.

"Sorry. Yes?" I answered.

"Welcome back. Mr. Fletcher would like to see you in his classroom for a moment." Patterson said.

"In the Chem lab?" I asked.

"Last I checked that was his classroom." Patterson answered, snidely.

"Right. Sorry." I stood up and gathered my things and moved toward the door.

"Saturday." said Mr. Patterson.

"Yes, sir?"

"You'll need a hall pass."

"Yes. Sorry." I said, grabbing the laminated pass off the wall and putting the lanyard around my neck.

"Hurry back." said Mr. Patterson. I stepped out into the hallway and walked toward the Chem lab. Chemistry with Mr. Fletcher was my third period class, right before lunch. Fletcher must have forgotten to give me something during class. I was pretty sure this was Fletcher's planning period, so that made sense.

Outside of the Chem lab I could see through the small window in the door that the room appeared empty, which was not unusual. I turned the handle and pushed the door open into the classroom. Fletcher always kept the lab locked up tight unless he was in there, so he must have just stepped out to use the restroom or something. The lab was a large room with high ceilings and expensive equipment. At the top of the exterior wall near the ceiling were ventilation windows about eight feet up in the air. They kept these windows open when the weather was nice, like it was today. They helped to remove some of the smells that accumulated in the lab during the winter months, a nice mixture of chemicals and stale air. As I entered the room, I walked toward Fletcher's desk to see if he had left a sticky note or something for me. The door slammed shut behind me.

I turned quickly, startled, and saw the person I least expected or wanted to see. Mannie stood there staring at me with a look of pure contempt, his body blocking the only exit.

"Well. Well. Well." said Mannie, walking slowly towards me, fully the predator.

"What are you doing here?" I asked, stepping back to put a large lab table between the two of us.

"Your boss made me look weak and I can't afford to look weak." said Mannie, stalking closer. "Os says I can't touch the old man, but he didn't say nothing 'bout you."

"Easy man. Let's talk this out." I knew the last thing Mannie wanted to do was talk it out, but I was trying to buy myself some time. My only hope was Mr. Fletcher coming in and discovering what was going on, but Mannie would probably just kill him too. So, all I could do was try to draw Mannie away from the door and rely on my speed to get out into the hallway.

Mannie gripped the table that stood between us, his arms flexed, and it looked like he was going to rip it free from where it was bolted to the floor. He snarled and swiped one of his beefy arms out towards me. Glass jars and beakers went flying across the room where they shattered on impact and glass shards spilled across the floor.

"You can run if you want. In fact, I want you to." Mannie taunted.

I turned and sprinted through the line of desks to my right toward the back of the classroom. I hoped to draw Mannie away from the door and then I would make a break for it. Mannie followed me, in no hurry whatsoever. He strolled down the row of desks toward me, and I pressed my back against the far wall of the classroom.

"There's nowhere to run, coward." snarled Mannie.

Finally, I saw my opportunity and made a break for it. I ran to the farthest point of the classroom and turned toward the door and ran as fast as my legs would take me, trying to use the desks as obstacles between the two of us.

I was steps away from the door when something solid smashed hard into my back, knocking me to the ground. I hit the floor with a crash, my head slamming into the solid linoleum floor. An involuntary grunt of pain forced its way out of my body and warm blood dripped down my face.

A moment later I felt myself being picked up roughly off the ground by my collar. Only then could I see what had hit me. Apparently, Mannie had launched one of the desks across the room at me. I hadn't considered desk throwing in my escape plan, and in hindsight this was a fatal flaw. Mannie flung me across the floor where I slid hard into the corner of the room. There was so much pain, especially in my back. I had never broken anything before, but I'm pretty sure the stabbing in my side was from a broken rib. My vision swam and my thoughts moved like slush. When I tried to move my body it wouldn't cooperate, all I could do was watch with futility as Mannie stalked toward me.

"So, you aren't as tough as your boss, that's too bad. I wanted this to last longer." said Mannie.

"Why are you doing this?" I asked through the pain, spitting up flecks of blood as I spoke. Every breath I took was laborious and painful. The blood from the cut on my head stung my eyes and blurred my vision. I raised my hand to wipe away the blood and when I pulled it back it looked like it was painted crimson.

"Because I can. Your boss walked you into my world, and he took something from me. I'll be damned if I let a human get one over on me." said Mannie, wrapping his hands around my neck and lifting me roughly off the ground. I tried to pry his hands loose, but it was useless, his grip was like a vice. Even on my feet, I still did not come close to meeting Mannie's eyes.

I don't know if it was courage or stupidity that caused me to talk through the pain, but I couldn't stop myself. "She's not a thing."

Mannie seemed surprised by my comment. The wheels

seemed to be spinning in his head. "What?" he asked, roughly.

"Maria. She's not a thing, and she deserves better than you."

Lizzy told me that one day my mouth was going to get me killed and here I was taunting a murder machine. Sadly, I didn't think I would be around to hear her gloat about being right.

A spark of recognition dawned in Mannie's eyes; he smiled a wide, vicious smile. "Oh, that is precious. Someone has a crush." said Mannie, drawing me in close. So close that I could feel his hot breath on the side of my face. Mannie's fingers tightened around my throat, cutting off blood and oxygen. "Let me be clear, human. She is MINE."

The door to the room opened and shut quickly. I glanced over Mannie's shoulder, hoping someone had come to my rescue. It was foolish. Mannie could have killed anyone who walked into the room, no one would have stood a chance. Mannie never even looked away from me. The man who walked into the Lab was vaguely familiar, I recognized him as one of the other people from the den. Another member of Mannie's pack.

"What do you want, Shark?" asked Mannie, his bloodshot eyes still focused intently on mine.

"Gotta roll. Someone's coming." said Shark.

Mannie emitted a low guttural growl. "I'll be seeing you around." Mannie released me and I fell to the ground violently. I dared to think that maybe it was over. I allowed myself a spark of hope that I wouldn't die there in the Chemistry Lab. I laid back against the cool concrete wall, blood pooling around me. Glancing around Mannie's large frame I saw that where Shark had been standing was now a large brown wolf who padded over to one of the open windows and jumped up and out of it. It was an impossible height, I had thought, for anyone to reach.

Mannie smiled. "The surprises just keep coming, don't they? You have no idea. Before this is all over, you are going to curse your parents for bringing your sorry ass into this world and then you are going to wish you had never met your buddy, Mallory. He's a dead man walking too, just like you. Here, I'll pass on a message to Maria for you. I'll be seeing her tonight."

Mannie smiled down at me and then in a blink he brought his knee powerfully forward and slammed it into my face. The back of my head smashed into the concrete wall and my world turned to pain and darkness.

SEVEN

When I opened my eyes, I was lying face up on a padded blue table in the nurse's office. It was a small office that I had only visited once in the past three years. Its whitewashed walls were adorned with bargain store motivational posters with annoying little sayings like "Your attitude determines your altitude" or "There is no 'I' in team." Unlike my last visit to the nurse's office, this time I did not come here under my own volition. Someone must have found me unconscious in the Chem lab and carried me here, but my rescuer was nowhere to be found. Even the nurse was not fussing over me, which seemed out of character, especially considering it was her job to do so.

Holy crap. Mannie had come to my school and tried to kill me. A werewolf had snuck into my school to kill me because I stole his girlfriend. If I still weren't terrified, I would have laughed. But Mannie hadn't come because of Maria. He had come to kill me because Mallory embarrassed him. That is what he said at least. It seemed impossible. This kind of thing didn't happen in the real world. For not the first time this week I considered that maybe I was stuck in a nightmare.

Nervously I brought my hand up to my face to survey the damage. Gingerly I ran my fingers down my forehand and along the padded bandage that covered the area just above my eye and across my temple. I could imagine the large gash that the bandage was covering. All I could do was hope that it wouldn't leave a lasting scar. With a slight hesitation I tried to rise on the table. I moved slowly and was surprised that it didn't hurt nearly as much as I expected so I moved my arms and back in a slight twisting motion to gauge my injuries. There was a dull ache in my back, but no loss of range of motion.

Lifting my shirt, I checked my side and there was a large purple bruise covering the right side of my ribcage and back, where the table had hit me. The bruise was sore to the touch, but nothing felt broken internally, the pain had subsided substantially, and while I was grateful for that, I was also confused.

The door to the nurse's office opened and Ms. Conley, the school nurse, walked in and she was not alone. Accompanying her were the principal, Mr. Houser, and the school resource officer. They all seemed surprised to see him sitting up.

"How are you feeling, Saturday?" Ms. Conley asked in a sweet voice. She took her job very seriously and her concern for the wellbeing of the students always took priority.

"Honestly, I feel ok, Ms. Conley." I told her. "Just a little confused."

"I am sure that you are." said Mr. Houser.

Ms. Conley reached into a small refrigerator and pulled out a bottle of cold water which she handed to me. "Here, drink up." she said, and I obliged. The water was cool and delicious, and I downed the entire bottle.

"Good. Now it's important that you tell us what all you have taken." she said.

"What I've taken?" I asked.

"Son, we need to know what you took to make you act that way." said Officer Stone "Did you bring it with you today, or did you purchase it at school?"

Officer Stone was the school resource officer, which essentially meant he was a police officer that patrolled the hallways of the school. Most everyone liked Stone, he took an active interest in many of our lives outside of school and seemed to genuinely care. His calm and friendly demeanor were nothing like his exterior.

His nickname was "Rock" and that is what many of the students called him, and it was appropriate. Rock was powerfully built and would willingly share with anyone about how he had turned away from a life on the streets to a life in uniform trying to change this city for the better.

"Rock. You think I was high?" I asked, not believing that they could honestly think I did this to myself. Before Rock could answer, Mr. Houser interjected himself. As beloved as Rock was by the students, Mr. Houser was not. Houser and his "holier than thou" tone did not ingratiate him with anyone. I was not a fan, and I had heard enough teachers complain about him to know I wasn't alone.

"Mr. Shepherd, allow me to lay the facts out in front of you and then you can regale us with your little story." Houser said snidely. "You were found unconscious in the Chem lab by Mr. Fletcher as he returned from lunch. The lab itself is completely trashed. The floor is covered in shattered glass and most of the desks have been flipped over and destroyed. According to the security tapes you were the only person to enter the Chem lab between the time Mr. Fletcher left for lunch and his return. Is any of this ringing a bell, Mr. Shepherd?"

I'm not going to lie; I was completely caught off guard. They weren't concerned for my well-being, they were furious. They thought I destroyed the lab on purpose, out of spite or something. I was in trouble, serious trouble, if I couldn't get them to believe me.

"That's not what happened at all!" I told them, unable to keep the fear out of my voice.

"What was this, Mr. Shepherd?" asked Houser. "Some poor excuse for an end of the year prank? Did you plan on destroying school property and then posting it online for your friends to get a good laugh at?"

"No sir. Not at all." I protested. "I was attacked, I swear."

They stared at me, unmoved by my objections. They didn't believe me. Rock and Ms. Conley seemed to at least take pity on me, Houser on the other hand just looked at me with contempt.

"You were attacked?" Houser asked incredulously. "By whom?"

"He doesn't go here." I said, knowing exactly how this was going to sound. "I know him from outside of school."

"I see," said Houser, patronizingly. "And how did this mysterious figure get in and out of the school without being seen?"

"He used the window in the lab. I think. That's how he left at least." I said.

"Saturday, that's just not possible," said Rock, predictably. "There is no way someone could exit through those windows without using one of the desks and even then, it would be extremely difficult. And none of the desks had been pushed up against the wall."

"Exactly right, so, Mr. Shepherd, before we have you arrested for destroying school property, why don't you tell us what really happened." the principal said.

"Arrested?" I groaned. The possibility of being arrested never even entered my mind. I've only been sent to the principal's office a handful of times and never for anything more serious than not paying attention in class. My heart pounded in my chest. My mind was racing frantically for some way to explain all of this. "No, wait! The hallway. The guy who attacked me had someone else with him and he came into the lab from the hallway."

"I see, so now you were attacked by two people?" asked Mr. Houser, sarcastically.

"No, or yes. I mean no. The second guy didn't do anything, he was just a lookout or something, but he was in the hallway. He would be on camera; you have to believe me." I pleaded.

"Mr. Shepherd, we've seen the video. You are the only person that entered the Chemistry Lab.," said Houser.

"No, that's not possible. Please just watch the video again."

Rock leaned over and whispered something into Mr. Houser's ear. They had a hushed conversation between them. I scrubbed my hands through my hair, in my head I urged them to believe me. Principal Houser sighed loudly. "Fine," he said. "Officer Stone seems to think we should give it another look. I think it is a waste of time, but I'm willing to humor him."

They motioned for me to stand so I did and surprisingly I felt pretty good. The pain was minimal, although admittedly the lack of pain did not help my case. Ms. Conley stayed in her office while the rest of us stepped into Mr. Houser's office. It was a large office, but where most administrators would have pictures of students from current and previous years, Mr. Houser's walls were covered with framed personal achievements and photos of himself with city officials and things like that. Only slightly megalomaniacal.

On one of the shelves on the wall was a small monitor currently displaying a live video feed of the front entrance to the school. Rock motioned for me to have a seat in a powder blue high-backed chair while Mr. Houser picked up a small remote from beside the monitor. Houser pressed a couple of buttons to bring up the feed from the lab hallway and then rewound back to the moment before I approached the door. Houser pushed play and we all watched the screen intently. Soon I approached the door to the lab, opened it, and walked inside. I wished I could turn around and walk away. Houser fast forwarded the recording and moments later I saw Shark speed down the hallway and into the room. It happened in a blur and Houser did not stop the tape, so it continued to fast forward.

"Wait!" I said, rising from my chair. "There he was that was him!"

I felt relieved, as if a weight had been lifted off my chest. Principal Houser stopped the tape just as Mr. Fletcher, the chemistry teacher, came into view of the screen.

"Go back just a bit and you'll see him." I said.

Houser turned and gave a shake of his head, obviously not believing a word I was saying. Nevertheless, the principal pressed rewind on the remote. Shark quickly exited the room and backed down the hallway in reverse. He was still a little blurred, but much clearer.

"There he is!" I said, excitedly. "Press play."

Houser pressed play on the remote and I watched again as Shark clearly snuck down the hallway and into the lab, pulling the door gently shut behind him. I let out a sigh of relief, sinking back into the chair. "There. I'm not crazy."

Oddly enough both Rock and Houser looked at me as if I were in fact crazy. "Don't you see? I wasn't lying and the other guy was in the Lab waiting for me." I explained, not really understanding how they weren't getting it.

"Son, what are you talking about?" asked Rock, obviously attempting to be comforting.

"The guy that just walked in the lab!" I shouted, standing up from the chair, my face flushing with anger. "The guy right there!" I pointed to the monitor.

"Where?" asked Houser.

"Here, give me that." and without thinking I grabbed the remote from him and rewound the recording to where Shark enters the frame. I pressed play and put my fingers on the screen and followed Shark into the room. "There! Right there!" I pounded my finger against the screen.

Houser and Rock exchanged a look and then they both turned toward me. "Son, there's no one there," said Rock, solemnly.

"No. He's right there. I saw him. I see him." My voice began to crack and fail. Houser and Rock continued to stare at one another. A brief silence fell over the room. All I could do was continue to stare at the monitor.

I was scared, I'm willing to admit it, and I made a quick decision to go for broke. I would explain everything the best I could and hope they would believe me. I didn't wait for them to say anything, I just started right in.

"Look I know this makes me sound crazy, but I swear there was someone waiting for me in that room, and he attacked me, and destroyed the room. His name is Mannie. I met him earlier this week when I was working. My new boss had to fight him to win a challenge and rescue this girl Maria and take her back to her mother. She goes to school here! She can vouch for that." I explained. "Mannie and Shark attacked me because Mannie was embarrassed that he lost the fight. For some reason you can't see Shark on the camera, but when he came into the room, they both... They... turned into wolves and jumped out the window."

Taking a breath, I looked to both men to try and gauge their reactions. They were looking at one another and some sort of silent communication transpired between the two of them. After a moment they turned back to me.

"Sit back down, son." Rock said. "Just breathe. It's going to be alright. We're going to step out for a second."

They both left the room, and I was alone with my thoughts. At this point I was beginning to seriously question my own sanity, and it looked like I was in some serious trouble. I was going to be arrested. How could this be happening? On the last day of school, no less. I wasn't exactly sure what to do or how to get out of this situation so I did the only thing that I could think of and texted Mallory.

Saturday:
Mallory. I don't know what to do. Mannie attacked me at school. I'm in serious trouble. Need help.

Immediately the dots popped up on the screen signifying that Mallory was populating a response. The three dots stayed there for what seemed like an eternity. I held my breath hoping that he would respond telling me what to do before Rock and Houser came back into the room. *Come on. Come on. Come on.* Finally, Mallory responded.

Mallory
K.

My face fell at the response. It wasn't helpful in the slightest, but I didn't have time to reply as the door to the office opened and I quickly shoved my phone back into my pocket. Rock came in and walked over to me, putting one of his massive hands on my shoulder. Rock looked at me with sympathy in his dark eyes.

"It's okay, Saturday." Rock said "You're not going to be in trouble. It is clear to us that this was not a prank. You need some rest."

"We've called your grandfather, he's on the way to pick you up. We will dismiss you early today and you can get an early start on your break. We've explained the situation and your grandfather agrees to take you to see someone. A professional. Someone who can help you work all of this out." Mr. Houser said.

"I'm not crazy." I said, leaning back in the chair, rubbing the palms of my hands against my eyes. Rock patted me on the back and helped me up out of the chair.

"We can wait out front for your grandfather," said Rock. I followed him out through the front office and into the lobby of the school. Rock motioned for me to sit down on a bench facing the front door.

"I'm gonna run some cold water over my face. I'll be back in a second." I said, walking into the staff restroom.

I flicked on the light of the small bathroom and locked the door behind me. The cool water from the faucet ran through my hands as I stared into the small mirror hanging above the sink. The face reflected at me looked much worse than I felt. There was dried blood matted into my hair and a large blood-stained bandage took up almost all the right side of my head.

Carefully I peeled back the bandage to get a look at the damage. The sticky medical tape came off cleanly, but not painlessly. I lifted the bandage free and gasped, dropping it into the sink. Where there should have been a nasty wound, there was nothing. There was no fresh blood, no scabbed over wounds, nothing. Only when I looked closer did I notice a faint white scar about an inch long that ran from my right eyebrow up my forehead. It had been an hour since the attack and based on the amount of blood in my hair and on the bandages, there should have been a gash, but there was nothing.

"What the hell is happening to me?" I asked softly to myself. I fumbled with the bandage and tried to put it back on the best I could. After I cupped my hands and took a long drink of cold water, I left the bathroom and found Rock was waiting for me in the lobby. We sat in silence for a few moments until we both noticed a car pull up outside. It was not my grandfather, instead a lithe middle-aged man stepped out of his car. Mallory still wore his long graying hair pulled back in a ponytail and he was wearing a black suit without a tie.

"Something tells me that this is not your grandfather," said Rock.

"Very astute." said Mallory with a smile. "Saturday's grandfather called me and let me know what happened. We both felt it would be best if I were the one to pick him up."

"Do you know this man, Saturday?" Rock asked protectively.

"Yeah, I do." I said. "It's fine."

Rock patted me hard on the back, causing me to lurch forward a bit. "Take care of yourself, Saturday. Have a good summer." Rock said, shaking my hand. "If you need anything at all, you contact me." I nodded and walked over to Mallory's car and got in. Mallory was already in the driver's seat and as soon as the door was shut, he took off.

"It sounds like you had yourself a day." Mallory said. "Let's talk."

EIGHT

"What's happening to me?" I asked immediately. "I should be in a hospital right now, but I feel perfectly fine. I have nothing to show for the beating that Mannie just handed me, except for a couple of bruises and a scar."

"You would prefer to be in a hospital?" asked Mallory, keeping his eyes straight ahead as he drove, only glancing over at me occasionally. "Because you don't look good, I must be honest. It looks like you've lost quite a lot of blood."

"Of course, I don't want to be in a hospital! And yeah, I lost some blood, the guy tried to paint the wall with my skull." I said dryly. "What the hell is going on?"

"Saturday, I am sorry. What happened to you today should not have happened. In fact, too much has happened too fast. Far too fast." said Mallory, cryptically. "There is so much that you need to know and understand, but before that can happen there is still much that you need to see. You must trust me when I tell you that things will become clearer. This is still just your first day on the job after all."

"I was almost killed and then I was almost arrested. That's not a great start!" I said. "They think I'm crazy."

"They won't be the last," said Mallory, and I knew he wasn't joking.

"They had part of it on video." I explained. "I could see them, but they couldn't, even when I pointed them out."

Mallory glanced up into his rearview mirror and I got the feeling he was making sure no one was following us. He didn't look nervous, just an old soldier always on alert.

"I told you; your eyes have been deceiving you, and I meant it." Mallory explained. "Your principal, your teachers, your friends, none of them know what you now know, none can see what you see. Their eyes and their minds have colluded against them to protect them from a harsh reality, that there are monsters walking among us."

"I don't understand, none of this makes any sense. Is Mannie an actual werewolf? That's impossible. How am I able to see these things now? Why couldn't I see them in the first place? What else is out there?" My mind raced and question after question forced itself out of my mouth.

"For the purposes of this discussion let's assume Mannie is a werewolf. You say it is impossible, yet you've seen what he can become. Why do you not believe it?"

"Because... Because werewolves aren't real. They can't be real." I said.

"I see, and why can't they be real?" Mallory asked.

"They just can't. If they were real, I would know, everyone would know. It'd be all over the news and definitely on YouTube."

"What if I told you that it was not just werewolves that were real, but also other creatures from lore, like vampires. Would you believe that vampires also exist?"

"Of course not." I said. "They can't really exist."

"I'm afraid they do, Mr. Shepherd. They exist as surely as you exist. You've not seen them before now because your mind simply wouldn't allow it."

"You said that before, what does that mean?" I asked.

"What would happen, do you think, if everyone truly believed in vampires and werewolves and all of the other creatures that go bump in the night?"

I thought for a moment about Mallory's question. I thought about how I felt when I saw Mannie transform into that creature with claws and fangs like something out of a nightmare. A tremor of fear ran up my spine.

"If everyone knew they were real then everyone would be afraid all the time. We'd be too scared to do anything."

"Yes, that is true. Fear makes humans act irrationally. If

humans truly knew about the dangers that lurked in the night, they would not rest until they had either destroyed the threat entirely or subjugated themselves in fear. So, you see, there is a mutual benefit in keeping the supernatural world obscured from the mortal population." Mallory explained. "A thousand years ago or so, the exact details are lost to time, an order of enchanters – Yes, they also exist- were tasked with creating a powerful bit of magic that would do just that. They created a magic veil that cloaks the supernatural world. This veil protects the mortal mind and allows it to explain away supernatural phenomenon, thus allowing the supernatural world to remain hidden in shadow."

"Wait, so you're telling me that not only do vampires and werewolves exist, but also there is some sort of magic spell that has prevented me from seeing them?" I asked. My brain seemed to be doing somersaults trying to comprehend everything Mallory was throwing at me. "That all sounds insane."

"Yes, I suspected you would say that and rightfully so. It would sound insane, had you not seen it for yourself. And you have seen it, Saturday. You broke through that spell and now you have true Sight. There is a world beyond the mundane, you just haven't been able to perceive it. In the den of The Strays the shroud covering your mind was broken. I am sorry that I was not more forthcoming beforehand, but by your own admission you would not have believed me. You had to see for yourself, like I once did."

My mind was racing. I could feel my pulse quickening. I thought about what I had seen, and I knew the truth in Mallory's words. It was real, all of it. Just as I had felt before, knowing this piece of information was like clicking the final puzzle piece into place. It was like a missing piece of information being revealed that allowed me to understand things I'd never understood before. It felt right. That didn't mean I was unafraid. I was terrified by it, terrified by everything else I didn't know.

"How did you come to be a part of that world? What are you?"

Mallory contemplated the question for a moment before answering. "I'm just like you, Saturday. I was brought into this world, unwillingly, by a vampire."

"So, that means Mannie really is a werewolf?"

"Yes." said Mallory. "But they call themselves 'shifters', not werewolves."

"The surprises just keep coming." I said mirthlessly.

"They will, I'm sorry to tell you, but only at first," said Mallory.

"That's what Mannie said to me, right before he introduced his knee to my face."

"Mannie will be taken care of, but in that regard, he was not lying. Best not to worry about him presently."

"Mallory, what would have happened if I walked into that den without you and witnessed Mannie turn into... whatever it was he turned into?"

"It's complicated, but if a mortal without Sight somehow stumbled into something like that their mind would find a way to rationalize it, like they were seeing a wild animal or having a hallucination. Because of the power and magic in the air the mortal would most likely see things that they would have believed to be impossible and that would be traumatic, but their mind would find a rational way to explain it so that they weren't broken by it. That den, however, and many places where supernaturals gather are protected with runes and magic to prevent humans from wandering in uninvited."

Mallory pulled the car into a parking garage; I sat in the passenger seat having an existential crisis.

"I'm way over my head here."

"If you just trust your instincts, everything will be fine." Mallory said, but I was skeptical.

"Where are we going now?" I asked as Mallory swung the car into a vacant spot.

"We are starting your in processing." said Mallory. "The first step is cleaning you up and outfitting you for your first night on the job. Where we are going tonight, it would be best if you were not covered in blood, dried or otherwise."

Together we walked out of the parking garage and into the sunshine. We walked for a few moments along a relatively busy sidewalk. It was an old part of town, there were no safety canopies denoting new construction and it was not as touristy as most parts of Manhattan, but the buildings looked well kept. Most of the buildings we passed by had aged well. They were old brick buildings with character, not the drab gray and silver and glass you see in new parts of town.

"I'm struggling to wrap my head around this." I said, gawking at people as they passed by me. The implications of this new reality were finally setting in. "Any number of these people could be supernatural?"

"It's possible, and you can just call them supers,'" said Mallory. "But it's highly unlikely. The numbers of supers are as high as they have ever been, but still, they pale in comparison to the number of mortals. It's barely a percentage, and for obvious reasons most supers are nocturnal by nature."

"Still, it's crazy to think about."

Our first stop was a barbershop where Mallory paid for us both to get haircuts and for me to get cleaned up. As the blood was washed from my face and hair it was as if the last remnants of a bad memory were swept away by the warm water. It was refreshing and cathartic. I was pleased with the new haircut as well. The barber shaved down the sides of my dark brown hair and he slicked the top over to the side with some pomade that looked to have been left over from the 1950's. It was different, but I liked it.

After leaving the barbershop we walked for about three blocks until Mallory stopped outside a large brick building which looked much like all the surrounding buildings, except it had a deep crimson paint trim along a white facade. It was a beautiful building with a large glass window. The sign perfectly centered above the window in large black lettering read "Iliescu's, since 1908".

"Here we are," said Mallory.

"Iliescu's? Is that a name?" I asked.

"As far as I am concerned, it's the only name when one is looking for a fine suit." Mallory explained, holding the door open for me to step into the establishment.

Iliescu's was the kind of place that I have seen in magazines and movies, but not the kind of place I could have ever afforded to walk into. The main room was an open space with a beautiful, marbled floor that both showed its age and held its shine. Numerous inviting gray and crimson plush chairs and worn leather wingbacks were positioned around the room. Along the walls were rows and rows of jackets and pants hanging symmetrically and color coordinated. Shirts and ties and other accoutrements were spread out neatly on dark mahogany tables and silver racks.

A middle-aged man of shorter than average height, wearing a fine grey suit greeted us at the door. The man held his hands clasped together in front of him as he strode across the marble floor.

"Mallory Moran. Is good to see you." the man said in a thick accent that sounded eastern European.

"Caius, old friend, how are you?" asked Mallory as the two men embraced.

"Am well, am well." said Caius, in a voice that was raspy and soft, barely above a whisper. "What can I do for you? Your suit seems to be holding up, no?" Caius reached out and adjusted the lapels on Mallory's suit, checking the insides and dusting off the shoulders.

"This visit is not for me I am afraid. Caius, allow me to introduce you to my protégé, Saturday Shepherd. Saturday, this is Caius Iliescu. His family has owned this establishment for over two centuries."

I offered my hand to Caius, who grasped it firmly with both hands. Caius looked over his large black rimmed glasses at me appraisingly, seemingly measuring me with his eyes.

"Saturday, this is an unusual name, no?" asked Caius and I held back the urge to comment that Caius wasn't exactly common, but I didn't think Mallory would appreciate me insulting his friend, so I bit my tongue. Instead, I just faked a laugh and said that I guessed it was unusual.

"Saturday will be starting work tonight and I need him fitted for a suit," said Mallory. "One like mine should suffice, in a color of his choosing, of course." My spirits rose slightly. I didn't often wear suits, but the idea of having a suit from a nice place like this was cool. Although I hoped Mallory wasn't planning on taking this out of my pay, because I had a feeling that would mean no paychecks for a while.

"My treat." Mallory added as if he had read my mind.

"Is good. You come to right place. Follow me, Mr. Shepherd." said Caius, turning and walking to the back of the store. The store itself was empty of customers at the moment, the only other people were a man and a woman who were folding clothes on the counter next to the register. The man, who looked to be a few years older than me, had the same stocky build as Caius as well as similar facial features. I pegged him as a younger relative. He wore a tight dress shirt that displayed more than a few muscles. I've never been one for lifting weights, but I've always been in pretty good shape, I just chalk it up to fast metabolism. The girl looked to be about the same age, but she did not have the same features as the two men. Where Iliescu was shorter with dark hair and features, she was tall and fair with red hair.

"Nicolae, Mira, I will be in the back with Mr. Moran," said Caius. "Continue to work as you are. If someone comes in, have them take seat. I will return soon." Iliescu then said something in a language I didn't understand.

I followed Caius and Mallory to the back of the store and through a heavy wooden door. On the other side of the door was a hallway with dark wooden walls, but the floor was a cold grey slate, instead of polished marble.

Caius flipped a switch on the wall and lights along the ceiling came to life. We passed by another door with a gold plate on it with the word "Arme" etched into it. It was not a word I was familiar with, but I'm not so dense that I couldn't guess it meant "arm" or "arms". Although why a room at a tailor would be labeled "arms" I couldn't imagine. The image of a room filled with detached mannequin arms came into my mind and I suppressed a laugh and a shutter.

"What language is that?" I asked Mallory quietly.

"Romanian." Mallory answered. "Caius is of Romanian descent. His grandfather, Decebal Iliescu came over to America from Bucharest at the end of the 19th century."

"Not Bucharest proper." Caius corrected. "But was close. Is called Pitesti."

"That's cool." I said. "I've never been to Europe, but I would love to go sometime."

Caius stopped at the next door. This door was labeled "Armură". Caius grasped the bronze door handle and pushed it open. Inside was a small hexagonal room with mirrors on four of the walls and the back of the door. The only wall without a mirror was a dark mahogany wood. The floor was a deep crimson carpet with a high pile and attached to two of the mirrored walls were benches for sitting in the same color and material as the wall.

Caius stepped over near the unmirrored wall and motioned for me to join him. Caius placed his hand on the mahogany and when he pulled it away the outline of his palm slowly faded away. As it faded a monitor blinked to life on the wall and a woman's voice said, "Good afternoon, Mr. Iliescu". The monitor displayed those exact same words before displaying a screen with a white background and a green button. "Press here to begin," it read. Caius pressed the button and a menu with many different options was displayed. I was trying to read all the options when I was spun around.

Caius stood in front of me and began taking my measurements. My arms were moved in many different motions and Iliescu used a small device that looked like a laser pointer to get my measurements. Apparently, the tailoring industry had caught up to the digital age.

After some more movements and measurements, Caius seemed satisfied. He punched some numbers into the display.

"What color, Mr. Shepherd?" Caius asked.

"Mallory, what do you think?" I asked.

"It is a matter of preference, but my advice to you is that while navy is en vogue, black is timeless, might I recommend a nice onyx." said Mallory.

Since Mallory was buying, I thought it best to take his advice.

"That sounds great."

"A fine choice." said Caius and he punched some more buttons on the display. Once he finished the display blinked out and once again appeared to be a normal wall. I could hear a humming noise coming from the other side of the wall that lasted just a moment and then to my surprise the wall slid open revealing a chamber about the size of a small closet. Inside of the chamber was a plain black suit. Caius reached in and removed the suit from its hanger and held it out for us to admire. It was a beautiful shade of onyx with a slight shine along the lapel. "This, Mr. Shepherd, is classic. Will never go out of style."

"I love it." I said, breathlessly, "I've never owned anything this nice before."

"Caius and his family are master craftsmen. They have no equal. Please, Caius, tell Saturday about his new suit." said Mallory.

"You are too kind." said Caius. "Mr. Shepherd what you have is called a British cut with notched lapels. Is no as trendy as Italian or as boxy as an American cut. Is a good fit to be sure. Feel now the suit in your hands. Merino wool is good fabric."

I took the suit jacket and ran my hands along the exterior for a moment and then handed it back to Caius who opened it up so I could see the lining. It was a charcoal black lining with numerous pockets.

"This is important part of the suit. You see this?" said Caius, pointing to the interior fabric. "This is a blend of silk Crepe de Chine and Spectra, carefully hand woven together."

I admired the texture of the interior fabric. It was smooth to the touch, but it felt more solid than it looked.

"While you are wearing one of Iliescu's pieces you will have some manner of protection. Think of this jacket as high society body armor." Mallory explained. "It will not make you invincible, but it will offer you some protection against blades and bullets and it will buy you some time, and that time could be the difference between life and death."

"That's... important." I said.

I tried on the jacket and the rest of the suit, and it was a perfect fit. When we returned to the main showroom Caius gathered up a few other things that I would need, like a dress shirt, socks, shoes, and other miscellaneous items. Caius typed it all up on an archaic machine that looked like something closer to an abacus than an actual register. Apparently, the high-tech devices were exclusive to the catacombs of Iliescu's place. I had no desire to look at the total price, so I just stood by silently holding the bag with my things in it while Mallory produced a card and paid for it all.

Once we were back in Mallory's car, I tried to get a better handle on what I should expect this evening.

"Are we going to some kind of party tonight?"

Mallory seemed to give it some thought before answering. "Something like that." he said, finally. "I think you will enjoy yourself, but it is very important that you keep your wits about you and practice proper etiquette."

"What kind of etiquette?" I asked. "Like, don't talk with my mouth full? Use a salad fork for salad and dinner fork for dinner?"

"Nothing like that at all, although both would be appropriate. Rest assured that I will give you the full run down tonight. For now, I will be dropping you off at home, where I am sure that your grandparents are eager to see you" He reached over and handed a small business card to me. Printed on the small index card was a phone number and a name. "At 8:00 PM I want you to call the number on this card. Hunter will come pick you up and drop you off where I will be waiting. Be sure and wear your new suit."

"Is Hunter a friend of yours?" I asked.

"Something like that."

Mallory pulled up outside of my grandparents and I collected my things.

"One more thing, Saturday," said Mallory. "Try and get some rest. It will help you recover from today and it could be a long night."

"Will do." I said, stepping into the house.

NINE

Dragging myself up to my bedroom I crashed down onto the bed. Complete exhaustion made sure I was asleep in moments. Apparently taking a beating and then performing a miraculous healing takes quite a toll on your body.

When I finally woke up a few hours later, I joined my grandparents for a quick dinner. Thankfully neither of them mentioned the call they received from my principal, and I certainly wasn't going to bring it up. As far as I was concerned, it would be fine if no one ever mentioned it again.

When I was back in my room, I decided to text Maria. I pretended like I just wanted to make sure we were still on to hang out tomorrow night, but also, I wanted to feel her out and see if she heard about my run in with Mannie. I waited nervously until 8 PM hoping to get a response, but she never texted back.

Before dialing the number Mallory had given me, I took a few moments to make sure I had everything I might need that night. Just as I was lifting my phone to dial it chimed to indicate a new text message. Unlocking my phone quickly I hoped to see it was from Maria, but instead the notification was from Wes.

>Wes
>Yo, dude. What happened today?

I cringed at seeing the question that I was dreading. I knew how crazy it was to think my little incident would go unnoticed. Freshman year one of the guys in my class, Chad, got busted for making up a fake girlfriend. People still gave him shit about it. Surely getting your ass kicked by an invisible werewolf on school grounds was at least as noteworthy as a fake girlfriend.

>Saturday
>Hey man. Had to bounce early.

I was trying to feel him out and see what he knew before I admitted to anything. My grandma didn't raise a fool.

>Wes
>People are saying you flipped out. You bust up the Chem lab? Everyone is talking about it.

Nausea. Immediate nausea. My first reaction was that my life was over. I would have to just change schools. I clung to the hope that people would forget about it over the summer, I prayed that would be enough time. I didn't want to talk about it, but I also didn't want to lie to my friends. Wes deserved a response, an answer that was as truthful as I could give, but I didn't want to do that over text. If I texted my friends the God's honest truth, they would have me locked away in a mental institution, and I wouldn't blame them.

>Saturday
>It's complicated. I'll explain later.

>Wes
>Whatever, man. See u later.

Phone still in hand, I punched in the digits to the number that Mallory gave me. Someone answered on the third ring. It was a girl.

"This is Hunter." she said, energetically.

"Hey, Mallory told me to call you. This is Saturday."

"Actually, no, it's Friday." said Hunter.

"Sorry, I mean my name is Saturday." I explained, more out of habit than anything else.

There were a few moments of silence on the phone and just as I was about to ask if she was still there, she spoke up.

"I know, man. I'm just messing with you." she said "Mallory told me about you. I'm giving you a ride to Sanctuary."

"I'll be honest, I have no idea what you're talking about, but yeah Mallory said you could give me a ride to meet him." I explained. "Do you need my address?" There was a slight pause.

"Nah I don't need your address. I'm actually parked out front right now." she said.

"Oh. Seriously?" I hesitated for a moment. "Alright, I'll be right out."

I gave one last look around the room to make sure I wasn't forgetting anything before pocketing my phone. I kicked myself for not thinking about trying to find some silver before now. Mallory probably had some that I could borrow, but I would seriously need to invest heavily in the metal going forward, if I hoped to avoid another beating.

The sun had long since set and the dark street was lit by intermittent streetlights and the porch lights of neighboring houses. The homes all down the block were peppered with lit windows where families milled about or sat stoically in front of their televisions. An unfamiliar vehicle sat in the driveway; the beams of the lights prevented me from seeing inside. It was a small black SUV that looked pristine except the front driver's side tire was missing a hubcap. I approached the vehicle apprehensively. The driver's window was rolled down, and a girl about my age stuck her head out of the window. She had mocha colored skin and close-cropped dark hair. She gave a big friendly smile.

"You called for a cab?" she asked cheerfully.

"Are you some kind of supernatural rideshare?" I asked.

She laughed a lot harder than I felt the joke deserved. "Oh man. That's a good one." she said after composing herself. "And yes, right now that's exactly what I am. You ready?"

"Yeah, I think so." I said. "Where are you taking me?"

She leaned further out of the window and beckoned me closer. I leaned in close so she could put her lips up to my ear and she whispered where only I could hear. "To Hell."

I drew my head back, goosebumps popped up all over my arms. "Where?" I asked, my voice unintentionally cracking.

She stared at me blankly for a moment and then the same wide smile cracked across her face. "Dude, I'm just messing with you again, you're too easy. Lighten up and hop in, I'm taking you to Mallory, who's not in Hell, I promise."

Ducking my head to hide my embarrassment, I walked in front of her car and slid into the passenger seat. Hunter was short and she had the seat pulled up close to the steering wheel. I studied her from the side. She was wearing a black tank top, which exposed her surprisingly toned arms, and her shirt had the words "I hit like a girl" printed on it in pink lettering. Hunter shifted the car into reverse and backed out of the driveway. A bright yellow smiley face emoji air freshener that was hanging from her rear-view mirror danced around in the air as she maneuvered down the street.

I peered nonchalantly into the backseat of the vehicle when I came face to face with a large pair of eyes and a gigantic open maw. I pulled my head back quickly out of fear, but the powerful canine teeth came after me. Hot breath and saliva misted the side of my face. I threw my hands up defensively, waiting for the beast to bite down, waiting for the pain when suddenly a warm wet tongue began to lap at my face and mouth.

"Holmes! Holmes, no!" Hunter said sternly as she used her right arm to force the dog off me and into the backseat. My face was covered in dog drool. I resisted the urge to wipe it away with my sleeve, seeing as how I was in my new suit and all, and settled for using my hands. The enormous black dog was now sitting on his hindquarters in the backseat, staring at me playfully. "Sorry about that. He wasn't trying to eat you, I promise. I fed him before we left."

"Is that... Is that a dog?" I asked, taking deep breaths trying to avoid a heart attack.

"Yes, he is a dog. You've seen a dog before, right?" she asked slowly, implying that she might think I was an idiot.

"Of course, I've seen a dog before, but I mean is he a real dog?"

"Well, he's been a dog as long as I've known him. So, if he's a shifter, he's a really lazy one." she said.

"Ok... cool." I relaxed a bit and leaned back in the seat. My heart was still beating rapidly, and I positioned myself to keep the dog in my peripheral vision, just in case. "I just haven't had good experiences with people who can turn into things. Just wanted to be sure."

"Don't blame you one bit. The Strays broke into your school and beat the hell out of you. I'd be jumpy too." Hunter said.

"You heard about that?"

She tilted her head towards me and flashed some serious side eye. "There isn't much that goes on in this world of ours that stays a secret for long." she must have seen me squirm in my seat because she added, "Relax, dude. Mallory filled me in on the details. He asked me to come by and watch your place in case one of those fur balls decided to show up and finish the job."

Um, what? So, Mallory thought there was a chance they might come to my house to kill me. A heads up would have been cool. And nothing against Hunter, all five-foot-nothing of her, but she looked like she weighed maybe a hundred pounds, tops. This was the protection Mallory sent for me. It was almost funny to think about. I didn't have much faith in Hunter being any help if we ran into Mannie and his friends.

"No offense, but you don't look like much of a bodyguard." I said.

"That's good." she said. "I hope to keep it that way. Now, listen up, pretty boy. If you ever come face to face with one of those mutts again, here's what you need to know.

You'll never out muscle a shifter, won't happen. You have to outsmart them, which isn't all that difficult because they think with their biceps."

"What would you have done if you'd been in my situation?" I asked.

She seemed to mull over the question for a moment. "First, I never would've walked into that den. Mallory is too brave for his own good. Secondly, the only thing more dangerous than a pissed-off shifter is a pissed-off shifter with wounded pride. I never would've left Mannie alive."

"Ok, but I mean at school, face to face with him, what could I have done to get away?"

"Hell, I don't know. Throw some protein powder and a shake weight at him and hope it distracts him long enough to get away."

The dog, Holmes, lay with his massive body sprawled out across the backseat. When I glanced back at him, he lifted his head up off his paws and gave a vigorous shake sending globs of drool all over the back of my seat. "Are you sure that's a dog, and not a horse?"

Hunter glanced up in the rearview mirror and back at the dog, Holmes, who sat back up inquisitively. "What do you think, Holmes? Dog or horse?" she asked. Holmes opened his mouth wide to reveal large, yellowed teeth and his long pink tongue stretched lazily out of his mouth in a big yawn. "I think he's bored with you now."

"What kind of name is Holmes for a dog anyway?" I asked.

"I don't know, what kind of name is Saturday for a human?" she retorted.

"Ouch. That's fair." I said. "Point to Hunter. So, on the phone you mentioned a sanctuary. Are we meeting Mallory at a church or something?"

"Not a sanctuary, the Sanctuary." she explained.

"What's the difference?"

"Well, for starters one's a proper noun. The Sanctuary

is a place, actually it's more of an event."

"Like a club or something?"

"The Sanctuary is a monthly event where supers get together and hang out and it's never held in the same place two months in a row." she paused, making sure I was following along. "It's called the Sanctuary because supers, supernaturals, whatever, traveling to and from the Sanctuary are protected and they are also protected while there."

"I'm confused." I admitted. "Who do they need protection from? And who protects them?" I found it difficult to imagine the guys from the Strays needing protection from anything.

She looked at me like upperclassmen typically look at Freshmen when they asked dumb questions. A look I'd received many times over the years. "They're protected by the Law, and from each other." she said, matter-of-factly.

"Do the shifters need protection from the vampires? Or is it the other way around?"

"Mallory hasn't explained any of this to you?" she asked, disbelievingly.

"It's all new to me."

"Wow. Alright then. Let me think about where to even begin." she said, taking a deep breath. "For the longest time there was just outright war among supers. Shifters and vamps fought each other and their own kind for territory and dominance. It came to a boil several decades ago when these warring factions of supers caused so much destruction that humans were starting to notice. A powerful vamp and his followers led a push to establish a cease fire among the groups. They knew that if enough humans were to discover the truth it would destroy the shroud which would have game over for everybody. At least that's how they pitched it. Salvatore De La Cruz and his protege Anton Moretti, both vamps, were ultimately able to bring representatives from all the factions together to create the New York Accords."

Hunter peered over at me to make sure I was following

along. I nodded my head.

"De la Cruz was old and powerful, while Moretti was young and cunning, and they were both ruthless. The Accords benefited the vamps more than anyone else, for sure, but it was seen by everyone as a step in the right direction. The Accords established laws by which all supers who wished to live in the area must abide. One of the most important things it established was the concept of Sanctuary, where once a month anyone who wanted could gather in a safe space to socialize and air grievances to a ruling council." she paused and must have seen the question hanging on my lips. "The Council is a small group of representatives from the three different factions. Vampires, shifters, and arcanists."

"How do they get those positions? Are they elected?" I asked.

"No, they're not elected. Supers very much abide by a plutocracy. Wealth and power are the only things that mean anything at all here. If you know nothing else, you should know that."

"Got it." I said. "What else? This is great!"

"Dude, temper that enthusiasm. You may think it's 'great', but you have no idea the shitstorm you're walking into. You are about to be in a room full of some of the most powerful creatures on Earth." said Hunter. "Things aren't all gravy just because of some document. A lot of supers would like to see the Accords done away with completely."

"Why? I thought you said it was a good deal for everyone."

"Sure, for many it's a good deal and it keeps things a lot calmer around here than it used to be, or so I hear, but there are many who want the chaos and anonymity of the time before the Accords. Some of them will be at Sanctuary tonight, but no one will dare to speak against it in public, only in whispers in dark places are such things talked about. The Council would quickly destroy any dissenters. There's no doubt about that."

I thought back to some of the stories I'd heard about in history class. It was completely unbelievable that a secret government had been controlling an entire city's worth of supernatural creatures all this time and I had never heard about it before today. *Wait, is this what the Illuminati is?* "De La Cruz and Moretti, are they still in charge? Like, as the heads of the Council or something?"

"Salvatore De La Cruz remains the most powerful vamp in the city, everyone essentially bends knee to him, willingly or otherwise. As for Moretti, he was killed shortly after the Accords were ratified."

"Who killed him?" I asked.

"No one knows, or at least no one has admitted to it. De La Cruz put a huge bounty on the head of whoever did it. A few out-of-towners and known assassins were questioned and some were killed in pursuit of the truth. It's commonly believed that whoever did it was killed, but I don't buy it. I wasn't around back then, but things don't add up for me, so in my mind it remains a mystery. Word is that De La Cruz is still secretly obsessed with finding Moretti's killer."

"Even though it was almost twenty years ago?"

"Twenty years is nothing to a vampire, that's like a long nap to someone as old as De la Cruz." she said.

"Thanks for answering my questions. Seriously, it's weird being so clueless."

"It's important that you know. Jake knew all of this, and it still wasn't enough to save him." said Hunter and I heard a slight catch in her voice. "But maybe it will save you one day."

"Who's Jake?" I asked.

"He was a friend." she said after sitting silently for a few moments. I took her words to imply that they were more than friends.

"I'm sorry." I said, and she gave herself a shake before punching me hard on the arm. "What was that about?!"

"Toughen up. You can't afford to be soft, especially

tonight. Weakness is like blood in the water to these people. If they get a whiff of it, they will sweep you up in one of their schemes, and that won't end well for you. Listen, the most important thing I can tell you, never let them catch you alone, and don't trust anyone."

I rubbed my arm where she hit me, trying to stifle the ache. When she looked over at me, I moved my hand away and tried to look like I wasn't in pain. The vehicle slowed and Hunter pulled up next to a small valet stand outside of a building with a coffee shop on the ground floor. We stepped out of the vehicle and a young valet handed her a ticket and started to get into the driver's seat. The valet jumped back out quickly with a shout, and I had a pretty good idea what startled him. "Hey! There's a dog in here!" the valet yelled at Hunter.

"His name is Holmes." she said.

"Whatever his name is, I can't take a car with a dog in it." the valet said.

"Just leave it running," said Hunter, turning to walk into the coffee shop.

From my limited experience, coffee shops come in two different varieties, they're either artsy and hipster or modern and sterile. This shop, called The Perk, was a form of the latter. It resided on the ground level of an over-priced residential building in Midtown Manhattan. When you first entered the glass facade of The Perk you were greeted by a steel railing denoting the line to order. While you waited in line you could view the large board with all their offerings on it. They served espressos, specialty lattes, expensive exotic coffees, and everything in between. You could peruse an assortment of many different magazines and newspapers as well as a moderate selection of fruits and bottled beverages all available for purchase.

Hunter and I bypassed the line entirely and stepped into the seating area, which looked straight out of an IKEA showroom, all modern and manufactured. Plastic chairs in all manner of bright colors, like yellow and orange sat up against whitewashed tables and black wooden benches. Mallory sat in the corner of the room in a black wooden booth reading a newspaper. He looked up as we approached.

"Here you go, one intern delivered safe, and sound as requested," said Hunter.

"Thank you, Hunter." said Mallory as he stood to greet us. "You are the best in the business."

"Not until you die, old man." said Hunter with a smile. "And unless there is anything else, I'll be going."

"Are you going to be at the Sanctuary?" I asked her.

"Nah, that's not my scene." she said. "But I'm sure I'll see you around. I better run before Holmes eats that guy." She turned on the spot and walked back toward the door. I noted the way that she carried herself made her seem much taller than she was. There was a confidence and fluidity in her movements that was captivating in a way.

"She's a good egg, that one." said Mallory.

"Yeah, she seems cool. I like her."

Mallory smiled. "Would you like some coffee?"

"No thanks. I'm not a big coffee drinker."

"Alright then, let's sit for a moment. Sanctuary is not far from here." said Mallory and I sat down in the seat across from him. "Did Hunter answer some of your questions?"

"Yeah, she did, but the more I learn the more questions I have." I said and Mallory laughed.

"That's good. An inquisitive mind and desire for answers will serve you well in this position." said Mallory.

"Hunter mentioned someone by the name of Jake. A friend of hers. Did you know him?" Mallory's face seemed to contort slightly at the mention of Jake's name.

"I did know Jake, and he and Hunter were very close. Did she mention anything else about him?"

"Just that he had died."

Mallory closed his eyes and nodded. "Yes, I am afraid that he did."

"How?" I asked.

"That is another story for another time. I believe that it is time that we embark to our destination." said Mallory.

"I understand." I said, having a distinct feeling that Mallory was ducking the question for some reason. "What are we going to do at Sanctuary?"

Mallory took a long drink from his coffee cup and when he returned it to the table it was empty save for a few remaining grounds. "We are going to do one of the most important things that we do in this line of work. Observe. Now let's get to it." said Mallory, standing up and swinging his arms into his suit jacket. On our way out of the door Mallory deposited his newspaper into the recycling bin and placed his coffee cup in the appropriate area. Together we exited the glass doors of The Perk and stepped out onto the concrete sidewalks of Manhattan.

TEN

Midtown was abuzz. The noise coming from the mass of people gathered only a few blocks away at Times Square carried undeterred through the skyscrapers and alleyways. We walked for a few minutes down the busy sidewalks and passed by numerous carts selling street meats, and tables where people peddled everything from postcards to phone chargers. It wasn't until Mallory pointed across the street to a large theatre set just off Broadway that I knew where we were headed. It was immediately clear that this theatre was our destination. While we were only a few blocks away from Central Park and it was not uncommon to see limousines in this part of town, the long line of them leading down the avenue was startling. Outside of the theatre security had set up a perimeter to keep tourists and gawkers from getting too close to the entrance.

As we made our way through the crowd and approached the front, one of the massive guards lifted his clipboard and marked it with his ink pen. Mallory gave the man a familiar smile.

"Moran." the large bald man acknowledged with a nod of his head. "Who's the kid?"

"Evening, Walsh." said Mallory, warmly. "This is Saturday Shepherd, my protege."

Walsh dropped his clipboard to his side and sized me up. I tried to lift my shoulders and stand up straight, but it didn't seem to impress.

"Finally taking on a new one, huh?" Walsh asked.

Mallory seemed to brush off the question. "Time and tide wait for no man." he said as he walked across the entryway and into the building proper.

I followed closely after him. Once inside we emptied our pockets and walked single file through a large metal detector. Once the security guard was satisfied that we were not carrying any weapons we were allowed to collect our belongings and step into the foyer.

The foyer opened into a wide room that seemed to circle the entire building, much like the walkways at Yankee stadium, except that it was all indoors. There were numerous doors that led into the central circular ballroom where it appeared that the Sanctuary was taking place. This first room was filled with what Mallory described as handlers and assistants, as well as some less important supernaturals or mortals. There were a few servers walking among the groups of people holding trays of drinks and appetizers, and for the most part everyone was dressed up. One of the servers came close enough that I could make out, with a shudder, bite marks on her neck.

Aside from the drinking of blood, Sanctuary reminded me a lot like a fancy party or fundraiser, or prom. Not at all like what I'd been expecting. Mallory led us through the crowd that was gathered near the front entrance and to the nearest door that led into the main circular ballroom. It was a double door with a metal pole running down the middle. Mallory pushed open the door and a loud roar of conversation hit me like a brick. It was the mixture of a hundred different conversations in a room built for its acoustics that caused the sound to carry like it did. All the noise seemed to converge together into an almost hypnotic chant.

"Holy..."

"Indeed." Mallory finished. "It can be quite a spectacle your first time."

My mouth was agape as Mallory led us to an empty table off to the side of the room and away from most of the crowd. "I need you to focus for a moment. While this place may appear to be glamorous it is just as dangerous as the Stray's den, in fact it is far more dangerous. Everyone here can manipulate and destroy you and most of them would lose no sleep over it. It is important that you stay close and just observe. Silently. Can you do that?"

I forced my attention back to Mallory and not on all the glitz and glamour that surrounded me. It was like something straight out of a movie. Occasionally someone so unnaturally beautiful would walk by it was unnerving. I had a good idea of what Mallory had just said so I nodded an affirmative and he seemed to accept this as an understanding.

The ballroom was circular, and the high ceilings were curved in the shape of a dome, it was like a large planetarium without all the equipment. Tables were set up on one side of a solid black rectangular dais in the middle of the room. On the dais were three large throne-like chairs where, I assumed, the Council would sit. For now, they were empty, but the sight of them was intimidating.

People milled about in small groups, large groups, or by themselves behind the dais in the open area or around the tables. Dozens of servers dressed in fine clothing passed by carrying trays of drinks of different colors as well as an assortment of hors d'oeuvres, only some of which I even recognized. Because I was sure that at least one of the items on the tray would be caviar I decided to abstain completely from eating anything I didn't recognize. I had no desire to eat fish eggs and in my estimation whatever else was on those trays was not worth the risk.

"Is this all of the supers in the city?" I asked Mallory.

"No, many of them are here, but not everyone attends Sanctuary," he said. "Most do not want to miss the event. In this world information and power are everything and Sanctuary is the best place to try and gather both."

"Hunter said some people don't like the Accords, is that true?"

Mallory hesitated and looked around for a minute before answering. "It is true that some view the Accords as nothing more than a power grab for the vampires, however there are some vampires who oppose them as fervently as anyone. Even still, few oppose it openly as I am sure that Hunter acknowledged."

Out of the corner of my eye I noticed a large man approaching and Mallory turned to greet him. The man was wearing blue jeans and a button-down shirt with a navy-blue blazer to give his outfit a more formal look. It was evident that this was not the type of man who normally wore blazers. He looked to be in his forties and his weathered face had the graying stubble of a day-old beard. Everything about the man was solid, and rugged.

"Mallory." the man said shortly. I pegged him for a man of few words and the pink skin around his knuckles said that he was also a man that talked with his fists.

"Briggs." Mallory acknowledged and held out his hand. Briggs extended his right arm, and the two men shook hands.

"Who's the kid?" Briggs asked and I made a mental note to track down a nametag somewhere.

"Charlie Briggs, this is Saturday Shepherd." Briggs held out his massive hand and I shook it. Briggs squeezed so hard I thought my hand was going to break. It wasn't clear to me who or what this guy was, but I was putting my money on half man, half rhinoceros.

"Hey kid," said Briggs. "Mallory, can I have a word in private?"

Mallory looked at me before answering. "Sure, but Saturday, stay close."

I assured him that I would. The two men walked together out of earshot, and I honestly had no desire to try and hear their conversation. I was about 97% certain that I wouldn't have understood it anyway, so I just stood there, taking it all in. It was impossible not to be awed by the glitz and glamour all around me. This was not the type of event a kid from my neighborhood attended.

I tried to see if I could identify the types of supernaturals that were around me. There were small groups of imposing men and women that stuck together in huddled circles. I assumed that those were the werewolves, or shifters and I made a mental note to avoid them at all costs. There were probably around twenty or thirty of them that I could see.

Dozens of individuals around me had unnaturally pale skin, a paleness that only comes from years without sunlight. These had to be vampires. A shiver ran up my spine at the thought and standing there without Mallory I couldn't help but feel exposed. All told there were probably close to a hundred of them in the room and they came in all shapes and sizes, which made sense considering they had all once been normal humans. Some of the vampires were dressed in styles that were popular in past decades, while others wore much more current fashions. The only consistent feature was the unhealthy paleness of their skin that was missing the pink blush of life. Many of them appeared to have used makeup to try and add color to their faces, and some of them had gone the other direction with it and added powder to embrace their white skin. There was a grace to the movements of the vampires, as if even the most mundane action was a part of a dance. There was a certain blasé attitude in their actions, a carelessness that can only come from someone assured of their place atop the food chain.

People were moving all around me, and it became difficult to focus on anyone. Servers walked in and out of my vision carrying trays of unrecognizable foods and sparkling drinks. I looked around, suddenly aware that I was alone. The crowd around me had swept me up like a river and Mallory was now out of sight. I cursed myself for being such an idiot and searched frantically for something familiar. Someone familiar. That's when I noticed I was being watched. It was as if the crowd parted around her and she filled my vision from where she sat across the room, alone. She was my age with wavy black hair that fell in strands upon her shoulders, she had a pale complexion, and her eyes were the color of ice. Her lips were as red as blood. She lifted her hand, her fingertips were entwined in the black lace of her dress, and she beckoned to me.

Effortlessly I walked toward her, my eyes unwavering as the crowd seemed to part around me. When I reached her, she brought her long black fingernail to her lips and a tremor ran up my spine.

"Aren't you adorable? I could just eat you up." she said with a wicked smile. "What's your name?"

I had to work moisture back into my mouth before I could answer. "Sa...Saturday. My name is Saturday." I said, finally.

"Saturday." she purred. "Such a lovely name." The way she said it, I almost believed it. She reached towards me and grasped my hand with hers. Her fingers were cold to the touch, but sparks ran up my arm, nonetheless. "Would you sit and talk with me for a while Saturday? These things can be oh so boring."

"I should probably get back to my friend, I'm sure he's looking for me." I said, but I had no desire to leave her side.

"We'll find your friend together once we're done talking." she said, and while all the alarms in my head were going off telling me to get the hell out of there, I couldn't. There was something about her eyes that made it very difficult to pull away. "My name is Irene. Irene Cross." There was lavishness in her voice as she pronounced each syllable perfectly. Her words were saccharine that made my mind go fuzzy. When she drew herself closer to me, I knew I needed to run away, but I couldn't. Instead, I sat down beside her.

"Do you know Mallory Moran?" I asked her.

"Oh, Mallory? That's your friend? Of course, I know Mallory, darling, he's a friend of mine as well." She smiled. "The stories I could tell you about Mallory. He was not always the gallant white knight he purports to be. Trust me." Irene still held my hand in hers and she gently pulled me even closer. Her perfume overwhelmed my senses. Underneath the artificial smell was a corruption that couldn't be masked. Not this close.

Irene peered deeply into my eyes. I recognized immediately that I'd made a mistake. Irene was not my age, not even close. Sure, she looked like she could be in college maybe, but she wasn't, she was older, much older. Everything about Irene was youthful and beautiful, except for her eyes. There was something unnatural about her eyes. It was as if an old woman was staring out of a youthful veil and those eyes seemed to cut through me and into my soul. Irene's lips parted slowly, and she spoke playfully.

"Saturday." When she said my name the hairs on the back of my neck stood up instantly. "Tell me everything about you."

"I'm not that interesting, to be honest, I would hate to bore you." I said and she laughed as if it were a hilarious joke. Irene smiled slyly as if she thought I was holding something back from her.

"Oh, you are anything but boring, my dear. In fact, I think you seem positively delicious. Your heritage, hmmm... Puerto Rican, unless I'm mistaken. It's been days since I have tasted that particular vintage." she said.

"Well, I'm only half, my father was-"

"Oh, a fusion. How wonderful." Irene said, cutting me off. "Come now, Saturday, don't play coy with me." she said this playfully, but there was no mistaking the threat in her words. She slid herself closer to me until her face was only inches away from mine, and her eyes, like round orbs of ice, were locked onto me.

How could I have thought even for a moment that they were anything but beautiful? "Who are you?" she asked again. The sweetness of her voice was so calming, and I could feel my fear fading away. It was silly, I realized, to not be upfront and honest with Irene. There was no reason I shouldn't tell her everything about me. She seemed pleasant enough and who I was is inconsequential anyway really.

"Irene, leave the boy alone." Mallory's voice snapped me out of my daze, and I glanced over Irene's shoulder where Mallory was standing. A sneer flashed across Irene's face, but it did not linger there for more than a moment before she was once again serene and happy.

"Mallory, there you are, your friend here was lost, and we were just about to come find you." She lied.

"I am sure that you were," said Mallory. "Luckily, I have found you both so there is no need for you to trouble yourself. Come along, Saturday."

I started to stand when Irene leaned in and whispered, "To be continued." She kissed me on the cheek. I shuffled over towards Mallory, my head felt fuzzy, and my cheeks felt like they were on fire. When I looked back to Irene, she was leaning forward in her chair applying a fresh coat of lipstick with a compact mirror, no longer paying attention to anything else.

Together we walked back over to the edge of the room. I waited for Mallory to explode and yell at me for disobeying him, but he did not say a word, only tapped his finger on his own cheek, motioning for me to wipe my hand across my own face. When I looked down at my hand it had vibrant red lipstick smeared across it.

"Did I get it all?" I asked.

"You got enough of it."

Just as I was about to ask him what he meant by that; a loud noise interrupted me. It was the sound of something hard clanging against stone or metal. It reverberated throughout the room in quick succession like a pulse, causing all the conversations in the room to cease until the only sound remaining were the echoes of the pulse. Silence hung in the air for a moment.

Standing on the dais in front of the throne-like chairs was a tall and lean middle-aged man wearing a black tuxedo with a white dress shirt and black bowtie. In his left hand was a long black cane with a silver spike on the end, and he leaned ever so slightly onto it. Once the room was completely silent the man addressed the crowd.

"Good evening and welcome to Sanctuary. "As he spoke, he turned his head slightly to connect with the audience, and I noticed a mark or a tattoo that ran from the side of the man's shaven head down his collar. It looked like a snake, but I could not make out all the details clearly. "All rise for the arrival of the Council." Only a handful of people were still seated, but they all stood up at his request, albeit some of them did so a little slower than others.

Mallory stood next to me facing the dais watching the ceremony begin. When Mallory spoke, it was low enough so only I could hear. "I considered Jake a friend as well. He and Hunter formed a deep bond, but they met while Jake was interning with me." Mallory said, directing me to keep my attention on the dais. "You won't want to miss this."

Across the room I could see the crowd part as an exterior door opened. A few people entered and formed a line leading to the dais. "Welcome, Lady Abigail Black, Enchantress of the Emerald Circle, Patron of the Shroud, Voice of the Arcane." the man on the stage continued. A smattering of applause broke out across the room as a woman was ushered through the door and down the line to the stage. She was tall and regal in a long dark green dress that trailed along the floor behind her as she walked. Her raven black hair fell down her back in a long single braid and the sides of her head were clean shaven. As she approached the stage the tattooed man offered her his hand, which she accepted, and gracefully she ascended the stairs. She was young, much younger than I expected someone in her position to be. As she took her place in front of one of the thrones the applause slowly died down.

"Jake worked with me on some of my investigations. I was involved in a particularly nasty one, in which a group of humans were being ritualistically slaughtered by a super and some very powerful figures cropped up on my suspects list." Mallory continued.

"Welcome, Michael Longfang, Alpha of the East River Pack, Master of the Silver Scepter, Voice of the Moon Children." The applause picked back up and a giant of a man entered through the open door, ducking his head as he did so. Longfang was wearing black dress pants with a white button-up shirt that was so tight that you could see every muscle on his immense upper body, and his dreaded hair was pulled tight in a bun that stood up on the back of his head. Several other shifters entered behind him and dispersed into the crowd as their leader mounted the dais in a single step and stood in front of one of the thrones.

"Someone knew I was getting close to solving the case and they tried to scare me away. They captured Jake and they killed him. They placed his body where I would find it, with a message clearly meant for me, explaining that he had been killed because of my work and that more bodies would pile up if I continued." said Mallory.

"Welcome, Salvatore De La Cruz, Sovereign of the Five Boroughs, The Eldest, and Voice of the Blooded."

I craned my neck to get a good look at De La Cruz, since it was a name I'd heard before, thanks to Hunter. De La Cruz was tall and lean, and he looked to be of Spanish descent with short black hair and a neatly trimmed beard. The vampire walked with a certain haughtiness to his step, stopping occasionally on the short walk to the dais to shake hands with certain individuals, one of them I recognized as Briggs. De La Cruz was wearing a very expensive looking suit, as did the men who flanked him on the walk toward the dais. Once De La Cruz took his spot on the stage, the man doing the introductions addressed the crowd once more. "I give you, your Council." he made a motion with his arms like an unveiling of a gift. Just about everyone in the sanctuary applauded the Council as the announcer left the stage.

"Call it cowardice, or call it something else, but I let fear sway me. I failed the humans who had been butchered. I failed Jake. Their killer was never brought to justice, though in my heart I know who was responsible. Maybe I knew from the beginning. I just can't prove it."

I was struggling to process what Mallory was saying and I couldn't understand why he was telling me now. I turned from the dais as the Council took their seats and I looked at him questioningly. The applause began to wane.

"Salvatore De La Cruz." finished Mallory, and I drew in a sharp breath.

ELEVEN

The shifter, Michael Longfang, stood and addressed the crowd.

"Welcome all, to Sanctuary. We will begin immediately and open the floor to your concerns or grievances. As always, you are reminded to maintain proper decorum and not speak out of turn."

Longfang took his seat and the room fell completely silent for a moment before a small man wearing a long black robe with red rings running the lengths of the sleeves approached the dais. The robed man was middle-aged, with long gray hair that was now only growing out of the sides of his head.

"The Council recognizes Philip Howe, Enchanter of the Crimson Circle." said Abigail Black.

"Thank you, Lady Black." said Howe as he gave a sweeping bow to the Council members. "Mr. De La Cruz, Mr. Longfang, I come before you today with a territorial dispute."

"We are prepared to hear your dispute. Continue." said De la Cruz in a silky-smooth voice with the slightest hint of a Spanish accent.

"Thank you." The enchanter began. "The Crimson Circle requires access to Hell's Kitchen Park. We believe that a powerful ley line runs through this area, and we would like to study it."

"Have you spoken with the owner of the territory surrounding the Park?" asked Longfang. "I believe it to be Charlie Briggs."

Howe nodded his head. "I have, and regretfully we have been unable to come to an accord with Mr. Briggs, who has thus far been unwilling to allow us even temporary access to his territory."

"Mr. Briggs, would you please come forward?" asked Abigail Black.

Briggs, the large man that Mallory had been speaking with earlier, stood up and walked to the front of the dais, stopping to stand next to Phillip Howe, who he dwarfed in comparison.

"The Council recognizes Charlie Briggs, vampire." announced Abigail Black. "Mr. Briggs, would you be willing to allow the Crimson Circle temporary access to your territory?"

"No." said Briggs, simply. The large vampire folded his arms and appeared bored by the whole situation.

"Mr. Briggs, I appreciate your position, but in the interest of cooperation I would ask that you reconsider. I am sure that the Crimson Circle is willing to make certain concessions in return. Am I correct in that assumption, Enchanter Howe?" said Abigail.

"Of course, Lady Black." said Howe. "We are prepared to offer a favor to Mr. Briggs from the entire Circle, as well as a personal favor from me."

Lady Black nodded her head. "Thank you. As you can see, Mr. Briggs, these are no small concessions. Surely, they are enough to warrant temporary access to a small portion of your substantial territory."

"No." said Briggs, again.

Lady Black held up her hands in exasperation, and turned back to her chair, black robes twirling around her as she moved. Longfang stood up to replace her, and I heard the faint creaking of the dais under the man's considerable mass. Even toe to toe Longfang would have been taller than Briggs, but up on the dais the shifter towered over the vampire.

"Briggs, we're wasting time, what do you want to make this happen?"

Briggs contemplated for a moment, sizing up the small enchanter who stood beside him. "Three favors from the Circle, and they will only be allowed entry during the night, and I will be escorting them in and out. If they do anything to upset the humans in my territory, I will expel them immediately. And I want a permanent right of feeding in their territory."

"Ludicrous!" Howe shouted, and quickly backed away when Briggs gave him a stern look.

Longfang laughed. "That's steep."

De La Cruz stood up slowly and I noted the man's impressive ability to command everyone's attention. The vampire didn't have to say anything or make any grand gestures, there was just a regal air to him.

"Briggs, you will allow the Crimson Circle access to Hell's Kitchen Park on a temporary basis. They can access it unaccompanied and unmolested for three nights." Briggs seemed like he was going to interject, but a wave of De La Cruz's hand cut him off. "In return the Circle owes you two favors, and you are hereby granted permanent feeding rights in the territory of the Crimson Circle, but exclusive to the Fordham campus." De La Cruz surveyed the two men to see if they would object. I could tell by the look in De La Cruz's eyes that neither man would.

"Fine," said Briggs.

"We accept your ruling," said Howe.

"It is done then," said De La Cruz returning to his seat.

As the proceedings continued several more disputes came forward that were similar in nature. Sometimes they reached a compromise and other times they did not. The Council offered input and settled disputes without resorting to violence, although it did seem like Longfang, who appeared to have a temper, wanted to punch a few people for wasting his time.

After a few moments of silence without any more disputes coming forward, Abigail Black once again stood and addressed the Sanctuary.

"Is there anything else that needs to come before the Council before we adjourn for the evening?" she asked.

No one spoke, but everyone was turning to look around and craning their necks to try and be the first to see anyone who would come forward. After a moment, the sound of a chair pushing away from a table echoed around the room and a woman walked forward. She was tall, doubly so with her long heels, and she had short brown hair that fell about halfway down her neck. She wore a charcoal black dress with a high neck and a hem that reached just above her knees. Her makeup was heavy, to cover up her pale complexion, with a red blush along her cheeks that made them seem more prominent.

"The Council recognizes Ms. Amelia Roth, vampire." said Abigail Black.

"Thank you." said Amelia, and she addressed the Council professionally. "I regret to bring this forward, but I was recently informed by a contact in my territory that a human was found murdered with obvious claw marks all over their body. My contact made it clear that the victim had obviously been destroyed by a shifter, who then carelessly left the victim's body where it could have been found by anyone."

I couldn't believe the callous nature in which she was talking about someone being murdered.

"As you all know, this is not the first time that this has happened recently and it is becoming something of a trend, and that trend cannot continue." continued Amelia. "In fact, within the past year, there have been four other instances of humans being discovered with claw marks all over their bodies. It is as if someone is not only being careless, but they are also flaunting what they are doing. Perhaps, Council members, this is an opportune time to remind everyone about why we do not kill humans, especially so carelessly where questions might be asked, and inquiries made."

"Thank you, Amelia." said Abigail, now addressing the entire room. "Her words are true. The Shroud that keeps the humans from discovering us can only go so far in protecting us. We must be vigilant and careful to do our part to maintain the illusion that we do not exist. That means that we do not kill needlessly. If you are caught killing humans you will be reprimanded, and if necessary, destroyed. For the sake of our city and our continued existence that sort of recklessness cannot stand. Thank you again, Ms. Roth. Mr. Moran?"

Mallory stood up when he was addressed by Abigail Black.

"Yes?" he asked.

"Can you take on the responsibility of investigating these murders?" asked Abigail.

"Of course. Amelia, if you could send over what you have and put me in touch with your contact, that would be very helpful, and I will add that info into my dossier of the previous murders." said Mallory.

Amelia nodded and returned to her seat; Mallory did the same.

"Thank you again for bringing this to our attention, Ms. Roth." said Abigail.

"Control your shifters, Longfang." said De La Cruz callously as he stood. Longfang growled under his breath and glared at the back of the vampire's head. De La Cruz snapped his fingers at the emcee who was sitting in the front row of tables and motioned for him to return to the dais. The man fumbled out of his chair and back up onto the stage. "That will do, let's get on with our evening."

"Yes, sir." said the emcee as he reached the center of the dais. "Ladies and gentlemen, that will adjourn this month's Sanctuary. Thank you all for being here." All three of the Council members stood and surveyed the crowd, which also stood and applauded the Councilors.

Mallory's phone buzzed and I watched him look at it momentarily with confusion before he answered it, speaking in a whisper. I could not hear what he was saying, and I was too distracted watching Salvatore De La Cruz. Something about the man awoke a hazy image in the back of my mind, like a memory long forgotten. I was working vigilantly to try and figure out what it was when De La Cruz turned his head and I saw with horror that the vampire's gaze landed directly on me. De La Cruz just continued to keep his eyes transfixed on me, and in turn I could not pull my eyes away from him. It was not until I felt a tugging on my arm that turned away and saw that it was Mallory who was pulling me out of the ballroom. "What's going on? Why was he staring at me like that?"

"We need to go." said Mallory as he pulled me along after him into the foyer and out into the street.

"Why, what is it? What happened?" I asked.

Once clear of the building Mallory broke into a run heading in the direction of the coffee shop. I picked up my own pace to stay beside him. "What happened?" I asked again, panic starting to set in. Mallory shook his head, obviously not wanting to have to say the words, but reluctantly he did.

"I'm sorry, Saturday. I just got the call, its Maria, and her mother... They've just been found. They're... They're dead."

TWELVE

Speeding down the street in Mallory's car I tried to will it to not be true. I couldn't believe it; I didn't want to believe it. Immediately I called Maria's phone, urging her to answer to prove that she was alive, and this had all been a mistake, but it went straight to her voicemail. Shock, almost like a distant numbness, set in.

Mallory said we were headed to the apartment Maria shared with her mother. Whoever tipped him off was keeping the area clear until we arrived. I couldn't imagine the scene in which we were about to walk.

Mallory pulled in behind a police car that was parked in front of a large apartment complex in Highbridge, near the Harlem River. The light above the entrance to the complex was busted, and the stoop was in total darkness. Mallory retrieved his bag from the trunk of the car and handed it to me to carry. There was a uniformed police officer waiting by the front door, which he was holding open. The officer looked overworked, the bags under his eyes told quite the story.

"Mallory." the officer said with a polite nod as they approached.

"Hey Clarkie, thanks for calling," said Mallory.

"Of course, this is some nasty business. Whoever did this did not try and mask what they are."

We stepped into the apartment building and followed the policeman up the stairs. "How long do we have?" Mallory asked.

"I haven't called it in yet, but I'll have to once I let you in. You should have about 15 minutes before the coroner arrives on scene. Mallory, this is bad. People are gonna ask questions." said the police officer.

"All the better that you called me first, Clark. Fifteen

minutes isn't much time, but we will make it work." said Mallory as we approached an apartment on the second floor of the building.

The hallway was dimly lit, the light overhead flickering intermittently, and the floor was grimy hardwood. The hallway walls were covered in filthy faded yellow wallpaper, desperately in need of replacement. The apartment number was 203, and the door was closed. Officer Clark reached over with a gloved hand and turned the brass knob, gingerly opening the door into the room. "It's all yours. The mother is in the living room, the girl is in the bedroom on the right. I'm going to step outside and call it in."

Mallory took the duffle bag from me and placed it on the hallway floor. Unzipping it, he reached in and pulled two pairs of shoe coverings out of it, the blue ones that you normally see surgeons wearing on TV. We put them on over our shoes before stepping into the room. Mallory pulled everything that he needed out of the bag before handing it back and I shouldered it. Stepping through the entryway, I entered my first crime scene.

The apartment was completely trashed, but there was an intentionality to the destruction that was clear even to my untrained eyes. There was a small kitchenette to the right once you walked in the front door. Immediately ahead was the main living area. To the left of the living area were two bedrooms and the bathroom. "It is important that we disturb this scene as little as possible in our search for clues. Stay close to me and prepare your mind for what lies ahead. It is never easy to stomach this, and it does not get any easier with time. That you knew these people makes it even more difficult." He patted me on the back encouragingly. "Also here is a bag, in case you need it." It was a large brown paper bag which I gripped tightly in my hand.

The only light that I could see was coming from a small lamp in the living room that lay on its side on the carpeted floor. Just peeking out from around the corner rested a woman's bare foot. A shudder rippled in my stomach and my breath caught in my throat. Mallory noticed as well because he returned his hand to my shoulder. "It's ok. It's ok." he said, reassuringly.

The taupe walls of the living room were covered in blood splatter. There were holes where large chunks of the walls had been smashed, and a coffee table lay busted and broken in the middle of the floor. Lying face up against one of the walls was the mangled body of Maria's mother. Ms. Álvarez's body was covered in deep crisscrossed gashes. The deep wounds across her arms and abdomen were stained with dark arterial blood which had pooled around her into the carpet. When my eyes fell onto her body, my head began to spin. Everything I had eaten that day threatened to propel itself out of my body and I brought the bag up to my mouth just in time to catch it. I forced myself to look away. The image of Ms. Álvarez's mangled corpse threatened to haunt my mind for the rest of my life.

"It's ok. There is no shame in that Saturday." said Mallory, reassuringly. "Just remember why we are here. We are going to find out who did this and bring them to justice, that is what we can do for her, and for Maria. Just take your time, when you are ready, we will begin."

I steadied myself, drew upon all my inner strength, took a deep breath, and turned back around. "I'm ready."

Mallory knelt gently as close as he could to the body without disturbing the pool of blood around her. I did so as well, just a little further back. Ms. Álvarez's eyes were open, staring emptily toward the ceiling. The light had long since left them. I resisted the urge to reach up and mercifully close them. Mallory took several photographs of her wounds and the apartment. "Do you see these cuts?" he asked, pointing to the ones across her arms. "They appear to be claw marks. Notice that the cuts run parallel and the jagged nature of the skin around the wound. A blade would leave a cleaner edge to its cut." Mallory explained.

"So that means it was a shifter?" I asked. "Mannie did this. It had to have been him."

"Easy." said Mallory. "We owe it to the victims to keep an open mind and to gather facts before we jump to any conclusions. The cuts along the forearms are what I would classify as defensive wounds, indicating that she tried to defend herself from her attacker. Now, human detectives would look for DNA or skin of the attacker in the fingernails of the body, but there is no DNA database of supers. Even if there was, I wouldn't trust it. Because of this, we must rely on other methods in our investigation." Mallory stood up, careful not to disturb any part of her body or the blood on the floor. "Are you ready?"

I took a deep breath and nodded. Mallory reached the bedroom door just ahead of me and slowly pushed it open. Along the far wall of the small bedroom a window stood open, and a slight breeze caused the sheer white curtains to tremble and wave. The only light was coming from a streetlight outside of Maria's window which washed the room in an eerily peaceful glow. It was not difficult to find her. Lying peacefully on her bed, atop her white comforter, was Maria Álvarez. Unlike her mother who had been butchered and discarded, Maria had been positioned intently. There was no pooled blood around her body. Her bed had been pristinely made and her body placed down on it in a way that did not even ruffle the comforter. No teenager kept their bed made that meticulously, I knew from my own experience as a messy teenager.

We stepped cautiously over to her bedside. She was dressed for bed. Strands of her beautiful long brunette hair fell delicately down her face. I could have almost forced myself to believe that she was just sleeping. Desperately I wanted her to just be asleep. There was a heat welling up behind my eyes, and somewhere down in my gut. Sadness and rage, two flames that fueled each other. Mallory's gloved hand gently drew aside her hair to reveal Maria's neck which was purple and bruised.

Mallory continued to check, without disturbing her body, for any more wounds or cuts, but saw nothing else. It was evident that she had been strangled, I did not need Mallory to point that out.

"These two murders are different in nature, Saturday, and I must confess my confusion," said Mallory. "Any number of those cuts on Ms. Álvarez's body would have been fatal, and yet her attacker continued to claw at her over and over repeatedly and unnecessarily. Maria, however, wasn't cut at all. Instead, she was strangled, which would normally indicate an intimate or personal relationship with her assailant."

"I'll be seeing her tonight." That was what Mannie had told me. It had been a threat. I cursed myself for not warning her, and my shame made it hard for me to look at her. I had only known her for a couple of days, but even amid the horror and chaos of the most stressful situation of my entire life I had been struck by her. We had plans to hang out tomorrow and I couldn't help the selfish 'what could have been' scenarios that were running around in my head despite my best efforts to quell them.

Now here she was, her body vacant of its spirit and fire. Her eyes were closed, mercifully. I didn't think I could have borne the pain of looking into them. Maria's once full red lips were now a shade of blue, but held a familiar pout to them, her hands lay peacefully across her chest, they... had something entwined around one of her fingers.

"What is this?" I asked Mallory pointing to Maria's fingers.

Mallory bent down and used his hands to gingerly lift her fingers. Gently he unwound the object free and brought it up to his eyes for inspection. "A hair. You wonderful woman. A hair!" said Mallory, joyously. "Now we have you. Well done, well done."

"I thought you said we couldn't get DNA from

supers?"

"I did say that, and it is true. However, we do have other means of using this to locate our suspect. It's costly, but I think that you would agree with me that it is worth it."

"Of course. We have to get him."

"Or her. Keep a completely open mind and allow the findings to narrow the narrative, or you will find yourself narrowing the findings to fit your own narrative." advised Mallory, before snapping a few more photos of Maria and the scene. Once Mallory was certain that he had checked everything and we could hear the sirens in the distance getting closer, he grabbed me by the arm and we both exited out of the open window and down the fire escape and back out onto the street. We were back in Mallory's car, speeding off down the street just as the flashing lights filled the scene outside of the complex.

THIRTEEN

It was closing in on midnight when Mallory's car pulled up in front of the small house that I shared with my grandparents. The street was dark except for the occasional porch light that dotted the block. Mallory rubbed his eyes with his palms, he looked as tired as I felt, probably more so.

"I meant to ask earlier, but everything kind of happened so fast." I said. "Why did you change your mind and tell me about Jake?"

Mallory looked at him contemplatively. "Talking about Jake is difficult. I feel more than a little responsible for his death. No, I was responsible for his death, I should have been able to protect him. Perhaps I should have told you before you agreed to come aboard, but the truth of it is that I was trying to protect you. I realize how foolish it sounds now, keeping you in the dark is too dangerous. I thought that maybe if I tempered all of this it might make it easier for you, but after seeing you with Irene and your innocence among that torrent of vile corruption of the Sanctuary, it made me realize that things needed to move faster than I was prepared. I hope that you will accept that answer, and my apologies."

I nodded my head. "I understand, and I do. I'm in this now. I can handle it."

Mallory smiled. "I am sure that you can. I still have a few things that I need to do before I can get some rest." Mallory said. "But you should try and get some sleep. We will meet in the morning and continue our investigation. Do you know where St. Paul's Chapel is?"

"Sure." I said.

"Very well, meet me outside of the gates to the chapel at 10 AM."

"Do I need to bring anything?"

"Just yourself," said Mallory.

I nodded and opened the door to get out of the car.

Mallory reached over and placed his hand on my arm. "Good work today. If you remember to just trust your instincts everything will be alright." he said. I didn't know what to say so I just smiled and stepped out onto the sidewalk. After I closed the door Mallory sped off down the street and out of sight.

When I pulled out my phone to check my messages, I was not surprised to see that I had a ton of them. Wes and Liz had blown me up. At first their messages were asking where I was, or how long I thought I would be, and they had gotten progressively nastier later into the night. I completely forgot that we were supposed to be getting together at Wes' house. Apparently bailing on my friends was my new thing, and I was not happy about that, but oddly it did seem crazy to be playing video games while so much serious stuff was going on.

Everything I saw at Maria's apartment was playing in a loop over and over in my mind, seeing her lifeless body had shaken me. Only a sociopath could see death up close like that and not feel something.

I sat down on the porch steps and typed out some replies to my friends, apologizing for missing out and hoping that they could forgive me. They would. They were great friends, despite the colorful names that they called me in their texts, "Ass Hat" being my personal favorite. After I sent those, I checked my other unread message, it was from an unknown number.

Unknown Number
Hey dude. This is Hunter. I dropped some heavy stuff on you earlier. If you need to talk, just give me a shout. Also, keep your head down, and try not to die. :)

I smiled. It was reassuring, in a way that I could not quite explain, to know that there was someone else out there that I could talk to about all of this. Someone who had been more forthcoming and honest than anyone else, including my own boss, the person who brought me into this thing in the first place. I saved Hunter's number in my phone and texted back, "Thanks, I'll try. :/" before creeping quietly into the house, being very careful not to wake up either of the sleeping occupants.

The light in my grandparents' room was turned off as expected. The television in the living room was also dark, meaning that my grandfather had long since fallen asleep in front of the TV, woken up, and then taken himself to bed. I quietly opened the door to my own bedroom and stepped inside. Shutting the door behind me I reached up to flip on the light to my room when something strong and vice-like clamped across my mouth and I was shoved violently back against the door.

I screamed, but it came out muffled, as I struggled to free myself from the hand around my mouth. The lamp on my bedside table clicked on, filling the room with a warm light. The terror at what stood in front of me silenced me at once.

A man in a white expressionless mask with pitch black eye sockets held a leather gloved hand across my mouth. The masked man held me in place with one hand, his strength was incredible, and lifted a finger to his mouth and made a shushing gesture with his index finger. Another man stepped away from the lamp that had just been turned on. There was no mask covering his face, instead he wore a suit and dress shirt with the top two buttons undone. There were numerous tattoos on the man's chest peeking up above his collar. The man with the tattoos had greasy light brown hair that was slicked back as he ran his fingers through it.

"Listen to my cousin and keep quiet." the tattooed man said with a thick eastern European accent. "We were sent to collect you, not to kill you."

"Who are you?" I tried to ask but muffled by the gloved hand of the masked man it came out as "murrr mur murrr".

"If Dukh removes his hand, do you promise to keep quiet?" asked the tattooed man, and I nodded. The masked man looked at the guy with the tattoos, who seemed to be the one calling the shots, and when he nodded the man in the mask removed his hand from my mouth. I brought my own hand up to rub my already sore jaw.

"Who are you?" I asked.

"I am called 'Mul', and this is 'Dukh'." the tattooed man said. "We are of 'The Family'."

Mul obviously expected me to know who "The Family" was, but I had never heard of them before, of course.

"You were sent to collect me?" I asked.

"Yes, to collect you, but if it makes you feel any better, we don't feel one way or the other about it." said Mul. "It's not personal."

"So, you aren't going to kill me?" I asked, just to be certain.

"No, that was not what we were paid to do," said Mul.

"Someone paid you to come get me?"

The man in the mask, who was called Dukh, turned to face Mul for a moment without uttering a single word and then turned back to face me.

"My cousin wonders if removing your tongue would fall under our current purview. Now, now Dukh, you know our rules." said Mul. "To answer your question, yes someone paid us a fee to collect you and bring you to them. They must have expected you to be better protected than you were. This is the only reason I can think of for why they would employ a chainsaw to remove a weed. Either way, here we are."

Suddenly the implications of the quiet house filled me with dread. "You didn't hurt my grandparents? Please, they don't know anything." I pleaded, my voice cracking.

"What kind of monsters do you take us for?" Mul asked, feigning surprise. "No, we did not need to kill your grandparents. We were paid $50,000 to collect you and bring you back unharmed. If you pay us $60,000, we will say that you were not here."

"I... I don't have $60,000. I've never even seen $60,000."

109

I said.

"While this is a shame it's not surprising giving your lodgings." said Mul, glancing around my bedroom. "I'm guessing that no one would pay a ransom for you either. Is too bad. Dukh, if you would."

I had just enough time to process what was happening when Dukh shoved a damp rag roughly against my mouth. It was impossible to not breathe in the strong fumes that caused my brain to go fuzzy and my vision to blur. Consciousness slipped away just as a thick black cloth bag was shoved over my head and I was picked up off the ground.

FOURTEEN

One summer I went with my grandparents to a park in upstate New York. We stayed in a two-bedroom cabin that was surrounded by trees on all sides. At night we sat around the campfire roasting marshmallows and talking about nothing in particular until the last remaining cinders winked out. I would sit there long after my grandparents had gone to bed, staring out into the night. It never got that dark in the city, but out there hundreds of miles away from the nearest streetlight the night was thick and heavy. I would stare out into the darkness and swear it was staring back at me.

When I opened my eyes, they immediately focused on the flames. The fire seemed to fight back against the dark that pressed in around it. Around the fire were a circle of half-rotten logs just big enough to sit on. Out in the night a wolf howled at the waning moon. I couldn't smell the smoke from the fire, that's how I knew this was a dream.

I reached into the fire and drew out one of the burning logs, there was no heat. I held the fire aloft and the light spilled out in front of me as I walked outside of the circle. The night retreated from me.

"I know you're out there." I said defiantly. "I know you've always been out there."

There was no answer, but out of the corner of my vision I could see movement all around me. They encircled me. I moved forward.

Holding the fire higher I saw the light fall upon something lying in the grass. Maria. Lifeless, her body lay neglected. Next to her was yet another body and another. My friends. Liam's arms were torn to shreds as if he had died fighting to the end. Further still in the darkness I found my grandparents lying next to one another looking up into the sky. I could have thought them stargazing except for the lifelessness behind their eyes. I felt heat behind my own as I dropped down to my knees beside them. I could hear a rustling noise all around me.

I held the firewood out and I heard the growls from the wolves behind me. The light fell upon Mannie who snarled at me, and I stood to face him. His pack stood beside him. They retreated away from the fire.

"Stay back." I ordered.

"What about them?" Mannie asked humorously, his voice slightly different than I remembered it.

I turned to see something edging closer to where my friends lay. When I turned and held the light out toward them, I could faintly make out creatures within the darkness skulking away from the light.

"What'll you do when the fire dies out?" Mannie asked.

The fire from my makeshift torch was already beginning to wane as it turned the wood to ash. Soon I would be alone in the darkness.

"You simply have to find the fire within." An unfamiliar voice said from the darkness. A tall, slender man dressed in black with a purple silk scarf draped over his shoulder stepped into the light. I had never seen this man before, but there was something familiar about him. It was he who spoke.

"How do I do that?" I asked, watching the creatures lurking around me.

The man laughed loudly. "Saturday, you already know everything you need to know." He said, stepping even closer to me until we were face to face. His eyes were the color of twilight. "It's in your blood."

He reached out and placed the palm of his hand over my heart, it lingered for a second and then he pushed me, and I fell backwards. At the same time, I lurched sideways abruptly, and I was awoken, blinded.

Panic set in. I could feel my surroundings, but everything was in complete darkness. It took a moment before I realized that my head was covered by a dense fabric that completely blocked out all light. When I lifted my hands to remove the covering, I found them held down by straps. I tried to remain calm and not panic, but my heart threatened to beat out of my chest. I could tell by the rhythmic swaying of my body that I was in a vehicle of some sort, but it felt like I was sitting on a hard metal bench. Everything around me was silent except for the sound of the engine and the occasional sound of metal clanging when we hit a bump.

When the vehicle came to a sudden stop momentum pulled me to the side and I was only able to hold myself up by the straps that held my arms down. The engine cut off abruptly and a door slammed shut. A door to my right creaked open and someone grabbed my hand. I tried to jerk away, but I was held tight. A moment later the strap was removed from one of my hands and then the other. Immediately I reached up to remove the hood from my head. The ghostly white mask of Dukh was inches away from my face. The vacant black sockets of the man's eyes stared into my own. We were in the back of a van, but not just any van, it looked like something out of a horror movie. The wall of the van on one side, the side that I was on, was lined with chains and bindings. The other side held enough guns and weapons to outfit a small militia.

Mul stood at the back of the van with the two rear doors open. Standing beside him was a bald man who appeared vaguely familiar, someone I had seen at Sanctuary. The bald man was not very tall, but he was very stocky. The navy suit that he wore was tight against his muscular physique. Further back behind him were two other men standing vigilantly and watching like hawks.

"Nice work." the man standing beside Mul said. "Come on kid, someone inside wants to meet you." He snapped his fingers at me and waved me forward.

Hesitantly I stepped toward him, but Dukh held out a hand to keep me in the back of the van. There was an immediate shift in the tension. The two men in the background unbuttoned their suit jackets and threateningly revealed two submachine guns.

"This is rude, no?" said Mul, gesturing to the two men. "In Russia you would be dead for less." Mul turned to face the stocky man. "Luther, if you want the boy, you will pay the agreed upon rate for him. First."

"Everyone just relax." ordered Luther. "Here's the $50K."

Luther offered an envelope to Mul who took it and pocketed it in his suit jacket without counting it. Dukh removed his hand, and I stepped down onto the concrete driveway of the large estate.

"For this insult the fee has increased to $60,000." Mul told Luther. "You will pay it or perhaps I should explain to Pakhan that you threatened his brother."

Luther gripped my arm and pulled me along beside him. "No. It's fine. The $10K will be sent." said Luther. "Let's go."

As Luther pulled me away, I glanced back over my shoulder at Dukh who was closing the back of the van. Before closing the doors, he brought his right hand up to his throat with his index and middle fingers forming the shape of the V. I didn't know what it meant, but it was obviously a threat, and I hoped it wasn't meant for me. The doors slammed shut, and Mul, who had gotten back into the driver's seat, sped off. Luther shoved the two-armed men forward in front of him.

"And that's coming out of your pay, you idiots." They buttoned up their jackets and fell inline walking up the large stone steps of the manor.

The house itself was massive, by far the largest home I've ever seen in person. I knew we must be just outside of the city, but I couldn't be certain exactly where because of the tall hedges blocking the front of the property. Dozens of stone steps led up to two double doors. Two large columns stood on either side of the door like stone guardians. One of the armed men reached the door first and opened it for the rest of them. I stopped hesitantly in front of the doorway, but Luther wasted no time in pushing me through it and into the entryway. The foyer was a large circular room with a gleaming marble floor with red and gold accents. The walls themselves looked like a painting that you would see in a museum, it was a myriad of gold and navy and red all working in tandem to form an expressionist piece that would have made my art teacher weep.

Luther yanked me around and turned to the two other men. "You idiots are back on perimeter duty." He spat at them. "Try to not screw anything else up tonight. Go!" The two men hung their heads and turned on the spot and went back outside.

"Talking like that to your henchmen never ends well in the movies," I said.

Luther glared and shook his head, pushing me into another room. The next room was even more impressive than the first. It had high arching ceilings, and the walls were lined with thousands of books all the way up. There was a staircase that led to a second level which was only a dark wooden walkway that circled the room where someone could go to access the higher up books. The floor level of the room had a large stone fireplace that currently housed a roaring fire. In front of the fire was a semi-circle of expensive-looking leather chairs and ottomans. There was a large rectangular mahogany table that took up about half of the room. The table was surrounded by high backed wooden chairs. Everything was meticulously placed and tidy.

"Sit down over there, he will be with you soon," said Luther, pointing to the chairs over by the fire.

"Who? Who will be with me soon?" I asked Luther, but the man left the room without another word. I took the opportunity to check my pockets, but they had been emptied.

No phone, no wallet, nothing. Awesome. Fantastic.

I didn't sit down. I was too wired to sit, like I'd just housed a double espresso. Even though I knew I should be scared, after everything that had happened with Mannie and The Strays, I was certain that I was all scared out. After coming face to face with a pack of creatures straight out of my nightmares, after walking among a crowd of vampires with fresh delicious blood coursing through my veins and living to tell the tale, after seeing a double murder, and after being kidnapped by some creep in a mask, I felt like there wasn't anything left to fear. This was just my life now.

Instead of sitting down, I walked over to the nearest bookshelf and picked up a random book and began to absentmindedly thumb through it. It was the Song of Hiawatha by Henry Wadsworth Longfellow. The book itself was frayed and in rough shape, but the pages were all intact. It had a copyright date of 1955. I'd never read it before, but I could vaguely remember Ms. Klein, my Lit teacher, talking about it. I placed it back on the shelf gently.

"In his crown alone was seated. In his crown too was his weakness." said a man's voice from behind me and I turned to see Salvatore De La Cruz, possibly the most powerful person in the city, standing across the room. De La Cruz's short black hair was slicked back, and he was wearing the same suit he had been wearing at Sanctuary. The light from the flames in the fireplace reflected in his eyes. "There alone could he be wounded. Nowhere else could weapon pierce him. Nowhere else could weapon harm him." The vampire crossed the room toward me as he spoke. "Have you read Longfellow's classic before?"

I had to work moisture back into my mouth as I immediately rediscovered true fear. Panic was all that I could process, my body was not responding to the shouts from my brain to run. Fear kept me in place, all I could do was stand there planted on the spot.

"Personally, I would recommend that you start with

'Evangeline' if you wish to begin a study of Longfellow and his works." continued De La Cruz. "We all can relate to the story of 'Evangeline' can we not? We are all searching for something, and it is torturous how often the thing for which we are searching is just beyond our fingertips." De La Cruz reached out and placed his hand on my shoulder. "You will excuse my ramblings; I have been called a romantic by those who know me well. Longfellow has that effect on many, although I knew him as a young professor at Harvard, and he was not always the romantic himself, he grew into the role. Seeing two of your wives die will do that to a man."

De La Cruz just continued to stare down at me appraisingly. I didn't look into the vampire's eyes, instead I watched his mouth. I was transfixed. Occasionally when De La Cruz drew out a word or hit a hard vowel the fangs of his upper canines were displayed. This was a stark reminder of just how far up shit creek I was, and there was not a paddle in sight.

"I'm being rude." De La Cruz continued. "My name is Salvatore De La Cruz." The vampire removed his hand from my shoulder and offered it to me. I hesitated for a moment before shaking his outstretched hand.

"I'm Saturday. Saturday Shepherd."

"Of course, you are." said De La Cruz, with a smile. "Welcome to my home, Saturday. Can I get you a refreshment?"

"No. Thank you." I said.

"Please, have a seat." De La Cruz gestured to one of the large leather chairs next to the fireplace.

I stepped into the ring of chairs and sat down in one of them. De La Cruz followed suit, putting his feet up on one of the ottomans and sinking back into his seat. "I trust that you were not harmed. The Family can sometimes be overzealous in their work." said De La Cruz.

"I'm fine, but who are those guys? And why did you hire them to collect me? And why am I here?"

When Salvatore spoke, he spoke with his hands, animatedly. Where the vampire had been direct and to the point at Sanctuary, he now appeared to be much more conversational. Between sentences De La Cruz's hands would come to rest in front of his mouth. When he paused for effect or was contemplating his next words, De La Cruz's index fingers would tap against his lips absentmindedly.

"I hired The Family to collect you because I do not know anything about you, and a man in my position cannot afford to be ignorant about anything. Not knowing anything about you meant that I could not be implicated and attached to you in any way before I knew exactly who you were. The Family, well they are just a tool, a useful and expensive tool, but a tool nonetheless."

My grandfather always told me that when life throws you a curveball, lean into it. So here I was, leaning into it. I threw caution to the wind.

"Are you going to kill me?"

For his part, Salvatore did a believable job feigning surprise. "Kill you? Why on Earth would I kill you?" Salvatore asked. "A man does not reach a position like mine by killing everyone that they meet. No, no, no. You could prove to be very useful."

It appeared that my life hung on my usefulness at the moment, so I stopped myself from telling De La Cruz that I was just a nobody high school student that couldn't possibly be useful for someone like him. Despite how true that might be.

"I can count on my hands the number of mortals that attend Sanctuary." De La Cruz continued. "That makes you unique. What I want to know is, who are you?"

Now, being used to this question, I just fell into my routine. "My name is Saturday Shepherd, I-"

"I know your name; I don't care about your name. I want to know who you really are." De La Cruz interrupted. "Why did Mallory bring you to Sanctuary? What is he up to?"

I detected a hint of agitation in Salvatore's voice when he said Mallory's name.

"I just started working with him. Honestly, I'm just trying to get school credit, that's all." I told him.

The vampire stared at me. I tried to survey the man's face for any reaction at all, but it remained stoic for several moments, before cracking into a smile. Salvatore De La Cruz, the most powerful vampire in New York City began to laugh. It was cacophonous and unnerving.

"Just trying to get school credit." De La Cruz mimicked, and the laughter stopped abruptly. "Oh, if only that were the truth of it."

Something changed in De La Cruz. It wasn't that he was angry, not outwardly at least, but when the vampire locked eyes with me it felt like my entire life was borne and exposed to him. Shame, doubt, fear, and despair flooded my mind in a torrent of emotion. Hopelessness washed over me, and I felt like I was sinking into the floor in a puddle of misery. De La Cruz slid forward in his chair and leaned in closer to me.

"What is your real name?" De La Cruz asked, his voice echoed and reverberated in my mind.

"Saturday David Shepherd."

"Tell me why you left the Sanctuary so suddenly." De La Cruz commanded, all feigned notions of free will were thrown out the window. This was no conversation, it was an interrogation, and right now, I couldn't see a way out.

"We went to investigate a murder." I told him.

De La Cruz seemed to perk up a bit. "Whose murder?"

"Maria Álvarez. A mortal girl."

De La Cruz scoffed. "And who does Mallory think killed the girl?"

I hated myself for talking about Maria with him. It felt like a betrayal of Mallory and of Maria, but I had no control. "He doesn't know yet." The pressure eased slightly for a moment. "But we will find them." I added quickly.

De La Cruz smiled. "I am sure that you will." The pressure released from my mind completely and I sank back into the chair with an audible sigh. "Relax, relax. We are just talking. Now would you care for a refreshment? When you are as old as I am you sometimes forget the need of humans to quench their thirst. I would hate to be thought of as an ungracious host."

"I'm... I'm fine." I said, trying to catch my breath. I wasn't fine. My lungs burned and sweat was beading on my forehead, but I didn't want to give De La Cruz the satisfaction of hearing me admit it.

"Very well. Then allow us to continue our conversation."

Immediately I was forcefully locked back into the now familiar trance with the vampire. The pressure built behind my eyes, and I sat up trying to fight it, but it was like fighting gravity itself. I had no more control over my body than a puppet has control over its movements.

"Let us continue talking about you." said De La Cruz, his voice was as smooth as honey once again. "I want to know about your family. What is your mother's name?"

"Isabel." I said. "Isabel Costa."

"Good. Very Good." said De La Cruz. "And your father, what is his name?"

"I don't know." I said, surprising myself. I wasn't sure why I said that my father's name was David Shepherd.

"You don't know?" De La Cruz asked, unbelievingly. "Do not test my patience, Saturday. Who is your father?"

The pressure in my mind increased, I could feel the blood pulsing against my skull. I knew the truth was the only way to relieve the pressure, but the words refused to form. Sweat rolled down my face and stung my eyes.

"I don't know." I said again, unwillingly. The pressure eased, only slightly, but De La Cruz's gaze intensified. My heart was pounding. I wanted to crawl under my chair and hide away from the vampire's unnerving stare. So many emotions were coming in waves like a torrent. At this moment I felt more alone than ever in my life.

"What are you?" De La Cruz demanded, rising from his seat.

I tried to fight the words, but I couldn't, doubled over in my chair. The words came out forced, but true. "I-Don't-Know."

Someone was shouting in the distance. The pressure released from my mind completely and I fell to the floor with a thud. Rolling up onto my side, weakly, I had to blink the fog away a few times to see what was going on. Salvatore stood on the other side of the room speaking with Luther and another man, a man that I also recognized from the Sanctuary. It was the vampire who Mallory had been speaking with. I remembered his name was Charlie Briggs.

"Sorry, Salvatore, but Briggs refused to wait," said Luther, using one of his hands to prevent Briggs from stepping fully into the room.

"Luther, if you like that hand and want to keep it, I suggest you remove it, before I do," said Briggs, dangerously.

De La Cruz stepped between the men. Briggs towered over Luther, but Luther stood his ground and did not back down. "If the two of you would like to compare manhood, I suggest you step outside and allow me to continue my business in peace." De La Cruz told them. Briggs and Luther continued to glare at one another, but after a moment they both took small steps back and the tension in the room subsided momentarily. "Good. Now, Mr. Briggs, why are you here?"

"I am not satisfied with how we ended our conversation earlier," said Briggs. "I came here to revisit it."

"You came all the way out here, unannounced, to discuss a minor territory dispute?" De La Cruz asked, incredulously.

"Nothing regarding territory is ever minor," said Briggs. "You of all people know that."

Slowly I made my way to my feet, trying my hardest to not draw any attention to myself. I looked around for an exit, but the only way out of the room appeared to be the doorway where the three men were now standing. There was no way I could escape without being seen.

"Fine." said De La Cruz "Let's discuss it further. If you would wait for me in my office, I will be with you shortly."

Luther motioned to usher Briggs into the room, but the man did not budge. "That won't work for me. I won't be put off for a mortal, you can make him wait, not me."

I was stunned. I couldn't believe the tone with which Briggs spoke to De La Cruz, and I wasn't alone. De La Cruz sneered.

"You are beginning to test my patience, Charlie." De La Cruz adjusted the knot of his tie while he seemed to contemplate the situation. "Very well. Luther, have your men attend to our guest and then join us in my office." Luther nodded and walked back toward the front door. Briggs seemed satisfied as he and De La Cruz walked across the room toward the other door. "We will continue our conversation shortly, Mr. Shepherd, and we will skip the pleasantries."

My heart pounded even harder. I sat down in one of the chairs and tried to clear my head, desperately racking my brain for a way out, but the more frantic I became, the more impossible it seemed. If I tried to go out of the front door I would be stopped by Luther and his goons. If I tried to go further into the house and out another door, I could walk right into De La Cruz, and that would lead to a world of pain.

Moments later, while I sat there locked in contemplation and frozen by fear, Luther returned with the same two men from earlier. I stood up nervously when they entered the room. "Um, can I get my phone call?" I asked.

"Very funny." said Luther, unamused. "Keep that sense of humor, you'll need it." Luther turned to the two men. "Now you two, stay here, do not allow him to leave the room.

Try to not venture into the realm of completely worthless."

The two men, one who was bald and the other who had a very 'preppy' looking haircut, nodded. Luther turned on the spot and went through the same door as De La Cruz and Briggs. "What about a bathroom break?" I shouted after him but got no response. "Man, that guy is an asshat. Am I right?" The two men said nothing, just shook their heads and went directly into patrol mode. One of the men stood in the center of the room, while the other in front of the door that was my only way out.

Slowly I walked around the chairs and toward Baldy at the center of the room. "Why do you listen to that guy? He treats you like crap." I had no end game in mind, no master plan, I was just trying to be friendly and empathetic in hopes they would let me go. I was grasping at straws at this point, but I couldn't think of any other way, and I had to try something.

"That guy is a killer," the bald man replied, "When someone at the top of the food chain tells you to jump, you ask 'how high', especially if you don't want to be eaten. Besides, they pay pretty damn well."

"Yeah, they do." The other man said, agreeing with his buddy.

I was desperate, I knew if I was going to escape it would have to be now before De La Cruz came back. I thought back to my conversation with Mallory to see if there were any nuggets of wisdom he'd given me that I could use. The only thing that came to mind was him telling me to trust my instincts. Trust my instincts? I didn't even know what that meant really. Right now, my instincts were screaming for me to get out of there, but what good did that do? I had to try something, and my window of opportunity was closing fast. My instincts said get out, so that's what I was going to do.

"Hey man. Look, I really need to get out of here, and fast." I said, but Baldy just stood there like a statue. "Seriously you gotta let me go. C'mon. One human to another."

"Not on your life, kid." he said. "Sit down and shut up."

"I'm sorry." I said, my heart pounding so hard that it felt like it was going to explode. "I can't." I sprinted past Baldy and straight for the door. The man guarding the door reached out a hand to stop me, but my instincts took over, and a fire was ignited deep within me. Everything slowed.

Reflexively I dodged out of the way of the man's hand. I leaned off to the side and gripped his arm with my right hand. Without even thinking my left elbow came crashing down against the back of his arm, right at the elbow. A sickening crack echoed across the room, and he let out a harrowing scream of pain. When the guard looked down to see his broken arm, I instinctively let go and grabbed a handful of his hair and brought my knee up to smash into the man's face. He fell limp onto the floor, knocked unconscious, his shattered arm lying at an awkward angle.

There was no time to feel remorse for breaking another man's arm and knocking him out, both of which were a first for me. Baldy had snuck up behind me and he had his submachine gun shoved into my back, using it to push me up against the wall. "Put your hands up!" he shouted. "I said, put your damn hands up!"

I lifted his hands up slowly. "Please don't do this." I said.

"Shut up!" the man shouted. "Don't make me kill you."

I could feel the blood surging through my veins. I could hear my own pulse pounding in my ears. The smell of sweat and fear in the room stung my nostrils. The second hand on the bald man's watch ticking the seconds away sounded as loud and prominent as my own thoughts. Tick. Tick. Tick. Time itself seemed to slow around me, as I was processing things at an unnatural speed. What was happening to me? Now was not the time for those questions.

I spun so fast that I was a blur. Effortlessly I ripped the weapon out of the guard's hand and launched a fearsome headbutt to the bridge of his nose. It shattered on contact. Hot blood spilled down the man's face as he fell to the ground clutching the injury. Without so much as glancing at the weapon in my hands I dropped it to the floor and ran. I ran faster than I've ever run before. I ran out of the front door and down the steps and onto the grounds of De La Cruz's manor. I ran down the long twisting driveway and out onto the street.

A black car appeared out of nowhere and came to a screeching halt in front of me, and I had to jump back out of the way to avoid it. The passenger window rolled down and I half expected to see Mallory in the driver's seat, but it wasn't him. It was someone I'd never met before.

"Get in!" The stranger yelled to me, and without thinking I jumped into the passenger seat and the car sped off into the night.

I fell back against the leather seat of the car, exhausted and out of breath. Coming down from an epic adrenaline high, I was crashing, and my body was begging for sleep. The driver gripped the steering wheel of the car and seemed to be paying me no mind at all.

"Who are you?" I asked, weakly. The driver of the car was a normal looking guy with his short cropped black hair and a beard of about the same length. He was wearing jeans and a plain white T-shirt, tattoos covered both of his arms.

"I'm the guy saving your ass, that's who I am." the driver said, not taking his eyes off the road. "But you can call me Lincoln. I'm a friend of Briggs. He told me that you would come running down that driveway in need of a lift."

"Wait, what? Briggs knew I was going to escape?" I asked. It had not dawned on me that Briggs could have been there to help, it seemed impossible, he hadn't even looked in my direction. "How'd he know I'd be able to get out of there?"

For the first time Lincoln gave me a once over. "Who knows? You don't look like much to me, but Briggs obviously knew you had a little something up your sleeve. I hope you appreciate the insane risk he took." Lincoln said.

"I do. I mean, I do now. I thought he was just there to

talk to De La Cruz, like he said."

"Hopefully De La Cruz thinks the same thing. If he suspects otherwise, Briggs will be the one needing saving, and we don't have enough guns for that."

"Briggs seems like he can handle himself. I met him earlier, he's strong as hell." I said, recalling the man's bone crushing handshake.

"Briggs is a bad mother, no denying it. I would take him in a fight over most people, but De La Cruz would crush him. The man has a century on Briggs, and it's hard to overcome that kind of power."

Apparently, size didn't mean as much in this world. That seemed like important information for someone looking to stay alive.

"So, kid, you gonna to tell me where to take you or should I just drive around until we run out of gas?" Lincoln asked.

"Oh, sorry." I said and prepared to give him my grandparents address when a warning flashed into my mind. It already seemed like too many people had my home address, it was probably not a great idea to go about broadcasting it to everyone I met. Instead, I made a snap decision to get out somewhere near Wes' house. "Um, you can just drop me off at the corner of Herring and Lakewood in The Bronx. I can make it from there."

Lincoln gave a half smile. "You're not as dumb as you look. No offense."

"None taken."

Lincoln reached over and turned on the radio. The Dropkick Murphys came on and Lincoln raised the volume. I relaxed and it was all I could do to keep myself awake. We rode the rest of the way without saying a word.

About an hour later we pulled up at our destination. The clock on the center console of the car said it was almost 4:00 AM. I was supposed to meet Mallory in 6 hours, and I desperately needed sleep. "Thanks for the lift, man." I said, before getting out of the car. Lincoln nodded.

I was crossing over to the other side of the street when I heard a car window roll down. Lincoln pulled up next to me. "Hey kid, has your boy Mallory explained to you how debts work among supers?"

I shook my head. "No, not really. Do I owe you a favor now?"

"No, you don't, but you should know that we take debts very seriously," said Lincoln. "They're like money, and you pay your debts, no matter what. Briggs wanted me to tell you that you can consider his debt to you to be paid in full. Got it?"

"But he didn't owe me any debt." I said. "I literally just met him last night."

"Like I said. Debts are like money, like a possession. When your father died, what was his is now yours."

It took a moment for what Lincoln said to sink in. Its implications slowly settled into my exhausted mind. I was frozen, unable to formulate a sentence or a question, or even a word. Lincoln nodded to me and sped off down the street.

Briggs had known my father. Briggs had owed my father a debt. How? So many things were running through my mind, and I couldn't process any of it. Lincoln said my dad was dead. It was like a shot to my stomach that knocked the wind out of me. I don't know why though. I always suspected he was gone. After all, wouldn't it be better if he were dead? If he weren't dead, it would mean he chose to stay out of my life. At least now I could pretend he wanted to be in my life but couldn't.

I would be lying if I said I didn't have some wild-eyed dream of meeting my father someday and piecing together some kind of relationship with him. That was over now, and the longing for that moment was real, however much I'd believed it would never have happened.

Had Briggs told Mallory that he knew my father? Was that what they had talked about at the Sanctuary? Did that mean that Mallory had also known my father? Surely, he would have told me. All these questions and more were running through my head as I shuffled wearily down the sidewalk toward Wes' house, where my friends were hanging out, most likely asleep by now. I was confused by all of this, but mostly I was just exhausted.

Wes' parent's house was a small split level with two bedrooms. Wes' room was on the first level, and I stood outside tapping on his window, hoping to wake up my friends so they could let me in. After a minute or so of progressively louder tapping, the curtains in the room were thrown back and Wes' face appeared in the window.

"Saturday?" asked Wes, his voice muffled by the double-paned window. He appeared disoriented as he unlocked the window and opened it up. "What's up man? What time is it?"

"It's like 4, bro." I said, climbing into the bedroom where Liz and Liam were now stirring. "Sorry I'm late guys."

Wes' room was a shrine to all thing's geek culture. Every inch of the walls was decorated with Star Wars, Marvel, and video game posters. The poster with the most prominent position in the room was her highness, Princess Leia, in the infamous gold bikini. Half of his bedroom was taken up by his gaming computer with three separate monitors and a cooling system. Wes' bed pulled down from the wall, but usually he kept it up and instead opted to sleep in a pile of blankets on the carpeted floor. The lights were currently off in the bedroom, but everything was illuminated by the glow of the TV, where the classic final scene from Blade Runner was currently playing.

"Dude. You look terrible." Liz said.

"Thanks Liz. You're sweet." I replied while sitting, or rather falling into a large blue bean bag chair on the floor. "I feel terrible."

"What happened to you man?" Liam asked. They were all staring down at me.

"Sorry, I know I said I would be here. I was working and then... Well... It was crazy, I'm just sorry." I told them, not sure how to explain it in a way that did not make me sound crazy or to drag them into my trouble.

"No, I mean what happened to you?" asked Liam. "You're covered in blood."

"I am?" I asked, looking down at my shirt and for the first time seeing the dried blood staining my new dress shirt. I paused for a moment and really thought about the events of the night and tried to imagine how I must look right now. "I'm sorry, It's a long story. Can we talk about it in the morning? I really need to sleep, and it's not safe for me to go home right now."

"Dude, are you alright?" Liz asked.

"I'm... I'm fine, I promise. Can I please just talk with you guys about it tomorrow?"

"Sure, no problem. Get some sleep, man." said Wes, with a hint of concern in his oft-sarcastic voice.

I knew they didn't believe me, and I wanted to protest and reassure them that I was fine and there was no reason to worry, but I could not keep my eyes open any longer. Exhaustion washed over me, and sleep came with ferocity. I felt safe here, among my friends.

FIFTEEN

The alarm on my watch began beeping at 8:00 AM. I felt like I'd just fallen asleep. Silencing my watch absentmindedly I sat up and rubbed the sleep from my eyes. My friends were still laid out across the floor of Wes' bedroom, fast asleep. Had it not been for my meeting with Mallory I would still be asleep too. My body felt like it had been run over by a truck that backed up and then ran me over again. Falling right back asleep would have been no problem at all, so I forced myself to stand up from the temptation of the surprisingly comfortable bean bag chair.

I snuck out of the room as quietly as possible and went into the bathroom to wash up a little bit. Wes' mom was infatuated with the ocean and lighthouses; therefore, their entire house was covered in trinkets and decorations in all forms of sea related paraphernalia. It was all a bit much and whenever Wes needed a good put-down; his mother's sea obsession was low hanging fruit that we all used to razz him.

Standing over the porcelain sink I stared into the medicine cabinet mirror that hung above it. My appearance was startling. I looked rough, and immediately understood my friend's concern. My hair was matted with dried blood, and it was crusted down the side of my face. There was a nice purple bruise above my right eye, which I assumed was from the headbutt. The fact that I had really given someone a headbutt was too crazy for me to even comprehend. I was not the type of person to go around passing out headbutts.

When the water warmed, I used it to wash my hair and face the best I could. When I finished, I went in search of a phone. The Fords still had a home phone, and while it was completely archaic and unnecessary, it was still very useful given my current predicament of being without my cell. Thankfully when I was a kid my grandparents required me to memorize their phone number in case I got lost, it was the only number I knew by heart. I needed to give them a call to let them know I was alive and not dead in a sewer drain somewhere, as my grandmother was probably imagining.

I was able to reach my grandfather and explain to him that I had come to Wes' last night and apologized for not letting them know. After a few words and a brief lecture on communication, my grandfather told me that he loved me and returned the gesture and hung up the phone.

I made sure to lock the front door behind me as I stepped out into the morning light. The air was fresh and clear, or as fresh and clear as it ever is in the city. The temperature was already rising, and the air was a little sticky, so I rolled up my sleeves and tossed my jacket over my shoulder. I wished there was time to run home to change before my meeting, but there wasn't. Mainly I just wished I weren't wearing slacks and dress shoes, which were not ideal for traversing the city.

Simply out of habit I reached into my pocket for my phone to request a rideshare, and once again found myself foiled by lack of technology, and I was forced to hail a cab like a barbarian. Thankfully, it was not long before I was on the way to St. Paul's Chapel in the back seat of one of New York's finest cabs, complete with sticky leather seats. I really hoped Mallory was waiting outside, because if he wasn't I was going to have to make a break for it. My wallet was also missing in action, and I didn't think about it until it was too late. I crossed my fingers that Mallory would be there because I had no desire to add "fare jumper" to my resume.

At about ten minutes until 10:00 the cab pulled up outside of the beautiful St Paul's Chapel on Broadway. The iconic brownstone columns stood tall across the front of the building and the black iron gate surrounded the popular tourist destination. One World Tower rose into the heavens just behind the church, the top of the skyscraper hidden among the morning fog that hung over the city.

To my great relief Mallory was leaning against the gate outside of the chapel, staring into the adjoining cemetery where workers were trimming back the old oak trees that were beginning to encroach upon the church. I opened the door and called for Mallory, who waved at me and walked over to the cab. Mallory was wearing his normal black on black suit, with the collar of his dress shirt unbuttoned. Mallory's eyes were constantly moving and scanning the crowd around him.

"Good morning." said Mallory, as he reached out to shake my hand. "Are you alright?"

"Hey, Mallory." I said, returning the handshake. "I'm okay, but I don't have my wallet. Would you mind paying for my cab?"

"You don't have any money?" the cab driver asked, angrily. "What the hell, I came all this way downtown!"

"Don't worry, I've got it." said Mallory, reaching into his jacket pocket and pulling out his wallet to hand some cash to the angry cab driver. Mallory even included a generous tip, which still did not change the look on the driver's face. Without a word the cabbie took off down the street, his "on duty" sign now turned off.

"Some people are just determined to be mad at the world."

"Sorry about that. I don't have a wallet or a phone. I didn't know what else to do." I explained.

"No wallet, no phone, wearing the same clothes from last night, and you have dried blood on your suit jacket." Mallory noted. "I suspect that your night did not end when I dropped you off." Mallory led me to a gate at the front of the chapel. We entered the grounds of the church alongside a small tour group following their guide. Right outside of the chapel, I stopped to read the historical placard in bronze that declared this church as "The Little Chapel That Stood." We entered through two beautifully ornate and sturdy wooden doors. The doors creaked noisily as they opened into the hallowed sanctuary of the chapel. There were six tall white columns, three on each side of the room, forming a large walkway that led to the altar and a collection of votive candles in red glass in a candle rack. The walkway was lined with chairs on both sides, all facing inward. Balconies on both sides look down upon the room. The spacious sanctuary was lit by the numerous silver chandeliers hanging from the ceiling and the natural light spilling in from the domed windows behind the altar. Mallory and I stood at the very back of the room next to a door that led into a separate section of the chapel. A few tourists were already in the sanctuary walking around by themselves or in groups, and more were trickling in to visit the famous church.

"Alright Saturday, tell me everything."

"I don't even know where to start." I said, hesitantly looking around at the people milling about within earshot.

"Begin at the beginning," said Mallory. "And do not worry about anyone hearing anything that they should not. Remember, their minds will not allow them to hear anything that they cannot explain. They are safe."

I took a deep breath and told him about the kidnapping, and about Luther, and the meeting with De La Cruz. I also told him about Briggs providing a distraction allowing me to escape. I told Mallory about how I escaped, how I had done impossible things. Mallory's eyes widened, but he continued to listen intently. Finally, I told him about Lincoln, but I didn't mention what he said about my father. I wasn't ready to confront that, not yet.

"What's happening to me? How was I able to do that?" I asked, as a short balding man wearing long robes that covered his hands squeezed between Mallory and I apologetically.

Mallory waited for a moment while the robed man passed by before speaking. "Do you know why millions of people flock to St. Paul's Chapel every year?" Mallory asked.

Mallory revealed a large skeleton key that he now held in his hand, and a distant memory of a key and a choice flashed into my mind. Mallory reached over and inserted the rusting bronze key into the lock of the door next to us and pushed it open. Mallory walked into the room discreetly and I, starting to get frustrated, hesitantly followed him.

I couldn't help but feel like Mallory was deflecting. "Yes, I know about St. Paul's, but what does that have to do with me?" I asked, impatiently. We now appeared to be in a small church library, completely alone. Mallory walked to the center of the room where a large well-worn rug rested upon the floor, it was threadbare and faded red and gold. Mallory pulled the rug back to reveal a door that had been cut out of the wooden floor. He lifted a large metal ring and opened the heavy door into the room with a loud creak. A hidden staircase was revealed. Mallory motioned for me to follow him and did, against my better judgement. We descended the stairs.

"People flock here because of what this place represents. On 9/11 every building in this area was damaged, many of them destroyed beyond repair." Mallory explained, grabbing a torch off the wall which he lit with a lighter produced from his pocket. "But not this Chapel. Not even a single window was busted out of the church. A large sycamore tree that stood for over a century in the cemetery of the chapel took the brunt of the damage, and the church was spared. Many believe it was a miracle. The tree itself was destroyed, but its roots were preserved in bronze and now sit outside of this very chapel, in honor of the tree's sacrifice."

While the story was fascinating it did not change the fact that Mallory was still not answering my question. "That's cool, it really is." I said. "But again, what does that have to do with what's happening to me?"

"Do you think the sycamore tree asked, 'why is this happening to me'? I doubt that it did, but perhaps I am wrong." said Mallory. "I am sure that when members of the church planted that tree long ago that they did so not with the intent to protect the church from such an event. They planted the tree to provide shade and shelter for parishioners and visitors to the church cemetery. Did that mean the tree could not serve another purpose when the time came? Obviously, it did not. When the tree was called upon to protect and shield, it did, dutifully."

The air grew colder as we walked down the damp stairway, goosebumps sprang up on my arms. The shadows from the torchlight danced along the stone walls that wept with water from the earth. "What's your point?" I asked, trying to keep the impatience I felt out of my voice.

"My point is that in life we may find ourselves called upon to serve some greater purpose if we are lucky. I was, and now you are as well." said Mallory, as he reached the bottom of the stairs and continued walking down a narrow stone walled hallway.

Although the underground hallway was cold and damp with its dirt floor and wet walls, I could feel the heat of anger rising inside of me. I was tired of Mallory's indirect and confusing answers.

"I don't want to serve a greater purpose. I just want to get things back to normal, like they were before I met you. None of this happened until I met you. I didn't ask to be a part of this, you forced this on me. I wanted out of your car, but you talked me out of it, knowing full well what was waiting for me."

I wanted Mallory to turn and face me, shouting at the back of the man's head took some of the venom out of my words. For a moment we walked in silence, the only sound was our breath echoing off the narrow walls. The hallway ended and opened into a small circular area, but Mallory stopped at the edge of that room and did not walk into it. When Mallory turned around to face me, he blocked my view of what lay beyond.

"I'm sorry." said Mallory, finally meeting my eyes. "I really am. I wish more than anything that you could have a normal life, ignorant of all of this, but you cannot. Whether you and I met or not, you are bound to both worlds, at home in one just as in the other. You say you wish you could go back, but we both know that to be untrue. In a way you have always felt like the mortal world, the human world, was hollow and empty."

I let the words soak in, and I knew that Mallory was right. I had always felt like something was missing inside of me. For as long as I can remember I always felt incomplete. My anger was too great to admit it, so I just shook my head.

"You can deny it if you wish." Mallory continued. "But I know the truth of it, because I once felt the exact same way before I found out what I am. What you are."

The words seemed to hang in the air right in front of me. "What you are." I felt as if I could reach out and snatch them from the air. The acknowledgement of a bad dream, of what had been poisoning my thoughts since my conversation with De La Cruz. "What am I?" I asked in a hushed voice, forcing the words out of my mouth.

Mallory rested a hand on one of my shoulders and stooped down to look into my eyes. "Truth, Saturday, always comes with consequences, in the supernatural world just as the mortal world. Truth can be inconvenient, and we can hate it, but it remains the truth regardless. Here, my boy, is your truth. You, Saturday Shepherd, are a son. The son of two people who loved each other, and loved you, that is what you need to know more than anything."

"Tell me."

"Your mother, Isabel, was a mortal, but you are not, nor have you ever been. You see, Saturday, your father was a vampire. And as the offspring of a mortal and a vampire, you are what is known as a dhampir." Mallory said matter-of-factly.

"A vampire? No, that's not possible, my dad wasn't a vampire."

"Your father was a vampire, I assure you. He was one of the most powerful vampires in the city, and his name was Anton Moretti."

"No, my father was David Shepherd." I yelled over the lump forming in my throat. "And I am not one of those... things!" My pulse was quickening, my vision swimming.

Mallory took his hand off my shoulder and placed his palm over my heart and pushed me gently back against the wall. Something about this moment gave me the feeling of deja vu, as if this had already happened once before, perhaps in the faint remembrance of a dream.

"Calm." said Mallory. "Breathe deeply and calm yourself. I am sorry that I must tell you these things. I hoped that we had more time, but things are moving much faster than I would like. Before he died, your father, Anton, entrusted me with your survival. I must train you to control your abilities, but first you must confront yourself. You must accept this truth and embrace it."

I took deep gulps of air and focused on a spot on the opposite wall, trying to calm myself. My pulse began to slow. Anton Moretti? There was something familiar about that name, something Hunter had said.

"Hunter told me about Anton Moretti, she said that he had been killed. Does she know about me?"

"No." said Mallory. "The only person alive that knows for sure that Anton Moretti is your father is me, and apparently Briggs, who approached me with the information at Sanctuary. I am not sure how he knew but keeping it quiet was the only way to keep you safe. Someone out there wanted your father dead, and if they knew he had a son they would have come looking for you."

"Do you know who killed him? Did they kill my mom too?" I asked. I'd been told my mom had died from complications during childbirth, but maybe that had been a lie too. Nothing would surprise me anymore.

"I have spent the last 17 years trying to hunt down whoever or whatever killed your father. The first couple of years after his death I did some things I am not proud of, all in the name of vengeance, not justice. I believed that an enemy of the Accords killed your father, so I started investigating any of the supers who voiced dissension. I made a lot of enemies, and I lost sight of my true purpose. Now, I have dedicated my life or whatever is left of it, to use my abilities to protect those who cannot protect themselves." said Mallory "I only met your mother once before her death. She was pregnant with you at the time. Your father introduced us. Towards the end he believed that someone was going to kill him. I did not think it possible, but he asked me to protect you both should something happen to him. Regretfully, I could not protect your mother from the pain and loss she felt after his death. She lost all hope and her body just shut down after your birth. I guess she felt like she had nothing left."

"She had me!" I said as warm tears spilled down my face. "I needed her."

"I know, son, and it is not your fault. None of this is your fault."

"I know it's not my fault. I didn't ask for any of this." I said. "All that I've ever done, has been in hopes of making them proud, but I didn't even know my own father's name. I've spent my entire life caring and missing people that didn't care about me."

"That's simply not true at all," said Mallory. "Your parents loved you. Your father could not have been more excited to have a son. He wanted a normal life for you, or as normal as possible, but when you were born, I knew that it would be impossible. Not all offspring of a vampire and mortal coupling are dhampir, in fact it is a very small percentage, but from the moment I first saw you there in the hospital, I knew that the power lay dormant within you."

I turned away from Mallory, using my sleeve to wipe away the tears that betrayed my emotions. I took a few deep breaths before turning back around.

"I'm tired of being lied to, Mallory. I'm tired of not knowing things that I need to know. I'm tired of being powerless." I said.

"I have not done a great job with any of this, I know, but I will do better. I will train you and together we will walk both worlds as a shield against those who would do evil. The blood in your veins is powerful and from what you told me about last night it is starting to manifest itself. I paid a great price for an enchantment that would shield you from your abilities, both the blessings and the curse, but now your blood calls to you. I will show you how to control it. Let's finish our business here and we will start your training immediately."

"What exactly are we doing here anyway?"

"We are here to collect a bargaining chip. I had to call in a favor to get access, but it was necessary to continue our investigation into Maria's death." Mallory explained, stepping into the open area and I followed him. It was a small circular room; the walls were made of the same stone as the hallways and the floor was also dirt. The round ceiling, which was almost low enough to brush against our heads, was also compacted earth. The only thing in the room was a tall basin, almost like a stone bird bath with a shallow pool of water in it. Hanging over the basin was a long singular tree root, glistening with beads of water.

While we were watching, a single droplet ran from the tip of the root and dripped down into the basin, causing ripples to disturb the still water. "This is the last remaining living root from the sycamore tree that saved the chapel. The event was declared a miracle by the church and therefore the water from this root has been ordained as holy."

Mallory reached into his suit jacket, pulled out a small vial and removed its stopper. He dipped the vial into the basin and skimmed it along the water, collecting a small sample of it. Mallory allowed the water from the outside of the vial to drip back into the basin and then stoppered it.

"So, this is holy water?" I asked.

"Yes, true holy water. It is valuable and rare and will afford us the cooperation of an arcanist." explained Mallory.

"Awesome, so I'm going to get to meet a real

magician?"

"Sure, if you are planning on attending a kids birthday party later today." Mallory said jokingly. "Enchanters and sorcerers are how they distinguish themselves, but best to use arcanist if you are not sure."

"Got it. Good to know."

Mallory pocketed the vial, and we made our way back topside. The church was full of visitors when we stepped back into the sanctuary. On the way out of the church Mallory deposited the skeleton key into a donation box next to the door. We walked to Mallory's car, which was parked on the street nearby. I couldn't be certain, but the air seemed crisper today than it had yesterday, the sun just a little bit brighter, and the sounds of the city just a little bit louder.

SIXTEEN

Mallory's sedan pulled up outside of an apartment building in Brooklyn. The building was not unlike the apartment complex that Maria lived in with her mother. We entered the elevator just inside of the building and Mallory pushed the button for the 13th floor. The elevator rumbled and shook, the pulleys sounding like they were in desperate need of repair, or maybe just a little grease. When it lurched to a stop Mallory turned his back to the door, which I thought was odd, until the back panel of the elevator opened wide, revealing a small landing and a door. We both stepped out onto the landing and Mallory pounded on the door with his fist. The golden plastic numeral one on the door of the apartment swung limply from a single screw and threatened to fall to the carpeted floor. We waited for someone to open the door, but no one ever did. Mallory pounded once more.

"Maybe they aren't home." I said.

"Oh, he's home, he's just ignoring us." said Mallory, continuing to knock. "Gadget, open up!"

A monitor on the door where a peep hole should have been blinked to life. A rail-thin man with a face that can only be described as having a weasel-like quality to it appeared on the monitor. Gadget's long brown hair was ratty and unkempt, and he had a pair of large headphones around his neck. He didn't look psyched about having visitors.

"Can I help you dudes?" Gadget asked in a nasally voice.

"Gadget, it's Mallory, let us in.," said Mallory.

"Dude, I know it's you, you think I don't recognize your knock? I'm busy right now, so kindly piss off." Gadget reached up as if to turn off the monitor but stopped short when Mallory pulled out the vial and shook it in front of him.

This caused Gadget to change his tone abruptly. "Whatcha got there?"

"You know what this is. All you have to do is let us in, do us a favor, and it's yours." Mallory explained.

"What kind of favor?" Gadget asked, nervously. "Your last favor almost got me killed."

"Just a simple locator spell, you won't even have to leave the apartment." Mallory assured Gadget.

Gadget seemed to contemplate the offer for a moment before he reached over to his right and tapped a few buttons on a keyboard. "Fine, but let's hurry, I wasn't lying when I said I'm busy."

The door made a hissing sound, like a seal being broken, and swung open. I had a feeling there was some supernatural technology or magic in play here. When we stepped into the apartment the door closed behind us and resealed itself.

It was a studio apartment, where everything was open except for the bathroom, which was blocked off with a couple of paneled dividers. Dirty dishes were stacked up in the kitchen sink and the trashcan was overflowing with take-out containers. Very much a bachelor's pad. Gadget was sitting in front of a massive collection of computer monitors, in a futuristic looking chair which he spun around in. The desk and floor were littered with empty soda cans and snack wrappers.

Gadget pulled off his headphones and sat them on his desk, atop what appeared to be an empty bag of chips. When he stood up out of his chair and onto unsteady legs, which I guessed was probably asleep from lack of use, I got a full look at him. Gadget was wearing pajama bottoms, but no shirt, and very skinny. Mallory used his foot to clear a path through the junk on the kitchen floor.

"Love what you've done with the place, Gad." said Mallory. "I might recommend a cleaning service to give it a once over, but other than that... It's great."

"Clean? Bro, who has time to clean? I stay too busy." said Gadget, stumbling toward them. "Alright, what do you have for me?" Gadget reached out to take the vial from Mallory, but Mallory drew it back. He reached into his jacket pocket and pulled out a small clear plastic baggy, which he handed to Gadget.

"I need you to find the owner of this hair." Mallory explained.

Gadget held up the bag and peered into it. I could not see the thick brown hair from where I was standing, but I knew it was there.

"Hmm." Gadget mused. "That's not much to go on, one hair means I will only have one crack at this, you know that right?"

Mallory nodded. "I do, I trust you."

I didn't share Mallory's faith, but I didn't have much to go on besides a terrible first impression of the man's lifestyle.

"And you know once the ritual is complete, I'll only know where they are at that exact moment?" Gadget continued.

"I do," said Mallory. "I will be prepared to leave at a moment's notice."

"Ok. Well, it'll take some time and I'll call you when it's done." said Gadget. "Now, if there is nothing else that you need..." he held out his hand to Mallory who placed the vial of holy water into it. Gadget carefully placed the vial into the pocket of his Cheeto-stained pajama bottoms. "Thanks for stopping by. See you later." Gadget began ushering them toward the door, but I couldn't pass up the opportunity to at least ask some questions first.

"So, you're an arcanist?"

Gadget glanced at me for the first time, as if he had just noticed that Mallory was not alone.

"Obviously," said Gadget. "I'm a sorcerer."

"What does that mean?"

Gadget looked at me as if I had a third eye growing out

of the center of my head. "You don't know what a sorcerer is?"

"I mean, I've heard of sorcerers in movies and books and things." I said. "But like, what's it really?"

"He is new to our world." Mallory explained.

Gadget looked back over his shoulder to his computer monitor and exhaled noisily to display his annoyance. "Fine, I have a couple of minutes. Being a sorcerer means I was born with the ability to access magic. You may have heard of this described as 'blood magic'? Or perhaps the more insulting term of 'dirty magic'?"

I, of course, hadn't heard of either, but I was very fascinated. Vampire lore and that type of thing never really did it for me, but I'd always been fascinated by magic. It was surreal to be talking to a real practitioner of magic, despite his unconventional appearance.

"What kind of things can you do?" I asked.

"The list gets bigger every day." Gadget answered.

"I remember at Sanctuary they announced Abigail Black as 'enchantress', what does that mean?"

"Mallory, is this guy for real?" Gadget asked, and Mallory nodded. "Well, basically there are two types of arcanists, you are either an enchanter or you're a sorcerer."

"What's the difference between an enchanter and a sorcerer?"

"The same difference between a broom and a vacuum." Gadget said. "One of them sucks." Gadget looked at us with a grin on his face, waiting for our reaction, but Mallory just shook his head.

"That joke would have killed in the right circles. I mean, not in any of the Circles, but... Well, anyway, thanks for stopping by." Gadget said, ushering us toward the door and as I was turning to leave, I got a good look at what was displayed on one of the massive computer monitors.

"Wait, you play World of Warcraft?" I asked, surprised.

"Do I play WoW?" Gadget snickered. "You've

probably heard of me, *GadolfTheWhite*, a max level mage. I'm kind of a big deal."

"And you play a mage?" I asked.

"Yep." said Gadget.

"But you can actually use magic...in real life."

"What's your point?" Gadget asked.

I was too dumbfounded to answer, and Mallory patted me on the back, leading us back into the elevator and out of his car.

"While we are waiting for Gadget to provide us with a lead, I believe that it is important to continue your training," Mallory said as we neared his office. "Hunter was telling me earlier about a case she is working, and I think that it might be best if you accompany her for its climax."

"Ok, that would be cool." I said. In all honesty I was only half paying attention to what Mallory was saying. After my conversation with an actual sorcerer, I was reflecting on what Mallory told me about myself, that I was a dhampir. I wasn't sure what that meant exactly, but something about it felt right.

When we finally arrived at the *Sifu Wok*, it was as greasy and hot as I remember. Entering Mallory's office, we were greeted nonchalantly by his secretary Violet, who sat behind her messy desk reading the newspaper.

"Someone called for you, Mallory. I wrote it down, but I've misplaced it." she said.

Mallory smiled. "Worry not, Vi. If it was important, I am sure they will call back."

Mallory motioned for me to close the door behind us. I took a seat in the same chair that I sat in for the interview, the interview before Maria's mom came in asking for Mallory's help, the interview that changed my life forever.

Mallory took off his suit jacket and placed it on a hook behind the door and rolled up the sleeves of his button-down shirt before sitting behind his desk with a sigh. As Mallory rubbed his eyes, I noticed the silver ring on his finger, and it sparked an unanswered question.

"When we were in the Stray's den and you were fighting with Mannie, at one point you seemed to create a silver blade out of thin air. How did you do that? Was it magic?"

"It was magic, but I did not create the blade." Mallory answered. "I won the blade off a shifter many years back, and since I cannot exactly walk down the street carrying it, I paid a sorcerer to attune it to this ring so that I may call upon it when I needed it. Observe."

Mallory held out his right hand away from me, palm up in the air.

"*Blad*" he said in a deep voice and just as it had in the den of The Strays, a brilliant silver blade materialized in his hand. Mallory wrapped his fingers around the hilt of the sword and swung it back and forth slowly, the sharp silver cutting through the air effortlessly.

"That's really awesome. Do I get one of those?" I asked, only half-joking.

"I'm afraid it isn't that easy and carrying silver around shifters is a great way to get yourself killed. They tend to take that sort of thing personally, considering how dangerous the metal is for them."

"Why do you carry it then?"

"Because I have earned their respect and because they know I will only use it when I have exhausted all other options. In the case of the challenge with Mannie, silver was the only thing that was going to get his attention and make him take me seriously. That does remind me of something though. *Slida*." Mallory said the last command and the blade dematerialized in his hand. He stood up out of his chair and walked over to remove a framed picture from the wall to reveal a built-in safe. Mallory spun the dial a few times and the door to the safe popped open. "Your father wanted you to have this, when you were ready."

My mind began to race. My father had apparently been

a powerful vampire, had he left me some kind of awesome magical object or a vast fortune? My high hopes were short lived, however, when Mallory turned around holding another small metal ring which he handed to me. I took the ring and examined it. It was heavy and gold and it had my father's initials raised along the top of the band. It was old and the initials were beginning to wear down into the metal.

"This was your father's ring." Mallory explained. "I believe that you are now old enough to wear it. Anyone who knew your father knew of this ring, he used it to seal his correspondence, and anyone who owed your father a favor will recognize this ring and will therefore know that you are his heir. He included a note for you." Mallory handed me a small envelope with a wax seal. My father's initials were pressed into the dried wax.

My hands shook as I turned the letter over and broke the seal. This would be the first time I saw my father's handwriting, the first message I read from him. Nervously I pulled the letter out and the envelope fell slowly to the ground. Unfolding the piece of paper, I read the single sentence that my father had left for me.

This will open many doors for you.
Anton Moretti

I let out an audible sigh of disappointment. Instead of the warm correspondence from father to son across time, the letter was cold and distant. He'd even signed it with his full name, instead of "dad" or something like that. My expectations for my dad were probably too high. Anton Moretti, my pops, had been an undead monster straight out of folklore, maybe he hadn't been capable of feeling normal fatherly emotions.

"Thanks Mallory." I said, not wanting to appear ungrateful. The ring fit perfectly on my right hand. The metal was cool, and it took me no time at all to get used to the sensation of having it on my finger. Mallory reached over and patted me on the back affectionately as Violet poked her head in the office to inform Mallory that he had a phone call.

Mallory stepped out of the office to take the call, the cord of Violet's phone stretching to its maximum length allowed him to stand in the doorway of his office. I watched him curiously, while absentmindedly playing with the ring on my finger. It seemed like the person on the other end of the call was doing most of the talking. Mallory just offered the occasional acknowledgement. At one point Mallory cupped his right hand over the phone and asked me to write down a number for him. "There is a pen in my desk drawer, somewhere." Mallory said.

I stepped to the other side of the desk and opened the drawer. It was full of loose fortunes from fortune cookies and miscellaneous office supplies. There were a couple of pens and one of them worked. I wrote down the number for Mallory on some scratch paper and handed it to him. When I went to put the pen back, I glimpsed my name on a handwritten letter that had been folded up and placed inside of the drawer. Looking to make sure that Mallory wasn't watching, I quickly grabbed the letter and pocketed it.

After Mallory finished up his phone call, he loaned me a few books to read in my free time and treated me to a late lunch at the *Sifu Wok*. I had some of the greasiest and most delicious lo mein I've ever eaten. Mallory informed me that Hunter would be picking me up the following morning and taking me for a ride-along with her. I was thankful for the chance to rest before the next adventure, assuming no one was waiting to kidnap me in my bedroom.

Mallory gave me a ride back home and even went inside to check everything out before leaving. I was reunited with my cellphone and wallet and took a minute to respond to my friends, apologizing again for the previous night, before having a quiet dinner with my grandparents. I even watched a movie with my grandfather before heading to bed. I did not, however, immediately drift off to sleep. Lying in bed, I turned the note I'd taken from Mallory's desk over in my hands and read it again, trying to grasp its implications.

> Mr. Moran,
>
> I believe it's time. Saturday is ready. As much as I hate to admit all of this is real, I cannot ignore the warning signs that you prepared me for. I'm sure Saturday has no idea anything is changing, but I've noticed. Part of me wants to move him away to keep him out of your grasp and away from the world we lost his mother to, but it's out of respect for her final wishes that I write to you now. It's time for you to meet Saturday.
>
> John Costa

There was no mistaking my grandfather's handwriting.

The last remaining piece of solid foundation upon which I was standing fell out from under me. My grandparents knew the truth of everything. It seemed they've always known, and they lied to me just like every other adult in my life. A mixture of anger and sadness welled up in me. It took all the restraint I could muster to not wake my grandparents up and confront them with the letter.

I swallowed it all down and tried to clear my mind of emotion. Hunter and her case were waiting for me tomorrow and my body and mind were desperate for rest. I needed my full wits tomorrow, so I forced myself to close my eyes and try to sleep. It finally came. I did not dream.

SEVENTEEN

I awoke in the middle of the night, wide awake, my body already beginning to acclimate to a more nocturnal schedule. Normally when I couldn't sleep, I would log in and play video games, but not tonight, I just wasn't feeling it. Instead, I reached over to the stack of old books Mallory loaned me and picked up the one off the top. The book was wrapped in solid black leather that was faded and torn and looked to be a strong breeze away from falling apart completely. The title of the book was on the front cover in faded gold lettering. *The Night Children*, by Augustine Calumet.

Carefully, I opened the book and began to read. There was no copyright date that I could find, but the use of words like "thou" and "yore" and "ye" told me it was old. The author, Augustine Calumet, seemed to have an intimate knowledge of supernatural creatures and must have spent a great deal of time researching vampires. The details were so in-depth that I began to wonder if it was possible that the author had himself been a vampire.

The first quarter of the book was dedicated to uncovering the history and background of vampires, and vampiric lore. Calumet gave several common beliefs about their origin but made sure to point out that none were confirmed, and they were all just conjecture. My favorite origin theory revolved around a tribal king from the Mesopotamian region who had butchered a rival tribe and a young sorceress had, with her dying breath, placed a curse upon the king and his family.

The young girl lifted herself off the dirt and up to her knees, her once white dress was now stained red from blood that poured from her wounds and the wounds of her mother who died trying to protect her. She lifted her bloodied hand and pointed her finger at the king who stomped toward her

"Blood alone will sustain thee, wretched creature. On the blood of my ancestors, I curse thee." the young sorceress spat. "Never again will thou see the light of the Sun." The king swung his vicious axe and the blood of the young sorceress sprayed across his face.

In a later chapter the author described the four known ways to kill a vampire. Surprisingly, none of them involved crosses or holy water. This was good information as I would have looked really stupid trying to ward off a vampire with a cross.

To kill one of the night children, I know of only four methods. One must remove the head of the vampire completely. Or one must drive a wooden stake through the heart of the vampire. Or one must burn the body of the vampire with fire. Or one must force the vampire into the sunlight.

According to Calumet, vampires sleep hidden away from the sun during the day and that is when they are at their most vulnerable. Calumet wrote that vampires were fueled by the blood of mortals and that it replenishes the vampiric blood in their veins, which allows them to live forever and gives them an unnatural strength and agility. I was most surprised to learn that vampires don't have to kill when they drink blood. Instead, Calumet wrote that they can simply drink what they need and leave the source alive so that they can feed from them later. Calumet did also point out that there are of course exceptions to this rule and some vampires will kill their prey just for the thrill or to satiate their monstrous natures.

Vampires, like humans, are not all the same. Some vampires walk among humans every night socializing with them because the vampire has learned to control and suppress its monstrous nature. While other vampire seclude themselves away and see humans only as cattle from which they feed. Worse more there are vampires who see humans as nothing more than toys for their twisted desires and pleasures.

The next section of the book dispelled the myth that the bite of a vampire transforms someone else into a vampire. In fact, according to Calumet, it takes great effort on the part of the vampire to pass on the curse to another. While the author did acknowledge he had never seen the ritual performed in person, he had discussed it in depth with an individual with intimate knowledge on the subject. Apparently, to create another of their kind, a vampire must drain the mortal of all of their blood and then replace it with a substantial portion of their own vampiric blood, which obviously leaves the creature temporarily weakened and vulnerable.

This process is incredibly dangerous to the vampire and often fatal for the mortal, thus the practice is not undertaken lightly. Vampires, by nature, are untrusting and granting immortality to someone requires a great deal of trust on the part of the vampire. Vampires, often, are forced to watch from afar as their mortal families wither and die, instead of passing onto them the curse.

I did wonder if advanced medicine and technology helped to alleviate some of the inherent risks of the procedure. The large number of vampires at Sanctuary seemed to speak for itself.

I read for hours, completely engrossed, despite the occasional word that I had to Google to figure out its meaning. Towards the end of the book Calumet dedicated a small section to what he called the "dhampir phenomenon". Calumet admitted he had never encountered a dhampir or anyone with direct knowledge of their actual existence, just conjecture and hearsay. He did go on to say however, that he believed that dhampir existed, he just lacked proof to back up the claims.

While I have never in my travels encountered a dhampir, it is my belief that they do exist, however rare they might be. The laws of nature dictate that for every action, there is a reaction. For thousands of years the vampire has fed from the human population, safely atop the food chain. I believe dhampir to be an evolutionary response. A half vampire who carries not the full burden of the vampiric curse. This has been discredited by fellow vampiric scholars who see vampires as unnatural and therefore not subject to the laws of nature. I hold fast to my beliefs and hope to encounter a dhampir one day so as to validate my claims and ascertain their place in our world.

I closed The Night Children and placed it back on the stack of books next to my bed. I was shocked to see sunlight peeking through my bedroom window. It had been a long time since I had sat down and read a book cover to cover that wasn't a comic book or graphic novel. I awarded myself a hearty pat on the back and got up to get ready for the day.

There was a knock on my bedroom door and my grandfather poked his head into the room. I could smell my grandmother's delicious pancakes and bacon cooking downstairs; it was one of the most pleasant smells in the entire world.

"Morning, son." my grandfather said. "Breakfast is ready, come on down and join us."

I hesitated for a moment. The raw emotions from the betrayal I felt the night before threatened to bubble up out of me. I tried my best to swallow them down.

"Saturday are you alright?" my grandfather asked.

"Yeah, I'm good, I'll be down in just a few." I said, but when my grandfather turned to leave the question that I had been holding in forced its way out. "Granddad?"

"Yes, son?" he said, stepping back into the room.

"Why...Why didn't you tell me that my father was..." The question was so ludicrous that I couldn't even say it. "...Why didn't you tell me the truth?"

My grandfather's face fell as he walked over and sat down next to me with a sigh. We sat in silence for a few moments before he put an arm around my shoulder and pulled me close.

"I'm sorry. I don't know what else to say, but I didn't

want any of this for you, and neither did your grandmother. Neither of us wanted to believe it at first." he explained. "We thought your mother had lost her mind or gone and gotten herself into drugs." He let go of me and I looked into his eyes. For the first time ever, I saw tears threatening to fall down his weathered cheeks. "Shortly before you were born, we met Mallory, and your dad, and learned the truth of your mother's words. You can imagine what that was like for us."

"Earth shattering?" I answered. "Life changing? Yeah, I know the feeling."

"Of course, you do." he said, wiping his brow with his sleeve. "When she died… It changed everything and you became our world, our responsibility. We wanted to keep you as far from all that supernatural nonsense as possible, but Mallory explained to us how dangerous it would be for you to remain untrained once you…you know, become what you are. We hoped and prayed for years that nothing would change, but last year I noticed a change in you. I hope that you can understand why I kept it all from you, son. I thought foolishly that if we never talked about it then it wouldn't happen."

Droplets of tears that had welled up in his eyes ran down his cheeks and his face was flushed red. Seeing my grandfather like this tempered any anger that threatened to rise in me. Instead of getting upset, I wrapped him up in a bear hug.

My grandparents were the only family I had. They took me and loved me and made sure I wanted for nothing. They always placed my own needs above their own. I refused to be mad at them, whatever they'd done, they did with love, I knew that.

When we joined grandma for breakfast, I gave her a kiss on her forehead and told her I loved her. Then I feasted. I ate my body weight in pancakes, not realizing how hungry I was.

After breakfast I went up to my room to wait for Hunter. I wasn't sure what we were going to be doing, but I wanted to be as prepared as possible, so I packed a backpack and made sure my clothes gave me a full range of motion. Tying my sneakers tight, I grabbed my backpack and stuffed it full of anything I thought I might need and waited for Hunter to call.

Shortly before noon the doorbell rang, and I was awoken from an impromptu nap. I made it downstairs in time to see my grandmother ushering Hunter inside. Holmes, the large mastiff who stood well above Hunter's waist, was trailing right behind her. Hunter was wearing skinny jeans and a black tank top with the words "keep NYC weird" on it in white letters. She was also rocking some sweet Converse All-Stars.

"There you are, Saturday." my grandmother said, "This young lady says she's a friend of yours."

"Hey." I said, nodding to her. "Grandma, this is Hunter. I'm gonna be working with her today. The small horse is Holmes."

"Hi there, Holmes." grandma said, scratching Holmes behind his large ears, which flopped side to side as he shook his head and panted happily in response.

"You ready to go, rookie?" asked Hunter with a smile.

I told my grandparents goodbye and loaded up into Hunter's SUV, with Holmes taking his usual spot stretched across the backseat. Hunter had a large wooden baseball bat holstered and easily accessible next to the passenger seat.

"Buckle up for safety," said Hunter, before pulling out of the driveway.

While driving to the destination Hunter filled me in on the details of her most recent case. She assigned herself to this case a few months back when she noticed something out of the ordinary. In the span of a month four different people, with just enough in common to catch her eye, went missing within a two-mile radius. She spent time investigating known supers with residences in the vicinity, but nothing came from that. It wasn't until the sixth victim went missing that she began to understand the pattern. The subject was taking a new victim every ten days and all the victims were from the fringes, either homeless or destitute, which was why the media or police hadn't picked up on it yet.

Hunter was investigating a rumor of a rumor regarding a newly arrived super, when she came across a dwelling that carried all the markers of a vampire's safe house. Today was the 10th day since the last victim was taken so she didn't have time to sit and watch the house like she normally would. We were going to breach the house during the day and see what we could find. If she were wrong and it was a mortal establishment we would leave quietly and clear everything up later, but if it were indeed the residence of the killer then we would operate with the authority to destroy the offender. I felt ill thinking about that possibility.

It was still early afternoon when Hunter pulled into a rundown parking lot just outside of a neighborhood in Queens. We hopped out of the vehicle, Hunter holding open the rear door for Holmes who jumped down and stretched his legs. Holmes' solid black fur gleamed in the afternoon sunlight. Hunter reached into the backseat and pulled out a small gray backpack which she strapped across her back. She withdrew her wooden baseball bat from its harness and sheathed it between her backpack straps. She looked like an awesome video game character, all five-foot of fury.

"Do I get a weapon too?" I asked.

"Sorry, bro. This party was BYOB. Bring your own baseball bat." she said smiling, and then patted her backpack. "Don't worry, we're loaded for vampire. Now let's go, dork."

Walking down the sidewalk we passed by a ton of normal looking homes. It looked like a typical middle-class neighborhood in Queens, and It's hard for me to believe that this was the type of place a vampire would live. I'd imagined them all living in high rises and mansions like De La Cruz, or coffins like Dracula, but apparently money and power were not as important to some of them as it was to others. From what Hunter described, it seemed as if this vampire found pleasure in killing humans, just like I had read in *The Night Children*.

Hunter stopped in front of a small brick split-level home with a one-car driveway and a small backyard. Nonchalantly she turned and motioned to me that this was the place. I looked up and down the street to make sure we weren't being watched. The tiny backyard was surrounded by a chain-link fence and Hunter went over to investigate it while Holmes and I followed close behind. She popped open the gate and we entered. From afar the house looked just like every other one on the block, but up this close I could see that it was not. For one thing, the windows were fake. While it looked like there were curtains and drapes hanging behind glass panes, there was in fact no windowpane at all, instead it was cardboard or wood with the image of a window plastered onto it. A clever design for someone who was trying to block out all-natural light without drawing unwanted attention.

The backdoor had a set of concrete steps that led up to a storm door. Hunter opened the outer door, but the wooden interior door was locked and wouldn't budge. Setting her pack down onto the ground, Hunter began to dig through it until she found a small metal crowbar. A devious smile crept across her face as if she were really excited about the chance to use it.

"Wait, wait, wait." I said, in a hushed voice. "What if this isn't the right place. Isn't that breaking and entering?"

"I think it's technically only breaking and entering if you steal something," she said.

"That doesn't sound right."

"Oops, too late," she said as she jabbed the sharp end of the crowbar into the wooden door frame. I winced at the sound of the wood splitting and glanced around nervously to make sure that no one was watching while she popped the door open. The wood splintered and cracked and when I turned back around the door stood open.

"Alohomora." Hunter said, smiling.

The door opened into the living room and the house itself seemed to recluse away from the light that poured in. The air inside of the home was warm and stale and smelled rancid. The living room had putrid green shag carpets and wood paneling on the walls. An old floral-patterned couch sat in the middle of the room in front of an ancient television with metal rabbit ears sticking out of the back. The stench of decay stung my nostrils. Everything just smelled wrong. My insides told me to run, to not step another foot inside of the house, and I desperately wanted to listen. Whatever I thought of the smell was nothing to what Holmes thought of it. The poor dog took a whiff of the air inside the house and let out a low moan, but bravely the dog was the first one into the house, with Hunter right behind him. I had no choice but to muster my courage and follow suit.

When the door closed the house returned to its normal state of complete darkness. Sure, enough, all the windows in the house were boarded up from the inside. Hunter dropped her pack in the middle of the living room and pulled out a few different items. The first item was a flashlight that emitted a red light, it was connected to a band she wrapped around her head. She handed me a handheld flashlight and in the unnatural darkness I clung tightly to the light source. Next out of the bag was a large belt that she wrapped over her shoulder and waist. It was like a bandolier that gunfighters wore in movies, but instead of bullets it held numerous sharp wooden stakes. So bad ass.

"We have to find where it sleeps." Hunter whispered. "And drive a stake through its heart, ideally without waking it up."

"What happens if it wakes up first?" I asked, nervously.

"We still kill it." said Hunter, confidently. "If it does wake up, we will want to drive it into the sunlight, it will give us an advantage. As quietly as possible let's take the boards off these windows, just in case." she pointed to the two windows in the living room.

While Hunter watched my back, I used the crowbar to remove the wooden planks off the windows, allowing natural light to enter into the room. The sunlight and fresh air that filtered into the home were a wonderful reprieve from the dark and decay.

"Shouldn't I have a weapon or something?" I whispered.

"You are a weapon." Hunter said.

"Then why do you have a baseball bat and stakes?"

"Because I can't kill this A-hole with my looks." she whispered. "Fine, I think I have something else in my bag." She reached down into her bag and pulled out a small hand axe, it was a little less than two-foot long, with a razor-sharp curved blade.

"Is this a tomahawk?" I asked. "Why do you have a tomahawk in your bag?"

"Because I couldn't fit a fire axe in there." she said as if it made complete sense and of course she would need to always have an axe with her. "Stop asking questions, rookie."

Hunter motioned for quiet and for me to follow her. She led us into the kitchen that adjoined the living room. The smell in the kitchen was even worse than in the living room. The light from the windows in the living room did not penetrate the darkness in other areas of the house, so the kitchen was still as black as night, and as silent. The only sound was the subtle hum of the refrigerator. There were no exterior doors in the kitchen and only a single boarded window above the sink. My shoes squeaked as they tried to stick to the disgusting linoleum floor. I shined my light around the room, half afraid of what it would reveal.

Hunter investigated a small pantry door, with Holmes by her side. Out of sheer curiosity I opened the fridge, and immediately regretted it. Damp, fetid air blasted me in the face, and a wave of nausea hit me hard. Inside the fridge were trinkets the vampire had kept from its victims. Fingers and ears and eyeballs all floated in clear jars like pickles. I'm not embarrassed to say I threw up right there on the spot. Everything I'd eaten for breakfast, all those delicious pancakes, spilled across the dirty linoleum floor.

Hunter shushed me from across the room as she closed the pantry door and walked over. While I composed myself, she looked inside the fridge. "It likes to keep trophies, and by the looks of it there are more victims than I thought." she said, giving me a rough pat on the back. "Get it together, rook, we have some justice to deal out."

Once we were certain the vampire was not hiding in the kitchen or living room, we made our way deeper into the house. Holmes led the way down the darkened hallway with his nose to the ground trying to sniff out the creature's resting spot. The dog stopped in front of a door on the right and Hunter quietly turned the handle, opening the door into the room. It was a small bedroom with half of the floor space taken up by a single twin-sized bed. I drew the beam of my flashlight across the room. The bed was made up perfectly without so much as a wrinkle in the sheets or bed skirt. On one side of the bed there was an old wooden dresser, beside it was an antique wheelchair with a blanket lying across the arm of the chair as if the person sitting in the chair had just gotten up and walked away.

Hunter tapped me on the shoulder, and I barely stifled the urge to scream out. Wide-eyed I looked to Hunter, who motioned toward the closet door and crept over to it. The closet had a small sliding wooden door. Hunter motioned for me to pull open the door and positioned herself, stake in hand, ready to strike. She counted to three silently with her fingers, and I pulled the door open vigorously, bringing my flashlight up at the same time.

There was nothing. The closet was empty except for an assortment of soiled clothes. Hunter looked frustrated. She looked around the room. There was nothing else in the room, except for the bed, which was also empty. After a moment of contemplation, I had an idea. I got Hunter's attention and with my hands I tried to relay what I was thinking. Gently lifting the side of the bed skirt, I revealed a small space underneath the bed. It was tight, but it would have been possible for someone to fit under there. Hunter nodded that she understood and motioned for me to trade places with her, and I did. She got down on her hands and knees with her red headlamp on and quietly lifted the bed skirt and looked underneath. I readied myself, but nothing happened. Hunter pulled out from under the bed and stood up, shaking her head; she turned to face me. She paused and I watched the blood drain from her face. I was trying to get a read on what was wrong, when I felt cold clammy hands grasp around my neck.

I couldn't breathe. I couldn't scream. My feet felt as though they were made of lead when I tried to turn around. The flashlight was ripped from my grasp and thrown against the wall where it shattered on impact, its light going out instantly. I waited for the bite, waited for the pain of the teeth sinking into my skin. I was in a daze.

"Duck!" said Hunter, and I was pulled back to reality. I did not so much as duck as I did fall, pulling myself free from the grasp of the undead creature. I hit the ground and rolled up to my feet. Now the only light in the room was the red light coming from Hunter's headlamp which bounced around as she ran at the creature, swinging her bat with great ferocity. The bat smashed against the vampire's skull just as Holmes' large body crashed into the creature, the dog grabbing a mouthful of undead flesh in its teeth. The creature let out a hiss like a serpent that sent chills through my body like ice water.

The creature kicked out its leg forcefully and sent Holmes flying across the room, a chunk of the vampire's flesh hanging from his maw. The dog hit the wall with a crash and fell limp to the floor with a whimper. Seeing this ignited a fire inside of me, and I closed distance with the undead creature, blood pulsing through my veins. The vampire resembled a human male, but it looked less normal than the vampires at Sanctuary had, it was monstrous and its visage frightening. The creature was tall and lean. Its pale skin was pulled tight across its face, giving it the appearance of a skull wearing a mask. The vampire's eyes were large white orbs, with no pupils that I could see. Its fingers were like long thin claws, with dirty yellow fingernails sharpened to a point. The vampire used them to lash out wildly at Hunter as the three of us fought in the cramped space of the tiny bedroom.

I hefted the tomahawk in my hand and looked for an opening to strike at the creature, but I knew I wouldn't be able to without hitting Hunter. I could feel my reflexes heightening, the wild strikes of the undead creature seemed to slow in my mind. I wondered if this was how Hunter was narrowly avoiding them, because she too was like me. A dhampir. It wasn't until this very moment that I knew for certain.

We moved to flank the creature, one on each side, fighting in tandem. As fast as we both were, the creature was just as fast, and it had the advantage of being an experienced killing machine. I narrowly escaped numerous strikes that would surely have killed me. Our only advantage was that there were two of us and the fact that the creature had just woken from its slumber. Since the creature was unable to focus on either of us it was distracted and not able to fully use its unnatural strength. But how long could we keep this up? Hunter dropped her bat and ripped a stake free from the bandolier across her chest. She waited for an opening and struck. The sharpened wood pierced the chest of the creature and she drove it back into the bedroom wall. For a moment, the only sound was the loud scream of the vampire. I waited for something to happen, for the creature to die, but it did not. Hunter hesitated, and it cost her.

"Missed it." she said just as the creature thrust both hands around her neck and twisted her body in front of it like a shield. It brought its long bony arm across her throat and held her tight, using its other hand to expose the skin at the base of her neck. The creature licked its lips and smiled a wicked smile at me.

"So fressssshhh." the creature hissed. Hunter struggled to escape its grasp, but she was held too tight. "So young."

"Let her go!" I said.

"No, I don't think I will." said the creature. "Instead, I will eat the flesh from her bones and add her to my collection."

"Hey, shit for brains, go ahead and bite me." said Hunter, continuing to taunt bravely and fight against the creature's grasp. "No seriously, do it, dummy."

"Oh, I shall, and your friend will watch me eat you piece by piece until it is his turn." the creature hissed.

"God, you're dumb." said Hunter.

"Hunter, what are you doing?" I asked, frantically trying to think of a way to free her.

"Only a complete idiot would turn their back on a mastiff." she said.

The creature said nothing, but it turned its head just as Holmes launched his massive body into the air. Reflexively the vampire let go of Hunter and spun out of Holmes' direct path. Instead of hitting him full on, Holmes just clipped the vampire's shoulder, knocking it into the wall. The creature, seeing its fortunes change dramatically, ran out of the bedroom. I followed right after it.

The hallway was dark and silent, and the creature was nowhere to be found. The only sound was our own breathing. Hunter used her headlamp to search the hallway, but it was empty. I clutched the axe tightly, knuckles white and palms sweating against the wooden haft.

"Where did it go?" I asked.

"Stay alert." Hunter ordered.

I swiveled my head around trying to watch both directions at once. I could feel the sweat running down the back of my neck, warm and sticky.

"Let's finish this, you coward." Hunter challenged, but only silence answered her. I wiped the sweat off the back of my neck.

"Saturday, take that axe and start busting out windows. All of them." said Hunter.

I lifted the axe up and stopped. The haft was covered in blood. How did it get bloody? I had not used it in the fight. Drawing it closer to inspect it I saw that my hand was covered in a deep crimson, but there were no cuts that I could see. Then everything fell into place. I grabbed Hunter and yanked her back just as the creature dropped from the ceiling. The vampire hissed loudly, baring its fangs, and stalking toward us.

Instinctively, I did the first thing that came to mind and launched the tomahawk at the creature. In slow motion the axe turned end over end in air. The vampire was just as surprised to see the metal blade cutting through the dark hallway toward it. The blade struck true, right in the center of the creature's chest. The vampire let out an ear-piercing shriek and flailed its arms wildly.

"Into the light!" Hunter screamed as she charged. I followed her lead and we each grabbed an arm of the creature and drove it backwards through the hallway and into the living room. The vampire fought madly against us, but our combined strength was enough to push it back. We forced it against the wall, fresh sunlight hit the creature's body for the first time in decades. The vampire's skin began to pop and hiss as blisters sprouted all over its body. The screams of the undead creature reverberated through my mind, but I closed my eyes and used all my might to keep it pinned against the wall. The vampire flailed, trying to bite at my arms, which were just out of its reach. Gnashing teeth and undead screams filled my ears.

"Just a little longer! Just a little longer!" Hunter repeated, and soon the thrashing stopped. I waited a moment and then opened my eyes, dropping what I held in my hands.

Where the creature had been there was now just bones and dust. The vampire had returned to the state of which it would have been had it died a mortal.

For a moment we stood over the creature's bones catching our breath, basking in the life-saving sunlight. The pile of bones was the first thing I've ever killed. I wondered if it could really be called killing if the thing had already been dead. There had been nothing human about that creature, but still it surprised me that I felt no remorse.

"We saved lives today." said Hunter, as she kicked the pile of bones and scattered them across the floor.

"I wish we could have stopped him from killing those people." I said. "There were so many."

"We can't bring back the dead and we can't change the past." Hunter said. "But we can give them justice, that's what we do, and we are the only ones who will. This is why you won't catch me hanging out and playing nice at Sanctuary, I know what these monsters are capable of. They can all hide behind their fancy clothes and their phony facades, but I've seen the darkness that lies within them. And when they cross the line, I'll be there waiting."

There was something in Hunter's voice, it was pained and yet it was resolute. I knew I couldn't fully comprehend the horrors of her experiences. I'd only been in the world for a week and already saw more than I could stomach. Finally, I understood the Shroud that Mallory spoke of, why the mind protected humans from reality like it did. The horrors of this world would break you and change you forever if you were not prepared to deal with it.

"What do we do now?" I asked.

"As much as I would like to torch this place, we just leave it. Eventually someone will come to investigate the smell." she explained.

"But what about all of this?" I said, pointing towards the bones.

"The Shroud still stands. We've done our part; the

threat is eliminated. The police will investigate, nothing will come of it, everyone eventually moves on."

I nodded and bent down to pick up the axe from where it lay in the pile of bones on the floor. I offered it back to Hunter.

"Keep it. You might need it one day." she said.

Thanks." I said. "Hey, did you know your dad?" I wasn't sure why I asked that, it just popped out.

"I did." she answered in stride, the question not seeming to catch her off guard.

"He was a vampire, wasn't he?"

She looked up at me and for a moment the carefree fun-loving girl that I had first met was gone and in her place was a girl trying to cope with the world that she'd been thrust in, just like me. For the first time her defenses were down.

"Yeah, he was a vampire." she said. "And I knew you were like me, by the way, just like Mallory. He didn't have to tell me; I just knew it."

"What was it like, being raised by a vampire?"

"I wasn't raised by my dad," said Hunter, with the familiar fire returning to her eyes. "After I was born my mother wanted my father to turn her, to make her immortal just like him. She had some twisted idea of us all being some happy undead Brady Bunch, as if that were possible. My dad rejected the both of us. He left us and came to New York, leaving my mother a shell of her normal self. He didn't kill her, but he might as well have. She was never the same. She died shortly before my sixteenth birthday, and that's when I fled home and came looking for him. He found me and had the nerve to welcome me with open arms as if nothing had ever happened. He told me what I was, what I could do. He trained me. He wanted to make me a weapon, a tool that he could use to destroy his rivals, but that didn't work out so well for him."

"I'm so sorry, Hunter. What happened to him?"

"I found his closet full of skeletons." she said. "I refused to let him use me, to make me a monster like him... So,

I killed him." I stood there in stunned silence, not sure what to say. "Be glad that you never got to meet your father, Saturday, that you never had to see the true monster that he was or would become."

I empathize with Hunter, she was projecting, which was understandable, but she didn't know who my father was. Hunter didn't know that it was my father who created peace in the city.

EIGHTEEN

That night, fresh off the exhilarating high of a fight with an actual vampire, I met up with my friends in Brooklyn at a popular arcade. With the money from my first paycheck in my pocket, I was really looking forward to a chill evening with friends.

The arcade, called Power Up! was a popular hangout for under 18s in the city. It had tons of vintage video games as well as some newer games modified into arcade cabinets. Power Up also served a wide variety of coffees, espressos, and chocolate. Part of the fun for our group was filling Wes up with caffeine and letting him loose, it was always entertaining.

Liz and Liam were locked in a fierce Street Fighter battle when my phone buzzed in my pocket. Mallory was calling. Just as I was answering the phone Liz kicked me in the shin with the back of her foot, without looking away from their game.

"I swear if you talk in my ear, I will fight you for real." Liz said, frantically mashing the buttons on the console to keep Chun Li out of the reach of Vega's claws.

"I don't mind, bro, talk all you want. It won't matter, I've got her right where I want her." Liam said lazily, trying to rile Liz up.

I stepped away from the game and over to a quieter corner of the arcade to answer the call.

"Hey Mallory." I answered.

"Saturday! Good to hear your voice. Are you out and about this evening?" Mallory asked.

"I'm in Brooklyn with a couple of friends. What's up?"

"Good news, Gadget says the locator spell will be finishing up tonight. I would like for you to go with me to locate the individual, if you are so willing."

I didn't even need to think about it. As much as I'd been looking forward to a fun night with my friends, finding the person responsible for Maria's death was far more important. I said as much.

"Good, I am glad to hear it. Send over your location and we will come pick you up." Mallory said.

I texted over the address to Power Up! before rejoining my group who had now moved on to Double Dragon. By the look on Liz' face I knew better than to ask who won the fight. Moving on to a cooperative game like Double Dragon was Liam's way of trying to make peace. Wes bounded over to them with a round of coffee for everyone. I was especially thankful since it seemed like I was in for a long night.

About 30 minutes later, after Liam had soundly pantsed me in Mortal Kombat, Mallory arrived with Gadget reluctantly in tow. Since Power Up! was mostly teens with a few college students sprinkled throughout, Mallory stood out like a sore thumb. Gadget however, fit right in.

The sorcerer was wearing a shirt this time, a black and white NWO shirt with a faded jean jacket pulled over it. His ratty brown hair was pulled up in a bun on the top of his head. When he saw all the video games and bright lights, he rubbed his hands together enthusiastically and started towards them, but Mallory grabbed him by the shoulder and pulled him back.

"Negative. Work now, play later." Mallory said.

"You sir, are a killjoy." Gadget replied.

I stood and shook Mallory's hand when he reached our table. Gadget offered a fist bump.

"Sup?" the sorcerer said, looking my friends and I over.

"Sup." Liz mocked.

I made the introductions and Mallory cordially shook everyone's hand.

"It's nice to meet you all, I have heard a lot about you, and I do apologize for stealing Saturday away from you all this evening. If you will allow me to make it up for you, I would like to finance your fun for the rest of the evening." Mallory said, pulling a roll of cash out of his pocket. He proceeded to count out two hundred dollars in twenties and handed them to Liam and Liz who were wide-eyed and thankful.

"Hell yeah." said Liz, smiling widely.

Out of the corner of my eye I noticed Wes stumbling toward the table with another tray full of coffee cups. All I could do was shake my head. Wes was out of control at this point. It happened anytime they came to a place that served flavored lattes. Wes had not been allowed to have caffeine as a kid and whenever we went out, he splurged and didn't know how to do anything in moderation.

"Coffee. Coffee. Coffee." Wes was chanting zealously when he bumped into another person and the tray of drinks twisted wildly in his hands and one of the cups of piping hot liquid flew toward the back of Mallory's neck. My eyes went wide. In the span of a heartbeat the older man spun in a blur and snagged the coffee out of thin air effortlessly without spilling a drop.

My heart pounded as I looked to my friends to gauge their reaction at seeing Mallory move at an impossible speed. Both Liz and Liam seemed stunned into silence for a sliver of a moment and then they seemed to shake it off at the same time.

"Nice save!" Liam said as he stood to take the tray to prevent any further damage.

"You idiot. No more coffee for you, you're cut off.' Liz said to Wes, who looked sufficiently rebuked. Mallory took a sip of the coffee and winked at me.

"Liz, do you like magic?" Gadget asked.

"No. No she doesn't. We should go." I interjected.

Minutes later Mallory, Gadget, and I were piled into Mallory's sedan heading back across the Brooklyn Bridge. The moon hung low over the Manhattan skyline and despite the city lights it shone brilliantly. Gadget was glaring at me.

"Soooo... Where are we headed?" I said, trying to break the silence of the car.

"You suck." Gadget said. "If you don't want people hitting on your friends, get uglier friends."

I turned to stare back at Gadget, who lounged across the backseat.

"That was you hitting on her? 'Do you like magic?'"

"Chicks dig magic." Gadget said.

"Sure, they do." I mocked.

"I'll have you know I do alright for myself." Gadget said, leaning forward to come face to face.

"Gentleman, if we could focus on the task at hand." Mallory interjected, and after a moment we both turned away from each other. "Gad, where are we headed?"

Gadget pulled out his phone and seemed to be typing something that I couldn't see from the front seat. "Looks like central park. Somewhere near the middle." the sorcerer said.

"How do you know that? Magic?" I asked.

"Oh yes. The magical art of GPS." Gadget said, turning his phone around so that I could see the map. "Moron."

"Gad." Mallory said sternly.

Gadget sighed. "I divined the current location of your suspect by fettering the hair that you provided to my blood. At the next full moon, which happens to be tonight, I'm able to locate the person in question. So, I now know the location of the murderer-"

"Alleged." Mallory corrected.

"Alleged murderer." Gadget continued "I know their current location within a hundred yards. Assuming they don't move around too much in the time it takes to get there, you should be able to find them."

"So, in a city where people are constantly on the move, we just have to hope that they don't move? That's not great." I said.

"It's a long shot, I'll admit, but at this point it is our best shot," said Mallory.

Central Park is 850 acres of fields and trees and bike paths where even the most seasoned New Yorker can get lost if they allow themselves. Sadly, this meant finding someone that didn't want to be found in the park was all but impossible. Since Gadget had been able to pinpoint a smaller section of the park there was a glimmer of hope we might be able to find Maria's killer. The three of us approached Central Park in the dead of night.

It was nearing midnight when we entered the park. Since it was closed to the public after 1 AM this was the latest I'd ever been there.

We walked for several minutes to reach the desired location. After a few moments of walking, we left the safety and familiarity of the concrete sidewalks and streetlamps and baseball fields and entered a wooded area thick with trees and growth.

"This is where I leave you." said Gadget, stopping in his tracks and refusing to leave the path.

"Where is your sense of adventure?" asked Mallory.

"I left it at home, thanks." said Gadget. "They're right through those trees. Good luck and so long."

"Thanks for your help, Gad.' Mallory said and started walking towards the wooded area, I followed him.

Mallory moved stealthily through the dense urban oasis, careful to avoid snapping twigs and dry branches. I did my best to follow suit, although my experience walking through this type of landscape was very limited. As we approached the edge of the woods, I noticed lights from fires up ahead and I could also hear the faint rhythmic beating of drums. Mallory held out his hand for me to stop and with his other hand he signaled the need for quiet. Mallory took the lead and moved forward at a slow pace, crouched low to the ground. I was careful to follow his exact steps.

We made it to the edge of the clearing and dropped down to one knee, hidden behind several large bushes. The clearing was an old rock quarry with an open grassy area surrounded on three sides by exposed rock. About twenty to thirty people encircled a single individual who was speaking to the group. The only light came from a couple of bonfires and torches, which I was sure were forbidden in the park. The ranger service tended to frown on forest fires.

I recognized some of the faces in the crowd. The tall and intimidating man addressing everyone was Michael Longfang, the Council member for the Shifters in the city. There were numerous other shifters in the crowd, and they all seemed to come in two different varieties, young or grizzled. The shifters who didn't look like fresh faced babies all carried numerous scars as if they had been through a war. One mangy looking shifter seemed to be hanging on every word that Longfang was saying, occasionally he had to pull his filthy blonde hair back out of his face from excitement.

I was unsurprised to see members of the Strays among the group. Their alpha, Osvald Steel, stood out among the crowd, and Waco the Strays' beta, The man I expected to see stood between them both. Mannie. Just seeing the smug look on the young shifter's face caused my blood to boil. Mallory's grip tightened on my arm. I hadn't noticed myself inch forward, but Mallory grabbed me and pulled me back.

"Easy. We can't just stroll in." Mallory whispered. "It's a Gathering, a meeting of Shifters. A very dangerous place to be an outsider." I took a deep breath to calm myself and settle the blood pulsing in my ears.

"I understand your complaints." said Longfang, replying to a question that I hadn't heard asked. "But we must look at the benefits. Many of you are too young to remember life before the Accords. It was war, pure and simple. We had to fight for everything! Every single piece of dirt was contested and bought with blood. Understand me, there's not any single vampire I would take in a fight over any of you, but they have numbers, and they have time. Politics and diplomacy are the weapons of the future, and we will wield them with the same deadliness that we do our claws and our teeth."

There was some head nodding among the crowd in response to Longfang's words, but there were an equal number of shifters who seemed uncertain.

"I can see that some of you disagree. Perhaps you think that you would be a better leader than I. If that's the case, I welcome your challenge. Strength still leads." said Longfang dangerously, pounding against his chest with his fist. His challenge was met with silence. The shifters in the crowd stared around at one another, looking to see if anyone would dare challenge Longfang. No one did. "Good. Then let's move on. Is there anything else?"

"Mallory." I whispered. "Should we go out and confront Mannie now?"

"No. We still do not know for sure that he did it. The hair that we found at the scene could belong to any one of these shifters."

I was about to protest when a rustling sound behind us caused me to jump. Mallory cursed under his breath as he turned around slowly. Two pairs of golden eyes peered at us through the darkness. The eyes belonged to two large black wolves, who with teeth bared advanced toward us and there was no doubt we were caught.

"My name is Mallory Moran, we are here investigating a murder, with authority derived from the Council. You will stand down."

One of the wolves growled intimidatingly and snapped its teeth as they continued forward moving to flank us on each side. Mallory put his hand across my chest and together we backed out of the woods and into the clearing. The two wolves were driving us forward. When we entered the quarry, every head snapped in our direction. It was super intimidating having several dozen predators stare menacingly at you. We walked among the crowd, which parted to allow Longfang to approach us.

"Found these two hiding in the woods, listening in."

said a voice behind us. The two black wolves were now standing in human form. The one who spoke was youthful with black skin and a shaved head. The other looked even younger than me, maybe 15 or 16 years old, with long blonde hair.

"Well, well, well. I don't remember inviting any half-breeds to this Gathering." said Longfang, circling around us as he spoke. Many of the shifters laughed. "What is it this time, Moran, did some trash cans get knocked over and you think one of my guys did it? Or is someone paying you to spy on us? Did you decide that detective work wasn't lucrative enough and decided to go full-on prostitution?"

I could tell that Longfang was trying to get under Mallory's skin, and to Mallory's credit he was keeping his cool. Longfang was pandering to the crowd, and they were eating it up.

"We apologize for interrupting, but we are here investigating a murder." Mallory explained. "Two humans, a mother and a daughter, were butchered in their homes. Murder, as you know, is a breach of the Accords and something that I take very seriously, just as I am sure you do."

"Irrelevant. No one here murdered any humans." said Longfang. "I'd check with your vamp buddies, sounds more like them."

"You see, that might have been my first instinct as well, but one of the humans had a history with some of your kind, and then there is the tricky business of a shifter hair being found at the scene. So, no, I think I am in the right place."

"Careful, Moran." said Longfang, dangerously. "I'm no pup that you can deal with so easily. I'll rip your heart out of your chest and eat it in front of you." I shifted nervously as I could feel the crowd getting ramped up. They were itching to see a fight. Mallory didn't blink.

"You heard Enchantress Black; the Council has given me authority to investigate these murders. A shifter is killing humans with impunity and hindering my investigation will not look good for you." said Mallory, diplomatically.

"I AM the authority of the Council." said Longfang, dangerously. "So, tell us the names of the humans so we can all deny involvement and get on with our Gathering and you can leave before you get yourself killed, owing me a favor for interrupting, of course."

"I find those terms agreeable." said Mallory, turning to face the crowd that encircled them. "One of the humans who was killed was a young girl named Maria Álvarez."

"Move!" said a voice from the crowd and shifters began to move, willingly or not, as Mannie pushed his way through, storming toward Mallory. "Maria's dead? Bullshit!" Mannie tried to push me out of the way, but I'd been expecting it and held my ground. Instead of allowing Mannie to push me out of the way, I lunged forward and punched him as hard as I could in his face. It was like hitting a brick wall. Pain shot up and down my hand and wrist, but Mannie fell to the ground with blood pouring from his nose. The look of surprise on Mannie's face turned into pure rage, and I realized I'd made a huge mistake.

Mannie jumped to his feet, and I readied to defend myself. Everyone started pushing each other back to encircle us, all except for Mallory who grabbed me and stepped in between us. Members of Mannie's pack grabbed him as the shifter fought to get free. Mannie looked murderous, and I felt it. I wanted to hit him again.

"You're a dead man!" Mannie roared.

"I know you killed her! I know it was you!" I yelled back, trying to incite him even more. "You think you're so tough. You're nothing! You're nothing!" Mallory held me tightly and would not let me go. Waco and Shark forced Mannie to the ground and were practically sitting on him to try and keep him down. Osvald Steel walked calmly over to Mallory.

"Calm yourself, Saturday," said Mallory. "This is not the time and definitely not the place. Calm yourself, for Maria and her mother. They deserve justice, not this." Mallory's words had an effect and I stopped struggling and he let me go.

"Explain." Osvald said.

"Maria and her mother were killed in their own home. The claw and teeth marks indicated a shifter. We also found a hair at the scene and a locator spell led us here. You can understand why this does not look good for Mannie." Mallory explained, looking at Mannie who continued in vain to struggle to get to his feet.

"When was this?" Osvald asked calmly.

"The night of the last Sanctuary," said Mallory.

"Yeah, the same day that he came to my school and tried to kill me." I said. "Did he tell you about that? He also told me he was going to be seeing Maria that night. Did you think I had forgotten that little threat, Mannie?"

"You talk to me, you do not talk to him." said Osvald, sternly. The alpha contemplated the information for a moment. "Mallory, you must continue your search. Mannie couldn't have killed the girl. He was with me all evening, after I heard about his adventure into the school he was punished severely."

"I don't believe that." I said. "I know he did it."

"Believe what you will, the truth is not swayed by your beliefs." said Osvald.

"It has to be him, Mallory, you don't believe him, do you? He's just covering for his packmate."

"I am sorry, Saturday, but I trust the word of Osvald. If he says that it was not Mannie, then I believe him." said Mallory.

Osvald turned back to his pack. "Let him up." he ordered. They picked Mannie up off the ground, his nose had stopped bleeding, but the dried blood caked around his mouth and chin only served to make him look more menacing. Mannie glared at me. "You will do nothing." his alpha instructed him.

"Are we finished?" said Longfang. "Moran you can

finish your investigation another time, you obviously have no idea what you are doing, which comes as no surprise to me. Coming from the stock that you do, you should dedicate yourself to more useful work, but you're used to being a disappointment. And Steel, I recommend you train your pup better. Getting knocked on his ass by a human? How embarrassing."

I was tempted to tell them that I was not just a human but thought better of it. Anything that brought Mannie some embarrassment was fine by me. "One of you killed, Maria. We'll find you." I said, emboldened by my anger.

"Moran, take your child out of here before I give it a spanking." said Longfang.

"I believe it is you that needs a spanking, Longfang." said a voice among the crowd. "That's what you must do to correct a wayward child, after all."

"Who said that!?" Longfang asked, furiously. "Which one of you gutless dogs said that?"

The crowd parted once more, this time for an old man who hobbled forward, bearing most of his weight on a thick twisted wooden cane. The old man looked to have once been powerfully built, but now his back was arched in near rigor mortis. The old man's long hair and unkempt beard were both white with age, his skin was stretched thin across his exposed face and was crisscrossed with white scars and one of his ears was half missing.

"Who the hell are you?" Longfang asked, laughing at the man slowly moving toward him.

"My name is Long Winter, and I am here to challenge you." the old man said.

I heard the man's name echoing through the crowd as everyone was repeating it in disbelief.

"Long Winter is dead." said Longfang, disbelievingly.

"I was as good as dead once, but I found a strength I had not thought possible. Our moon mother showed me the way, the true way, the old way." Long Winter explained.

"Now I have returned, and what a sad state I find here. You all have completely abandoned the ways of our people. You are led by a leech puppet who bends his knee to a fanged master. Shameful."

The shocked looks on the shifter's faces in the crowd seemed to mirror my own feelings. They either could not believe that this man was standing before them alive, or that someone was speaking to Longfang in such a way, or both.

"I recommend that you crawl your old body back into whatever den you crawled out of, because strength still leads in New York." said Longfang, pounding his chest brazenly.

"Ah, I see. You challenge a boy, but do not honor the challenge of a warrior. Perhaps you need your master's permission?" asked Winter.

"Warrior? I see no warrior." said Longfang, playing to the crowd. "I see only an old dog that needs to be put down."

"This wolf still hunts, boy," said Winter. "I challenge you."

"Very well." Longfang sighed "You should have stayed dead, Winter." Longfang stalked toward his challenger arrogantly.

Winter said nothing, he tossed his cane to the side and stood himself up straight. The large black cloak draped around Winter fell to the ground revealing thick arms and a barreled chest. Winter reminded me of old Viking warriors I'd seen in movies. Longfang stopped short, hesitating at seeing the transformation of the old man. The shifter's mind seemed to be questioning whether he had been duped.

Longfang's eyes began to glow a golden yellow, his body began to shift and change, becoming more animalistic and imposing. Winter reached down and dug his powerful hands into the ground, razor sharp claws growing in place of his fingers easily punctured the earth. As the rest of his body began to shift into its monstrous form, Winter used his hands to launch himself forward at Longfang. They hit each other in midair with the sound of a thunderclap that sent a shockwave throughout the crowd, which pressed back away from the combatants. A tremor spread throughout my very bones, and I had to keep my jaw clenched to prevent my teeth from chattering.

Longfang and Winter, both now nearly seven foot tall and more powerful than I could imagine, were ripping into one another with great ferocity. There was no illusion of defense or evasion, it was pure unadulterated violence. Winter was more than holding his own. Gone was the frail and withered old man, and in his place was an old warrior who fought with experience.

Longfang was all power and offense. The only shifter I'd ever seen fight was Mannie, and Longfang was on a completely different level. He wasted no movements, there was a purpose behind all his attacks. He would swipe low with his claws to draw Winter's hands, and then use his jaws to snap at the exposed neck.

Blood poured from both men. There was a wicked gash along one of Longfang's arms, the result of a successful counterattack by Winter, who had even more wounds on his own body. The most concerning of Winter's wounds was a deep gash on his neck where he had been forced to rip it free from Longfang's jaws.

"Who exactly are we rooting for here?" I asked Mallory, unable to look away from the violence. Mallory watched the fight intently.

"Shifter politics being what they are, I couldn't even begin to know," he said.

I noticed the four members of Longfang's own pack who stood off by themselves. I had heard them referred to as the East River Pack. A few of them looked concerned, probably because they thought their alpha would make short work of the old wolf. I wondered what they would do if it looked like Longfang was going to lose.

Long Winter appeared to be slowing from his wounds, and Longfang noticed. Winter gave himself some distance and began to rely more on counter strikes. Longfang launched fewer strikes with more precision, laughing a raw and wretched laugh as he did. "Draw your blade." Longfang roared.

"I don't need it." said Winter, his altered voice was grating like rocks being dragged against stone.

"You mean, you don't have it." said Longfang, continuing to laugh. I looked to Mallory to ask him what Longfang meant, and noticed him shift nervously, unconsciously rubbing the ring on his right hand. "You are not worthy, old wolf."

"I am more worthy than you, dog." Winter spat, wiping the blood from his face, and drawing himself up for one last effort. Longfang held out his right hand, with his fist pointing toward Winter. "*Klo.*" The word was deep and powerful and unfamiliar, but a silver blade began to materialize in Longfang's hand. It was a long-curved blade, its sharp edges gleaming in the moonlight. The blade curved like a long sharp tooth, befitting the name of its owner.

Winter went right for Longfang's blade, but the younger man was a step faster. Longfang sidestepped Winter and brought his blade around in a blur, swinging the sharp silver right for the older man's neck, a killing blow. Luckily for Winter, his momentum took him out of the curved blade's reach. Longfang spun around and closed the distance, raising the blade high and bringing it down with ferocity. Winter turned just in time, and he raised his hands, grabbing Longfang's blade hand and twisting the blade harmlessly away from his own body. Winter pulled Longfang into his grasp, so that the two monstrous forms were face to face, hand fighting to gain leverage over the blade. Longfang used all his might to try and bring the blade down onto Winter, who was trying to pry it away from the younger man's hand. Neither of them gave an inch.

It seemed for a moment they had reached a stalemate and that whoever's strength held out the longest would be the victor. I watched intently with my hands clenched together tightly, anticipating, and waiting for Winter to falter, but to my surprise the older man did not relent. In fact, it was Longfang who appeared to be waning, his cocky expression was replaced with sweat and a look of intense focus.

In an instant of weakness, the blade hand of Longfang was pushed back and Winter, sensing an opening, lunged for the taller man's throat. I thought I saw a look of satisfaction sweep across the face of Longfang briefly before he leaned his upper body back and kicked the legs out from under the older man and then used his right hand and the hilt of his weapon to smash into Winter's face. The blow reverberated through the crowd with the sound of a sledgehammer hitting bone. With a sickening crunch Winter spun in the air and landed face down in the mud and blood, unmoving. Longfang laughed mirthlessly as he walked over Winter's body and raised his sword high in the air.

"That's enough, he's finished." said Osvald, stepping away from the crowd. Longfang looked over at him and smiled before he brought his silver blade down and shoved it into the earth so close to Winter's face that the silver rested against the older man's cheek. Longfang released the blade and held his hands up, drinking in the howls and shouts of victory from his pack and some of the others in the crowd.

"I could have killed him, but he is beneath me, " boasted Longfang, triumphantly. The shifter put one of his feet onto the back of Winter and grabbed the hilt of his blade and slowly unsheathed it from the earth. The blade came out pristine and unstained by dirt or blood. Longfang hefted it into the air victoriously and the blade slowly faded and vanished as he returned to his human form. Winter's body also returned to its normal state, and the once massive beast was now an old man lying face down in the mud, with nasty looking wounds all over his body.

"Strength still leads!" Longfang shouted and others joined him in his celebration with howls and chants. I was enthralled by what I was witnessing but knew that this was probably our one opportunity to get out of there before Longfang took an interest in us again. Mallory who seemed to be thinking the same thing.

"We have a list of suspects; we will continue our investigation." Mallory said reassuringly. "For now, let us tactfully retreat."

We walked quickly, but did not run, back to the wooded area. I looked back and saw that everyone was too caught up in the celebration to have even noticed, all except Mannie who was staring furiously in my direction. I was too full of hate for Mannie to notice the other person in the crowd watching us leave.

NINETEEN

"I just don't buy that Maria was killed by a shifter other than Mannie, it doesn't make sense, it's too much of a coincidence," I said to Mallory, who sat across from me at an all-night diner where we were rehashing the nights events over runny eggs and scorched coffee. Mallory also wanted to talk about my experience with Hunter and my first fight against a vampire.

"I understand why you feel that way, I do," said Mallory. "But I trust Osvald. He would not lie to cover up for one of his packmates, not for something serious like this."

I started to protest, but Mallory held up a hand. "You will just have to trust me on this one, Saturday." he said.

I wasn't ready to let it drop, but I knew continuing further wouldn't do any good. Mallory seemed to have said all he was going to say on the subject. I trusted Mallory's judgement and resigned myself to drop the matter for now and put my grudge against Mannie on the back burner, temporarily.

"What do we do now?" I asked.

"We revisit the photos from the crime scene, and make a list of suspects, and we see if anyone had a motive to harm Maria or to frame a member of the Strays."

I felt ill. I did not want to look at the photos from the crime scene again. As it was, I saw them every time I closed my eyes. "You think someone killed Maria and her mother just to frame The Strays?"

"It is certainly a possibility," said Mallory, sipping his coffee. "I will reach out to Osvald to see if he can think of anyone who might benefit from something like that. You, on the other hand, will continue your training. At the next

Sanctuary I would like to formally recognize you and for that to happen you need to be ready."

"How do I get ready?"

"You will be studying," said Mallory.

I groaned. It was summer break, the last thing I wanted to do was study. Mallory could obviously tell what I was thinking by the look on my face.

"I know, I know, but you will also be training with Hunter in the evenings. She will help you learn to harness the power you have inside of you so that you can control it and use it when you need to."

"Why won't you be training me?"

"I will be continuing the investigation, besides, I thought that you might prefer working with someone closer to your age. If you would rather I train you I could-."

"Nah it's cool, I like Hunter. She's a trip, it should be fun."

"A 'trip' indeed." said Mallory "I know she has some fairly radical ideals about vampires and supernaturals in general, but she means well. She is jaded from past dealings and quite honestly it is understandable, but do not let it cloud your own judgement."

"I won't."

"Good. I am glad to hear it, and I think it's been an exciting enough evening for us, let's get out of here." Mallory said, motioning for the waitress to bring over the check.

"Who's Long Winter?" I asked, the question had been nagging at me.

"Long Winter was or is something of a legend among the supernatural community, at least here in New York." Mallory answered. "He was the leader of the shifters in the city back before the Accords. He was not a politician; he was a warrior, and he led the shifters in the war against the vampires. When your father and De La Cruz first brought the proposal for the Accords to Winter, he wanted nothing to do with them. Winter refused them and forbade any other shifter from signing. It was his belief that it was a trick by the vampires to leash the shifters for their nefarious purposes."

"Obviously, the Accords were eventually signed, so did he change his mind? What happened?" I asked.

"Winter was challenged and defeated and left for dead. Control of the shifters fell to someone else, a puppet."

"Longfang?"

"Yes. Michael Longfang was nothing more than a young upstart at that point, but he was a fierce warrior and already the alpha of his own pack. Your father had Longfang's ear and together they outmaneuvered the shifter's rivals. Longfang took control of the shifters, signed the Accords, and culled anyone who resisted."

"Was it Longfang who challenged Winter?" I asked.

Mallory shook his head. "Winter was full of pride. He believed that any shifter could match any vampire in single combat, so when a vampire challenged him, he accepted immediately. Winter did not hesitate when the vampire raised the stakes and brought a human in to fight alongside him. Winter had no idea that it was no mere human but was instead a dhampir. This deceit allowed the vampire and the dhampir to overwhelm Winter in the public challenge."

"But that's cheating!" I said louder than intended. Our waitress raised her head up from her phone and looked startled.

"In a sense, yes it was," said Mallory calmly. "But it would not have mattered. Winter was too arrogant, he would have accepted any challenge thrown at him if it were made publicly. He would not have wanted to lose face among his people."

"Who was the vampire?" I asked, fearing that I knew the answer and that it would sully the image I had of my father as a great diplomat.

"None other than Salvatore De La Cruz himself," said Mallory. "And the dhampir was me."

I almost choked on my coffee. Something about the

way Mallory spoke about Winter made me suspect that he had been the dhampir, but the thought of him working alongside De La Cruz was too much.

"Wait, you and De La Cruz were friends?"

"Hardly." Mallory answered. "I was a means to an end for him, a way to help him get what he wanted, which happened to be the same thing that your father wanted, and I respected your father."

"That was how you won your silver blade?"

"Yes, Moonsbane. After the challenge, the blade went to the victor. De La Cruz did not want a shifter weapon, so he gave it to me in return for a favor. I can assure you the blade was not worth being in his debt." said Mallory.

The waitress brought the check and Mallory paid. We loaded back up in the car and headed to my house. The sun was just starting to come up when I walked inside. It appeared that I had officially become nocturnal as I told my grandparents goodnight just as they were waking up and I went into my room to try and get a little sleep.

The next couple of weeks were a complete blur, but I finally sank into a routine. At about 2 in the afternoon, I would wake up and have a late lunch before heading down to the local library to study. I read the books that Mallory had given me with a ferocious appetite. Mallory showed me the supernatural section in the library where I could find copies of books on unusual subjects like *History of Hidden New York: through 1941* and *Mother Moon* which was a type of religious text for shifters that I didn't understand at all. I would power through them the best I could until dinner, which I tried to always have with my grandparents. After dinner I would hang out with my friends playing games or venturing out into the city.

Mallory checked in on me every couple of days to check my progress and update me on the investigation. At this point most of what Mallory was doing was surveying some of the shifters from the Gathering that he did not know. Mallory also spoke with Osvald and Mannie and neither of them were very forthcoming nor helpful. Mallory hadn't seemed surprised by this, he said shifters always preferred to handle their conflicts internally.

"Don't expect too many shifter clients."

Mallory didn't take me with him to that interview for obvious reasons, but he did take me to speak with some of Ms. Álvarez's neighbors. One neighbor, an elderly woman named Freda, provided us with our first break in the case.

Simply put, Freda was something of a cat lady. While I didn't ever actually see a cat, she just had a cat lady-like quality about her. Freda's hair was so gray, it was practically white, and it was so frazzled it looked as if she'd recently been shocked. As crazy as she appeared, when she spoke, she seemed very lucid. During our conversation with Freda, she mentioned she hadn't seen or heard the Alvarez's leave their apartment at all day before the murders. She did, however, say that she heard a lot of commotion the night their bodies were discovered.

"What kind of commotion?" Mallory asked.

"Oh, well there was glass breaking, and then I heard something smash against our shared wall. I would have thought that they were fighting, but there was no yelling or anything, and Ms. Álvarez, well she could get loud when she needed to." the woman explained.

"I see, and did they fight a lot?" Mallory asked.

"Oh, no, hardly ever. That's why I was scared to go over and check on them. I was afraid that something was wrong."

"What happened after that?" I asked.

"Oh, well I don't have a phone, so I went downstairs and walked outside and flagged down a policeman and told him what was going on."

"And what time was that?" asked Mallory.

"Oh, probably around 9 PM, I had just finished watching one of my stories, so yes right around 9." she said.

"And did you see anything out of the ordinary when you went back upstairs?" asked Mallory.

"No, not really." she said. "The policeman, he was quick to that apartment. Well, he stopped for a second when a homeless man came stumbling out of the alley next to our building, but then he was right up the stairs, and I couldn't believe it when he told me. Those two beautiful girls were murdered. I just can't believe it."

"I see. Well, thank you so much for talking with us, it has been very helpful." Mallory told her. "I have just one more question. This homeless man, do you remember anything about him? Can you describe him?"

"Oh, well they all look a lot alike, don't they?" she said.

"Anything at all that made him stand out?" asked Mallory. "Any little detail could help."

"Well, he had long dirty hair that covered most of his face." she said. "And he was tall, and big. He looked like he could find a job if he got a haircut of course. Most of these folks just need a job if you ask me."

"I'm sure," said Mallory, politely.

After we concluded the conversation with Freda, Mallory seemed satisfied. He was convinced that this homeless person was more than just an innocent bystander.

"I believe that we have just heard the description of our killer, Saturday."

Every night around midnight I joined Hunter in different places around the city to train. She, always accompanied by Holmes, worked to help me control my abilities. After just a few nights I was already getting better at speeding up my reflexes when I needed to do so. Free running and climbing were also becoming easier for me. The hand-to-hand combat stuff was coming along with a little more difficulty. I had zero experience fighting, outside of video games of course. Despite how good it felt to punch Mannie in the face, I also recalled the pain that had shot up my arm and it wasn't something I was interested in doing again.

One night we met out near the Hudson. Hunter had us standing on a thin beam to work on balance. On one side of the beam was a 15-foot fall onto the concrete and the other side was a much farther fall into the filthy and frigid water of the Hudson. Holmes sat safely down on the concrete staring up at us curiously, his black fur blended perfectly into the darkness.

"Alright, focus," said Hunter.

"Focus on what exactly? I can barely see my own feet. The only thing I can focus on is the fact that I'm a gentle breeze away from falling to my death."

"Quit complaining. A time may come when you must fight in total darkness." she said.

"Yeah, but how often do you fight in total darkness above a river? Probably not a lot, right?"

"Enough talking, rookie. Catch!" she said, tossing something at me. Instinctively I reached out and caught it, swaying nervously as I did so. It was a long wooden practice sword.

"What's this for?" I asked.

I couldn't see her very well, but I could imagine the look that she was giving me. "For hitting each other." she said.

"I'm not going to hit you with this. Are you crazy? I could seriously hurt you with this."

"You're right. You're not going to hit me with that, because I'm too fast for you. But you ARE going to try, or I'm going to knock you in the water."

"This is crazy, not to mention needlessly dangerous. Here, look, I'll attack you. Boop!" I reached out playfully with my wooden sword, but she knocked it aside with her own effortlessly.

"And now it's my turn." she said and charged at me swinging wildly. I freaked out, not knowing what to do. The water loomed ominously below, and I retreated carefully, my sword up defensively to block her blows. The wooden swords smacked against one another, and it was all I could do to keep her from knocking me into the icy depths of the waiting water.

"Stop! Stop! Seriously!" I pleaded.

"No." she said simply and swung at my head. I ducked just in time as she brought the sword back around and swung for my legs. Instinctively I jumped back to keep her from sweeping my feet out from under me. I landed deftly on the thin beam, and she was laughing gleefully. Once I realized I was not dead and was not going to die, I laughed too, and then playfully charged at her, trying to knock her in the water.

This was how we trained every night and every night I learned more about myself and what I could do. I was not mastering anything, but I was becoming more confident in myself and in my new world.

TWENTY

The night before Sanctuary Mallory called to tell me that there had been a breakthrough in the Álvarez case and that he wanted to meet. Mallory asked to meet at his office, so I hopped on the bus and headed to Chinatown.

When I walked into his office, I noticed immediately how exhausted Mallory appeared. He was sitting behind his desk leaning back in his chair munching on a fortune cookie with his eyes closed.

"Knock, knock" I said hesitantly.

"Saturday!" said Mallory, sitting up in his chair and dusting the crumbs off his shirt. I noticed the dried blood around his neck and on his collar.

"Mallory, are you alright?" I asked.

"Of course, my boy, of course. Nothing a little sleep won't fix." said Mallory, smiling and rising out of his chair gingerly.

"Should we do this tomorrow so you can get some rest?"

"No, this is important. We are nearing the end of our investigation and I have something I need to show you." Mallory walked out of his office and into the waiting area where Violet sat reading a magazine at her desk. "I am taking Saturday to the Tombs. We will be back shortly, Vie."

"You need to take yourself to bed." she said, looking at Mallory sternly over the bright orange rim of her glasses.

"Your mothering, as always, is noted and appreciated, Vie. There will be plenty of time for sleep later." said Mallory.

Mallory opened the only other door in the small office, what I assumed was a closet, with a key from his key ring. When the door opened it revealed a hidden staircase leading down. Together we descended the old stone steps for a few minutes until we reached the wooden landing. Mallory opened another door which led into a dimly lit stone tunnel that ran far off into the distance in both directions. This had to be one of the secret underground tunnels below Chinatown I'd heard about. I followed Mallory to the right, and we walked along in darkness, the only light to guide the way was Mallory's flashlight.

"Up above us is Canal Street. This corridor was developed hundreds of years ago, like many others underneath the city." Mallory explained. "Their intended uses were varying, but ultimately, they were used by gangs and organized crime families to hide out and move illegal goods in secret. As far as I know, I am the only person who uses or even knows about this particular tunnel that runs down Canal and under the Manhattan Detention Center."

After walking for a few minutes, we reached a metal door with iron bars blocking the way. Mallory pulled out his keys and used a large brass one to open the door. The inside was filled with empty cells and catacombs that branched off in numerous directions like a cave. The stone walls of the old prison were damp and cool to the touch, probably having not seen sunlight in over a century. I could hear dripping water echoing from the caverns and a train passing by in a nearby subway tunnel rumbled against the walls. I braced myself against a steel door and covered my ears to drown out the screeching sound of the metal cars grinding against the tracks. There were small runes etched into the steel door.

"Here, you take this." said Mallory, handing the flashlight to men as he lit a torch on the wall and removed it from its bracket. "What I need to show you is just down here."

We passed by a few more empty cells before Mallory stopped and turned toward a darkened chamber. As soon as the light landed on the bars, I could see that it was different from the others. The metal was not iron, but instead a brilliant silver, and the bars ran on all four sides like a cage, even the ceiling above the cell had silver bars. Inside of the cell, sitting in the middle with his legs crossed and his head bowed was a shaggy and wild looking man. When I approached the prisoner raised his head and through his matted blonde mane he growled ferociously. It was a warning growl and instinctively I felt compelled to back away.

"I give you, our fugitive," said Mallory.

Rage bubbled up inside of me, rage, and confusion. Here I was face to face with Maria's killer, but I'd been so certain it was Mannie. It didn't make sense; it didn't fit the narrative I'd created in my head. Mallory seemed to understand and placed a comforting hand on my shoulder.

"How did you find him?" I asked.

"Even in a city this large, shifters stand out if you know what to look for. Once I had even a few small details about him it allowed me to narrow my search. I found him stalking some humans near the docks. I was able to capture him, but it was not easy. Once I had him under wraps and brought him here, he confessed his involvement in the murder of our friends."

"What do you mean by 'involvement'?"

"That's why I have brought you here because I wanted you to hear what he has to say. He says he has information for us he will provide if we allow him to leave the city and never return. I suggest we hear him out."

"Fine."

"I appreciate your open mind," said Mallory. "Alright, it's time to talk. What do you have to say?"

The man lifted his head, his golden yellow eyes peering out through the shaggy hair that fell across his face. He pushed himself up onto all fours like a child learning to crawl. His clothes were ripped and stained varying colors of brown and yellow. He was barefoot, and his toenails shared more than a passing resemblance to long yellow claws. They scraped against the concrete floor as he crawled toward Mallory and me.

"Seen you, I did." he said, snapping his teeth as if

biting off each word. "Came looking for a killer. Found many killers, you did. Made to kill, teeth to rip and tear flesh, so easy."

The man's movements were feral, more animal than human. Being around him was unnerving and even with the silver bars between us I was uncomfortable.

"What is your name?" asked Mallory.

The man cocked his head to the side. "Am called Rat. Rat. Yes. Rat." he said, "Rat has story, and you let Rat go."

"What do you have to tell us, Rat? Did you kill those two women?" asked Mallory.

"Women?" asked Rat.

"Yes, the women we were asking about at the Gathering," said Mallory.

"No, not kill them. Rip them, tear them, break things, but Rat don't kill them."

"I don't understand. You hurt them, but you didn't kill them?" I asked.

"Didn't hurt them. Already dead when Rat get there. Rip them, tear them, break things, but Rat don't kill them." said Rat, almost chanting the last sentence.

"Who did kill them?" asked Mallory.

"You thought wolf kill them. Rat done good." said Rat.

"You wanted us to think that a shifter killed them?" I asked.

"He did. Said it could bring war and blood and fun if Rat clean up messes." said Rat.

"What messes?" I asked, frustrated.

"Oh yes. Little leech just can't control himself." said Rat, laughing as if he had told a very funny joke.

"Give us a name!" I shouted at the creature.

Rat lurched forward with supernatural speed and hit the bars with his head, bone and flesh clanging hard against the solid metal. Rat's sizzled and burned where the silver touched it, but he continued to throw himself against it trying to get at me.

"Luther. Luther. Luther. Luther. Luther." Rat chanted every time he slammed into the silver bars with a sickening thud. "Luther. Luther. Luther." The words followed us out of the Tomb.

TWENTY-ONE

"You know what this means, Mallory. You know what we must do." said Hunter.

We were all standing around Mallory's cramped office later that same evening. Mallory had called Hunter and asked her to join us. Mallory was sitting in his chair with his head in his hands rubbing his temples. I was sitting in one of the chairs on the opposite side of the desk, still trying to wrap my mind around everything. Hunter, on the other hand, was pacing around the small room. Holmes was enjoying a bowl of greasy noodles in the waiting room, which had Violet all up in arms.

"Can someone please explain it to me?" I asked. "What do we do? What can we do?"

"We have to kill Luther. He broke the law; God knows how many times. Not only that, but he's also been having a shifter cover up his mess in an attempt to restart the war." said Hunter.

"We can't kill Luther," said Mallory, exhaustion evident in his voice. "Not on the word of an obviously mentally deranged shifter. Our lives would be forfeit. He's De La Cruz's man."

"I know who he is, Mallory. I haven't forgotten. Are you sure you aren't letting things cloud your judgment here?" asked Hunter.

"Are you sure that you are not letting things cloud yours?" Mallory retorted.

"This is bigger than me and you, this is bigger than De La Cruz. We have to take this guy out before he starts a war. No one wants that. I wasn't old enough to be around back in the day, and I don't want to experience it if even half the stories are true. We have the ability to stop this, we must act."

"All of the stories are true!" Mallory snapped. "But our word is not enough to keep De La Cruz from destroying us and no one would question it."

"I'm not afraid of De La Cruz," said Hunter.

"You should be. Both of you. All of us." said Mallory.

I ran my hands down my face. The cool metal of my father's ring brushed against my skin. I thought about my father and what little I knew of him. I wondered what he would have done in this situation. My father had been a leader, and brave, at least that is what I had been told. There's no way he would have let something like this stand. The Accords were part of his legacy, he helped to broker peace in a time of war and Luther wanted to destroy that. I had to stand up and protect the city from that, to protect what my father created.

"You say that De La Cruz would dismiss us." I said. "So, we have to let everyone else hear us. If we bring this up at Sanctuary and let the shifters and other vampires hear our claims, maybe they won't be as dismissive, and the pressure will force De La Cruz to at least hear us out. We can always keep Rat locked up and they can hear it from him if they need to."

Mallory looked up at me and smiled. "There is still no guarantee that anything will come of it, but yes, the political pressure alone could be enough to force De La Cruz's hand. Hunter, your thoughts?"

Hunter stopped pacing for a moment and looked around at both of us. "I don't like the idea of this going down at Sanctuary when I'm weaponless, but it's probably the best chance of getting a captive audience."

"Even if he doesn't like what we have to say, he wouldn't dare attack us at Sanctuary. It would destroy the illusion of safety, which would put an end to Sanctuary all together." said Mallory.

"I hope that you're right." said Hunter. "For all our

sake."

"Me too," said Mallory. "Now, I suggest we all try and get some sleep. Sanctuary is in less than 24 hours, and it would be best if we had our wits about us. Hunter, I would ask you to take young Saturday home, if you would be so kind. We will meet outside of Sanctuary tomorrow night."

The following night Hunter and I waited outside of a swanky hotel in Midtown. The entire venue was rented out for Sanctuary, which was taking place in the grand ballroom. The reception and cocktail hour had just kicked off. Limousines and taxis were lining up outside of the venue dropping off patrons in all manner of attire. Some were dressed in expensive suits, while others wore clothes appearing to have not been washed this month. It was quite a dichotomy.

The two of us stood off to the side watching everyone pass through security while we waited for Mallory to show up. I did notice some familiar faces arriving at the hotel. Briggs and Lincoln rolled up together, Briggs nodded slightly in my direction as he passed by. Irene Cross, dressed all in black like a widow attending a funeral, walked haughtily toward the front of the hotel. She was trailed on all sides by three men in suits who were going out of their way to swoon all over her. Amelia Roth, the businesswoman, stepped out of a limousine along with several others in expensive suits and jewelry.

The East River Pack, led by Michael Longfang arrived in force, as did The Strays, and several other packs I recalled seeing at the Gathering. Enchanters from the Crimson Circle, led by Enchanter Howe, all arrived together wearing black robes with red trim or stripes. They stepped out of a door which appeared out of thin air in the side of the building near where Hunter and I stood. I jumped in surprise at seeing people walk through a wall.

Obviously, I kept my eyes peeled for any sign of Salvatore De La Cruz and his entourage, which was sure to include Luther, but they had yet to arrive. It was likely they would be fashionably late. Abigail Black however, the head enchantress, arrived promptly with her own entourage of arcanists. I was surprised to see Gadget among the crowd vying to get in the front door, the sorcerer had even dressed up for the occasion in a navy-blue jumpsuit.

Up ahead the crowd forming around the entrance began to part for a small group of people. My breath caught when I saw the haunting white mask of Dukh, one of my captors. With Dukh was Mul and two other men and a woman I did not recognize. I guessed they must be The Family. Hunter informed me that the head of the Family was called Pakhan and pointed out the man in the suit who was walking at their head. Outwardly there was nothing about him that stood out, but his reputation and the reputation of the Family obviously preceded them because of the uneasiness of the crowd around them.

Countless other vampires, shifters, arcanists, and humans with Sight showed up for the biggest supernatural event of the month. Many of the people who were arriving I had never met or even seen before. Hunter tried to give me a rundown on the individuals that she knew, but it was difficult to keep up. It really gave me perspective on just how big this community was, and just how much I still had to learn.

It wasn't long before Mallory joined us. Mallory was also wearing an Iliescu suit like me, his was charcoal black with a matching shirt underneath. Mallory's gray hair was pulled back behind his head in his signature ponytail.

"Are you both ready?" asked Mallory.

"I'd feel a lot better if I had my bat, and that duffle bag of yours," said Hunter.

"I'd be lying if I said I did not feel the same way," said Mallory.

"I'm ready." I said.

The inside of Sanctuary was set up similarly to last time. There was a public area where people milled about in small groups socializing with one another, while servers carried trays covered in a variety of refreshments. For the vampires, the servers themselves were the appetizers, many of them had fang marks on their necks where they had already been sampled. I just hoped they were paid well.

The three of us found a corner where we could talk. The loud buzz from all the voices in the room ensured we would not be overheard.

"Once the Council members take their place they will make their announcements, once that is finished, they will open the floor for grievances. That is when we will bring our accusation forward." said Mallory.

Hunter and I nodded that we understood our roles and how everything would go down. I just hoped a war didn't break out when the shifters learned the truth. I also hoped De La Cruz didn't decide to kill me on the spot for running away from his house after the last Sanctuary.

Right at 9:00 PM the doors to the ballroom opened and the crowd began to file into it. The three of us joined the mass of people heading in, and we found a nice spot with a good view of the dais where the Council members would sit. The ballroom had a high curved ceiling with numerous, currently vacant balconies. All the tables, with their white linens and fancy dishes, had been moved to one side of the room. Some of the supers went directly to the tables and began to take their seats. The onyx black dais was not in the center of the room like it had been at the previous Sanctuary, but instead it sat back against the wall with the three throne-like chairs placed uniformly across it.

The whole spectacle was awe inspiring. Knowing that there were this many people in the city who were either vampires, shifters, or arcanists blew my mind. After a few moments, the same master of ceremonies as last time, with the smooth voice and the serpent tattoo, took the stage. According to Hunter, the middle-aged man was a vampire and before his turning he had been a moderately successful DJ.

The man tapped his cane against the dais floor

ceremoniously and the room went silent. The emcee again welcomed everyone to Sanctuary and began to introduce the Council members. First, he introduced Abigail Black and then Michael Longfang, who were led to the dais and took their places in the thrones to the left and right. Lastly, he introduced Salvatore De La Cruz, who came in flanked by his bodyguards and assistants, including Luther. I didn't focus on De La Cruz, but instead glared at the smug look on Luther's face and the man's arrogant smile. I held out hope that soon I would be able to wipe it off his face.

De La Cruz finally made it to the dais and took his place on the middle throne. When the vampire sat the crowd finished their applause and the emcee took his own seat at one of the tables and Sanctuary officially began. Abigail Black arose and welcomed everyone.

"As always, we encourage you to take this opportunity to forge new alliances, to break ground on new relationships, here under the protection of Sanctuary." the enchantress said. "It is in these walls and in this hour that we can build a better future for everyone."

Abigail Black was the only Council member that I hadn't met in my brief time living among the supers. She seemed nice enough, but I knew from my limited experience to take nothing at face value.

I sat nervously through the announcements, most of which made no sense to me anyway, or involved supers I didn't know. The butterflies in the pit of my stomach fluttered wildly. Thinking of Maria and giving her the justice she deserved helped to take my mind off of the fact that I would soon be the center of attention for the entire room.

After a few moments Longfang stood up and addressed the audience. The shifter was so tall that he would have had to stoop down to speak into the microphone, so instead of using it he moved it off to the side and relied on his booming voice to be heard.

"The floor is now open for you to address us. I will

remind you to remain respectful and to be prepared to face anyone with whom you level an accusation." Longfang said before returning to his seat on the dais.

The crowd fell silent, waiting for someone to stand. I looked over to Mallory, who nodded. Mallory was the first to stand before Hunter and I followed. In the silence, the sound of our chairs moving against the ballroom floor was grating and all eyes in the room immediately fell on us. The three of us walked around the tables and the people in chairs to reach the base of the dais to address the Council.

"The Council recognizes Mallory Moran, and Hunter King, dhampir, accompanied by someone unknown to this city," said Abigail Black.

Up this close, I could feel Salvatore De La Cruz's gaze, it was focused directly on me. I felt as if I could wilt under the intense pressure but stood fast and bolstered my resolve.

Mallory cleared his throat. "Thank you, Lady Black. This young man is Saturday Shepherd, also a dhampir."

"Another dhampir?" said Longfang, incredulously. "I thought you were supposed to be rare?"

"Why is it that you bring the child forward, where is the father?" asked Abigail Black.

"Saturday's father was recognized by the city and this very Council, but he has since met his death. The progenitor of this dhampir was Anton Moretti." said Mallory.

When Mallory said my father's name several things happened all at once. A murmur of disbelief ran through the crowd, and it quickly turned into a shout as people talked loudly over one another, and everyone craned to get a good look at me. De La Cruz's eyes widened, and though the shock was quickly replaced by his normal stoic facade, there was no denying it had been there.

"Silence!" Longfang shouted and everyone slowly obeyed, but there was still a low buzz in the ballroom that would not be suppressed.

"We will of course need proof of these claims,

Mallory." said Abigail.

I held out my right hand, as Mallory had directed me to, and showed them my father's ring. Lady Black stood up and walked over to the edge of the dais where she peered down at the ring. She took my hand gently into her own and examined the initials which were embossed on the metal surface. She looked up and met my eyes and gave a warm smile, which served to raise my spirits immensely.

"I can verify that this is the ring of Anton Moretti." she said, standing and returning to her seat.

"We will need more than a trinket to verify lineage, Moran." said De La Cruz, breaking his silence. "You could have easily stolen the ring and placed it on the hand of another dumb, young, dhampir."

"To what end?" asked Mallory.

"To your own ends, whatever they are. We will not rely solely upon your word in this manner." said De La Cruz.

"A simple spell could be used to verify this information. That is easily done at another place and time." said Abigail. "For now, the Council and the city recognize Saturday Shepherd, dhampir."

"Indeed, we do, Saturday Shepherd, dhampir." said De La Cruz, biting off each word. "Now, if that is all."

"I'm afraid it is not." interrupted Mallory. "We have a charge to bring forward."

"Of course, you do." said De La Cruz. "What is your charge and whom does it involve?"

"We are here to level a charge of murder and sedition against Luther Wright." said Mallory, and again the room grew loud as everyone began to talk to one another, and again Longfang attempted to silence the crowd.

"What are you playing at, Moran?" asked De La Cruz. "Luther is one of my men."

"Does that make him above the law?" asked Mallory, dangerously.

"You test my patience, boy," said De La Cruz, and I

would have laughed if De La Cruz had not looked so angry. Mallory was in his fifties, someone calling him boy was funny.

"The accused will come forward," said Abigail.

I watched Luther rise from the table he had been sitting at with De La Cruz's other men. Luther buttoned his suit jacket as he sauntered haughtily across the room. Stopping a few paces away from us, Luther turned to face the Council.

"Continue, Mallory." said Abigail.

"During the course of an investigation into two murdered humans we have uncovered what appears to be a habitual killer. All the evidence at first led us to believe that a shifter had killed the humans, the markings and a hair found at the scene most prominently pointed in that direction. However, once the shifter was located and interrogated, we were informed that this goes even deeper than we could have imagined. A vampire fed from these two humans, butchered them, and then paid a shifter to mutilate their bodies to draw suspicion away from the vampire and onto a shifter." an audible gasp erupted from the crowd, but Mallory continued. "That shifter identified the vampire as none other than Mr. Luther Wright. Upon further reflection I was able to deduce that based upon unsolved crimes of a similar nature from the past, under the purview given to me by this very Council, Mr. Wright has killed fifteen humans in the past five years and used a shifter to clean up his mess all to satiate his evil needs and to fracture the shifter's standing in the city."

A shocked silence followed Mallory's words. Luther was smiling and snickering under his breath.

"That's a very cute story." Luther said.

"These are very serious claims, Mr. Wright," said Abigail Black.

"Serious?" barked Longfang. "I should come down and break your neck with my bare hands, Luther, you worthless bloodsucking scum."

"That's quite enough, Longfang." said De La Cruz, rising from his seat. "There is no basis to these claims. They are simply the fanciful tales of a play detective well past his prime trying to cause a stir. You are dismissed, return to your seats."

"Like hell." Longfang said, again jumping to his feet. "One of your men is trying to undermine my people and you refuse to act? I won't let that stand."

"I am telling you, Longfang, Moran is a known liar. Several years ago, he came to me with some wild idea about a vampire conspiracy much in the same vein. It is just his way of keeping himself relevant and appearing to be something that he is not to impress the young children he keeps in his company."

"That is a lie!" said Mallory "You claim to support the Accords, but you continue to be dismissive of any claims against your men."

"Careful, Moran. We both remember what happened last time." said De La Cruz just loud enough for those around the dais to hear. "I wouldn't hesitate to kill one of your pets again. Even Moretti's boy if you force my hand."

I saw the blood drain from Hunter's face. I saw her lips move, mouthing the word "Jake" under her breath. Mallory reached out and grabbed her arm to keep her from doing anything rash.

"Now, I will say again this matter is settled and you will not mention it again. You are dismissed." announced De La Cruz.

The three of us held fast, but Luther smiled smugly and moved to return to his seat. Before he had gotten very far Longfang barked an order for him to stop.

"This is not over. I will speak to this shifter accuser and hear the words from him directly. If I believe the truth of it, Luther, you are a dead man." said Longfang. "East River Pack, rise." The four members of Longfang's pack stood in unison. "Hold this man until I return." They moved to flank Luther who looked to De La Cruz. The vampire was shaking his head.

"Enough of this, Longfang," said De La Cruz. "I said

'enough'! Do not force my hand on this."

When De La Cruz said those words, Longfang seemed to immediately interpret them as a threat, and he was not the only one. Shifters across the room stood up, ready for a fight. The temperature in the room seemed to rise by about 20 degrees.

"Your words hold no sway over me, bloodsucker. If you are looking for a fight, just say the word." said Longfang, dangerously, turning to stand toe to toe with De La Cruz.

"Gentlemen, stop this!" said Abigail Black. "Remember the Accords, remember the laws and the sanctity of Sanctuary."

De La Cruz smiled. "It appears that I gave my dog too long of a leash. A common mistake when trying to break a puppy. Time to start over."

I wasn't sure what words could have calmed the situation, but I knew those were not it. Abigail Black seemed to sense it as well, because she walked quickly off the dais and several other arcanists fled the building entirely. Mallory pulled Hunter and I back to a safe distance. The East River Pack surrounded Luther, who made no movements to fight or flee.

I had no idea what to expect. Longfang had proven that he was a ferocious warrior, and he dwarfed De La Cruz, and yet De La Cruz looked extremely confident. I had heard tales of the vampire's power; I just didn't see how it could possibly match Longfang's.

De La Cruz carefully removed his suit jacket and folded it over the back of his chair. Longfang did not wait for him to finish before he charged at the vampire, transforming into his monstrous form as he did so. De La Cruz, with the speed and fluidity of rushing water, evaded Longfang's wild tackle attempt. De La Cruz grabbed the monstrous shifter by the back of his neck and used the beast's momentum to throw him to the ground. The remaining crowd, the ones who were not fleeing, gasped as De La Cruz wrapped his arms around the neck of the flailing shifter, and with a sickening crack the vampire snapped Longfang's neck. The hulking beast's legs stopped flailing, its body lying broken on the dais and the shifter's silver blade materialized harmlessly beside it.

Longfang's pack stood in disbelief staring at the broken body of their powerful alpha who had been dispatched so quickly. De La Cruz rose and brushed himself off before casually kicking the body of his fallen foe off of the dais unceremoniously. The shifter's large body hit the floor with a thud that silenced the remaining supers in the ballroom.

"The time has come for a change," said De La Cruz. "I am disbanding the Council, and I now speak with supreme authority. You will follow me, or you will be destroyed."

I looked to Mallory, nervously, to see what we should do, but he was completely focused on De La Cruz, and I saw an unfamiliar emotion on his face, fear. Most of the shifters in the crowd were using the chaos to flee, choosing to not stick around to see what De La Cruz's proclamation meant for them.

"As for you." said De La Cruz, returning his attention back to Mallory, Hunter, and I. "What to do with a wayward child. Such a disappointment to your father."

I couldn't contain myself any longer. "You are the only one who would have disappointed my father. You have destroyed everything the Accords stood for, everything he worked to accomplish."

De La Cruz turned his head just enough to look at me, his expression full of mockery. "It is cute that you believe yourself informed, but I wasn't referring to your father. Instead, I was speaking to Mallory. He has disappointed me greatly." said De La Cruz, turning to face Mallory. "I allowed you too much time with your human mother, that was my first mistake. It made you weak. That you would waste your gifts on such a foolish errand. So disappointing."

"Mallory, what's he talking about?" I asked.

"Your little friends don't know, Mallory?" asked De La

Cruz, slyly. "Go on, tell them. Tell them who your father is, or are you ashamed of me?"

Mallory stood in stunned silence for moments that seemed to stretch into an eternity.

"It's true." he said, weakly, his head hanging low, chin against his chest. "Salvatore De La Cruz is my father."

TWENTY-TWO

My breath caught in his chest, and Hunter cursed. Shock and a feeling of betrayal rose in my throat like bile. I trusted Mallory and he kept this from me. He kept so much from me.

"Yes, and now once again I have to punish you, Mallory." said De La Cruz "You see, Mallory has never been able to betray me. As much as he may want too. Perhaps he sees some redeemable quality in me. Perhaps it is just another of his weaknesses. Even after I killed his former pupil, he would not betray me. So weak. Now, Mallory, I will offer you the choice. Which of them shall I kill, the boy or the girl?"

Hunter's eyes were full of blind fury, I couldn't believe any of it. Mallory continued to stare at the ground.

"Which of your pupils shall I destroy? Pick or I will kill them both." said De La Cruz.

"I'm not afraid of you." said Hunter, stepping forward to face the vampire.

"Oh, we have a volunteer," said De La Cruz, smiling. "How disappointing. I wanted to kill the son of Moretti, since the opportunity to kill my former rival was taken away from me. Perhaps I will kill you both after all."

"No!" said Mallory, lifting his eyes to face De La Cruz. "No more. This is between you and me, no one else must die. Leave them out of this."

De La Cruz contemplated all of this for a moment, straightening his tie and slicking back his hair before making yet another proclamation.

"Dhampir blood is now forfeit. They are banned in my city, and the culling begins now, starting with these three." De La Cruz pointed down at the three of us standing at the base of the dais.

"Gadget, now!" Mallory yelled and I looked at him, confused, when a brilliant beam of light sliced through the air beside us. Mallory thrust his hands into the hole in the air. I had no idea what was going on.

"It's a portal, bro!" said Gadget, who was standing against the far wall, holding his hands out toward us to keep the spell active. When I turned my head back around to Mallory, he was pulling his trusty duffle bag out of the portal and dropping it onto the ground. The portal winked shut.

"*Blad!*" Mallory boomed and his brilliant silver blade formed out of thin air. "Be quick about it. I can't take him alone." Mallory said, before closing distance with De La Cruz. The East River Pack, awoken from their shocked state by the sight of the silver blade, ran at De La Cruz as well, one of the shifters picked up their fallen alpha's blade and hefted it high as they charged. Hunter reached down and threw open the duffle bag and rifled through it until she found a long wooden baseball bat with steel spikes jutting out of the end of it. She smiled encouragingly at me before charging into the fight.

I shook myself out of a daze and reached into the bag myself. Quickly I found the tomahawk and wrenched it free. It felt familiar and as good as anything, so I moved to join the fray when I was grabbed around the back and thrown roughly to the ground.

Luther stood over top of me, the vampire's short muscular frame stalking toward me slowly as I tried to crawl back to my feet. The vampire hoisted his own large steel blade with the intent to drive it down into my stomach.

"So, it was your girlfriend I killed? That's funny." Luther said, standing over me. "I saw her hanging around with that shifter and I just couldn't help myself. She really was beautiful. Well, before you die, it might help you to know she was delicious."

Cold rage washed over me. I rolled to my left and came up ready to fight. The vampire brought down his blade in an arching slash, but I parried it away with the blunt iron band wrapped around the haft of my axe. Metal clanked on metal causing sparks to flash briefly in the air. Luther used the momentum of the blade to swing it wildly back around and I deftly danced back away from the razor-sharp edge of his sword.

"You're out of your depth, boy." mocked Luther as he stalked toward me arrogantly. Before he could get close enough to take another swipe with his steel blade, Luther was tackled to the ground by a blur of hair and teeth. Mannie came up on top of the vampire, claws and teeth gnashed, clothing and flesh and blood were flying in all different directions. I could just make out Luther's screams over Mannie's ferocious roars of vengeance.

I had just a moment to fully observe the chaos going on around me. A full-on war had broken out in the supposedly safe confines of the Sanctuary. Vampires and shifters were fighting each other, some just trying to escape the room alive. It looked like the peace of the past two decades was finished. The Accords, my father's legacy, were dead.

De La Cruz's other goons moved to help their leader, but the Strays and their alpha Osvald Steel, were blocking them from getting onto the dais. It looked like De La Cruz didn't need the help anyway, the vampire was more than holding his own against four shifters and two dhampir. I was desperate to get into that fight to help my friends, but out of the corner of my eye I could see that Luther had made it back to his feet and was now taking the fight to Mannie. Both men were pouring blood from various cuts and gashes, but neither appeared slowed by their wounds in the slightest.

Mannie towered over Luther, but their strength seemed to be equal. Mannie was propelled on by his fury, Luther his arrogance. I knew that I could tip the balance if I joined the fight, but first I had to swallow my hatred for Mannie. I had to set aside the animosity I felt for the shifter and fight alongside him. It wasn't something I wanted to do. Mannie, who had almost killed me, Mannie who I believed had killed Maria.

I thought back to the moment when Mannie had learned about Maria's death at the Gathering. He hadn't wanted to believe it, much like I hadn't wanted to believe it. Mannie had loved Maria. The way the shifter showed his affection was possessive and dangerous and when Maria was taken away from him, he lashed out. Sensing even that tiny bit of human emotion in Mannie was enough to spur me into action.

My pulse quickened and my senses heightened. I ran at Luther as fast as I could and caught the vampire unaware as I shoulder checked him into the wall of the ballroom. Luther's bulky frame crashed through the wall and into the lobby of the hotel where dozens of people were scrambling to escape the fighting. Mannie looked at me, his shifted visage making it impossible to get a read on what he was thinking, before howling a ferocious challenge to Luther, who was stepping back through the splintered wall.

"Rivals becoming friends, how touching." mocked Luther.

"For a henchman, you talk too much." I said and Mannie grunted his approval.

"Come catch these hands, boys." Luther challenged, dropping his sword to the ground, and baring his fangs menacingly. Mannie shifted back down into his human semblance and up this close I could see the youthful features of his face, the pain from his physical and emotional wounds were more evident.

"I want to enjoy this." Mannie said.

I dropped the axe, sensing that this fight was too personal for a weapon. I circled around to one side of Luther while Mannie moved to the flank on the other side. Luther didn't wait to make his move, he went right at Mannie, sensing him as the greater threat. He was, so I didn't take it personally.

Mannie swung savagely at Luther's head, but the

vampire ducked, and Mannie's fist smashed into the wall sending chunks of drywall flying. Luther came up swiftly, slamming his foot into my chest sending me staggering back. Mannie wrapped Luther up around his chest, but only for a moment. The vampire powered free by flipping the shifter over his head. I came flying back in as Luther pulled himself free and threw rapid fists at Luther in quick succession, but the vampire was able to block them with his forearms.

I ducked to avoid a feint from Luther and found myself wrapped in tight headlock. The vampire slammed his knees toward my face, and I was just able to get up a hand to dampen the blows slightly, but not enough to prevent my lip from busting open. Luther's grip on my head loosened and I was able to slip free as Mannie wrapped the vampire up in another lock. This time Luther didn't try to break free, instead with an unnatural speed and fluidity the vampire turned in Mannie's arms and sank his razor-sharp fangs into the shifter's neck.

Mannie yelled out in pain and released his grip on the vampire, instead focusing all his effort on prying himself free. Luther shook violently and tore a deep wound in the shifter's throat, which bled profusely. Mannie brought his hand up to cover the wound and left himself exposed for Luther to slam his fist into the shifter's face causing him to drop to the ground in a pool of his own blood.

I could only stand in horror, alone against the vampire who turned his attention to me with blood dripping from his mouth. In one impossible motion the vampire closed the distance between us, his hand sweeping across the ground and lifting his sword as he did so. I couldn't move. Luther grabbed me around the throat with his left hand and slammed me back against the wall, using his other hand to lift the long steel blade into the air.

"The good guy doesn't always win. Not in this world." taunted Luther, blood and flesh covering his face. The vampire's eyes were cold and emotionless. I struggled to free myself from the vampire's crushing grip around my throat. Fire and hatred erupted in the vampire's eyes as he brought his sword down to kill me. The blade fell toward me violently, time seemed to slow. I waited for life to flash before my eyes, but it didn't, only Mannie's blood covered fingers appeared before my eyes as they gripped Luther's sword hand keeping the razor-sharp blade inches away from my neck.

Mannie struggled to prevent Luther from bringing down his sword further. The vampire and shifter were locked in a battle of strength, both using all their focus to maintain control of the blade. I used all my own might to pry Luther's hand away from my neck. The instant that Luther divided his attention Mannie wrenched the blade free from the vampire's grasp and I twisted the vampire's other arm behind his back. Deftly Mannie spun the blade in his hand and swung it violently, severing Luther's head cleanly.

Luther's body immediately turned to dust and bone, returning to its proper state of decay. I stepped back, dropping the bones I held in my hands. Mannie stared emotionlessly at the pile of dust where Luther had been standing for a moment before looking back up at me. Mannie dropped the sword and motioned toward the dais.

"Go kill that son of a bitch." he said before running to aid his pack.

I obliged.

TWENTY-THREE

De La Cruz was encircled by combatants when I joined the fray. The shifters of the East River Pack had tactfully flanked the vampire and were moving in and out swiftly to keep him off guard. The problem with this strategy is their pack movements did not allow for the dhampir to coordinate an attack. This meant Mallory, Hunter, and I couldn't find any opening to attack, and De La Cruz was only fighting four instead of seven, and the centuries old vampire seemed confident against those numbers.

De La Cruz was unbelievably powerful, and with speed to match. His raw power and centuries of experience made him more than a match for the shifters, despite their coordinated efforts. In fact, after a few moments De La Cruz seemed to find a pattern in their attacks. The vampire caught one of the shifters with a backhand sending the wolf flying against the far wall which they crashed into and fell limply to the floor with a whimper.

De La Cruz grabbed one of the other shifters, which used its sharp teeth to rip a large gash down the vampire's arm, and bit into the wolf's neck. De La Cruz ripped a chunk of the shifter's flesh and blood poured out of his mouth. The vampire threw the shifter into one of its packmates, and both slid across the dais, painfully landing in a heap. Mallory called out to the remaining shifter, the one who held the silver blade, to try and get him to fall back and coordinate an attack, but the fury on the shifter's face was unmistakable. The shifter charged; silver blade held high. Mallory rushed in as well to try and draw De La Cruz's attention, but he was too late. The vampire dodged out of the way of the blade, ripping it free of the shifter's hand in the process and shoved the blade through the young wolf's stomach. Mallory yelled out just before the killing blow landed. The shifter fell to its knees, clutching the mortal wound and looking in vain for someone to help him, before doubling over in the throes of death.

De La Cruz turned on the three of us, blood dripped from his mouth and down his neatly trimmed beard. He opened his mouth and spat out a chunk of shifter flesh and hair, causing Mallory to stop in his tracks, still about ten feet away from De La Cruz.

"Come and die, son." the vampire said, ominously, drawing a long steel sword from a scabbard attached to his throne.

Mallory looked back to where Hunter and I stood. "You two, get out of here. I'll hold him off." he said.

"Not a chance, old man," said Hunter.

"We're with you, Mallory." I said.

Mallory nodded and turned back to face his father. "You hold no sway over me. Not any longer."

"A father and child should not have to kill one another, especially considering how powerful we could be together." said De La Cruz, sighing. "But make no mistake, there is nothing romantic about how I will kill you, and your friends."

"I may die, but before this night is over, you will be humbled." said Mallory, and he charged. Hunter and I followed right behind him, moving off the sides to find an angle to attack from. The vampire just laughed. I knew that De La Cruz underestimated us and after seeing the man fight, I understood why, I just hoped we could use that to our advantage somehow.

"Draw defenses, look for an opening." Mallory shouted instructions over the chaos of the battle. My heart pounded in my chest, and I embraced it. I allowed my instincts to take over. "If this creature still has a heart, we will find it."

Mallory swung out with his blade and with his other hand he jabbed a sharp wooden stake up at the vampire's chest. De La Cruz saw the feint and chose to allow the silver blade to bite into the skin on his arm. The silver did not harm him, but the blade did deliver a clean slice down his forearm. The wound healed itself immediately. When De La Cruz moved out of the way of Mallory's attack, he presented his back to me, and I did something very stupid. I jumped on. This seemed to surprise everyone, including myself, who couldn't believe what I'd done. I wrapped my hands around the vampire's neck to prevent De La Cruz from throwing me off.

De La Cruz bucked wildly but didn't dare use his hands to remove me or else he would open himself up to an attack from Hunter or Mallory who both circled the vampire probing for a weakness. Instead, the vampire swung violently with his blade to keep the other dhampir at bay. There really was nothing I could do but hold on for dear life. I dared not slacken my grasp at all, I had seen De La Cruz's power and had no desire to experience it firsthand.

Hunter seemed to have found an opening finally. She swung her baseball bat right at the back of the exposed knees of De la Cruz. The vampire took the blow square and his knees buckled from underneath him, but he did not fall over. Instead, the vampire caught himself by driving his blade deep into the dais floor and bracing himself against it. De La Cruz spun quickly away from both encircling dhampir before they could attack again. The vampire jumped very quickly and launched himself, back first, into the nearest wall. This meant that I took the brunt of the impact and was smashed between the powerful vampire and the solid concrete wall. I groaned and was momentarily knocked unconscious as my skull bounced against the wall. My vision swam and my grip loosened, and I fell off the vampire's back. My senses were knocked back into me when I hit the floor. Knowing that I was vulnerable I rolled away quickly, and Mallory and Hunter were already on the vampire again trying to draw its attention.

I shook the cobwebs out of my head and pushed myself

up to my feet. As I dropped everything when I jumped on De La Cruz's back, I was now weaponless. Mallory's duffle bag sat nearby, so I ran for it and the first thing I pulled out was a long wooden torch with oiled cloth wrapped around the end of it. Seeing the torch reminded me of something I had read. The only ways to kill a vampire were to remove the head, sunlight, a wooden stake through the heart, or fire. *Fire!* I dug back into the bag and found a lighter and lit the clothed end and immediately fire sprang to life.

De La Cruz seemed to be toying with the three of us but seeing the fire in my hand seemed to change the equation in the vampire's mind. Everything became much more serious for him, and he came right for me. I waved the flaming torch trying to catch his clothing. De La Cruz moved around the flames deftly, trying to reach me, but I spent every ounce of energy I had remaining to keep out of the vampire's grasp. Hunter reached De La Cruz and stabbed his heart with the stake. She had to jump to reach De La Cruz, but his back was exposed, and the sharp wooden tip was primed to come down right into the creature's heart. In a split second the vampire turned away from me and caught Hunter in mid-air. The vampire's long undead fingers closed around her throat, and she dropped the stake and tried to pry his hands free.

"No!" Mallory shouted as he ran to help.

I could only watch in horror as De La Cruz smiled evilly and heaved Hunter across the room. She crashed through one of the dining tables and fell to the floor limply, unmoving. From this distance I couldn't tell if she was still breathing or not. De La Cruz caught Mallory with a powerful blow that sent the elder dhampir sliding against the dais. I screamed at the vampire as I shoved the lit torch against his suit, where it immediately burst into flames. The vampire lashed out wildly trying to free himself from his flaming clothes, ripping his jacket off his body and tossing it aside.

When De la Cruz turned back around to face me, he leveled his gaze and hate colored his face.

"Your father did not know his place either. I wanted to be the one to kill him so badly. I wanted him to suffer. Instead, someone stole that from me, and when I find out who that was, they will pay desperately." De La Cruz, spat stalking toward him. "For now, I will have to settle for destroying his offspring."

"My father was a better man than you, he would never have done what you have done." I said defiantly.

"You have no idea what kind of man your father was." De La Cruz laughed. "I alone knew the lust for power in his heart. Almost enough to match my own. One of us had to die, we both knew it, and as always, I came out on top, I alone rule, and once I rip you limb from limb the last bastion of Moretti's blood will spill on the ground and his memory will be erased forever."

I hefted the torch and stake in my hands. "Then stop talking and come do it." I said, bravely.

De La Cruz again laughed at me, but this time there was no mirth in it. The vampire charged in a blur before I even had time to register what was happening. The long-sharpened fingernails on the vampire's hand were splayed out dangerously ready to slice. The vampire brought them down in a swift motion, I tried to move, but all I could do was lift my hands defensively.

An instant before De La Cruz's hands came down; I was knocked roughly out of the way. I spun in the air to land on my back and saw Mallory standing where I had stood, completely exposed. De La Cruz brought down his hands with wicked precision, slicing across Mallory's neck, and blood blossomed from the deep gash. Mallory clutched his throat and fell to the ground, dark red blood already beginning to pool around him.

"No!" I heard myself screaming, distantly. Everything seemed quiet and slow. The fighting around the room stopped for a moment as everyone looked to see what had happened. I picked myself up and ran to Mallory's side. The older dhampirs' eyes were already glossing over, but they flicked toward me with recognition. I knelt beside Mallory who struggled to take my hands in his hands which were now covered in blood.

"Sorry." said Mallory, weakly, his voice barely able to rise above a whisper. "So, sorry."

"It's ok, It's ok. Just hang on" I tried to reassure him.

"No. Need you. Fight." said Mallory, each word a struggle. Mallory lifted his hand up, clutching my hand, tapping the metal ring with his blood-soaked hands. "Use. This." Mallory tried to smile; his eyes struggled to remain focused on my face. "Proud." he said, as the light slowly went out of his eyes. Mallory's own silver blade, Moonsbane, materialized next to his body. Mallory was gone.

I held my mentor's- no, my friend's-lifeless body in my hands and gently lowered him back against the dais floor. Hot tears filled my eyes and ran down my face. I swallowed pure rage over the lump in my throat and lifted Moonsbane before turning back to face De La Cruz, who stood a few feet away watching with a smile on his face pulling his own blade free of the dais.

"It will comfort you to know that you will join your friends soon." the vampire said wickedly, hefting his own sword.

"No." I said. "No!" I charged at De La Cruz with every ounce of energy I had remaining, I just charged. Every muscle in my body burned like fire. My blood burned like fire. I leapt at the vampire and tackled him. Both of us were lifted in the air by my momentum and we crashed hard against the ground, but only for a moment. Despite the noise of the battle and the roaring inferno of fury bubbling up inside of me, I heard the faint clanking of metal as my father's ring hit the floor of the dais, and then I felt myself falling again. I had just enough time to look to the side and see the brilliant beam of golden light shining around us as it appeared we were falling through the dais itself.

We fell through the darkness for a moment until we landed hard on a cool concrete floor in a pitch-black room.

TWENTY-FOUR

The abrupt and hard stop caused me to lose my grip on De La Cruz. Rolling to my side, I grunted in pain. The fall knocked the breath out of me, but I didn't seem to have any broken bones. It took a moment to realize the seriousness of my situation. I was in an unknown location, in complete darkness, with an ancient vampire who wanted to kill me. Quickly I scurried to my feet and gave myself some distance. I backed up against a cold, damp wall.

"Where have you brought us?" said Salvatore De La Cruz from the darkness. I debated answering him but decided to keep my mouth shut and not give away my position. The truth was I did not know where I had brought us if I in fact had been the one to bring us here. Mallory had said to use the ring, but I thought he meant in a less literal sense. The light that appeared around us as we fell had been the same as the portal that Mallory used to retrieve his bag. That had been a spell cast by Gadget. I wondered if it was possible that my ring could have had some magical ability attuned to it that Mallory knew about. A question for Gadget, should I survive this experience.

"It matters not; your death is inescapable." said De La Cruz.

"Actually, old friend, it is your death that is inescapable." said a familiar voice from the darkness. I covered my eyes as a fire erupted from the area where the voice had spoken. The light from the torch spilled across the room and the unknown person lifted the light until their face and most of the room was lit. The torchbearer had a youthful, but pale face with short brown hair and dark eyes. He was tall and lean like De La Cruz, but where De La Cruz was smooth and calculating, this man was stern and edged. I'd seen this man twice before in my life, once in a picture in Mallory's office and once in a dream.

"Moretti?" said De La Cruz, disbelievingly. "Impossible, you're dead. What is this sorcery?"

"What?" I said, breaking my silence, but I might as well have been invisible to the two other men who glared at one another.

"I have waited and dreamed about this moment for the past 17 years. The look on your face has made it all worth it." said Moretti.

"What game are you playing at, Anton?" said De La Cruz.

"We both know you wanted me dead. You knew it was me that everyone wanted to lead them, and you saw me as a threat. I was not going to be able to best you in single combat, not then at least. So, I devised a plan, with the help of your own child. Mallory hid me away and I've spent nearly two decades in seclusion, growing stronger and wiser." explained Moretti. "When the time was right, we chose to enact our plan and destroy you and I will take my rightful place."

Could this really be my father standing here in front of me? It seemed impossible. De La Cruz rubbed his blood-soaked chin as he contemplated the situation, and then he began to laugh, and it was blood curdling.

"This was your grand plan?" said De La Cruz between fits of laughter. "I thought you were dead all this time; I thought the pleasure of killing you was taken away from me. What a delightful surprise this is, because Moretti, whether it be two days, two decades, or two centuries, you could never defeat me."

"Perhaps that is true." resigned Moretti. "But I am not alone." Moretti finally looked over to where I stood with my back up against the wall. "Hello, Saturday. It's nice to finally meet you, son." For the first time I looked into the eyes of

Anton Moretti and in that moment, I knew that it truly was my dad, back from the dead. A weird cocktail of joy and sadness whirled around in my stomach. "And as you once showed Long Winter." my father continued. "A vampire and a dhampir of their own blood are a deadly combination."

For once there was a slight hesitation that flashed across De La Cruz's face, but he quickly composed himself. "Once you are dead, and for good this time, I will parade your remains and the remains of your son through the streets as an example of what happens to dissidents under my regime." said De La Cruz.

Moretti dropped the torch against the concrete wall and flames erupted all around the room, washing everything in a bright firelight. Finally, I could see that the room we were standing in was in fact a large concrete cell outfitted with numerous fashioning's, like a bed and an overstuffed leather reading chair and many books. All these things had been pushed unceremoniously to the corner of the room to create an open area now surrounded by a roaring inferno. In his other hand Moretti held his own sword with a hilt of wrapped leather.

De La Cruz and my father circled one another, each careful not to get near the flames. I held tight to Moonsbane and grabbed a wooden chair from off the pile and smashed it against the ground. Picking up one of the legs of the chair I sliced down the end of it with my blade creating a sharpened tip. Now, wielding my blade and stake I moved to join my father in flanking De La Cruz. Around and around, we circled, De La Cruz hissing in defiance, no one willing to make the first move.

Finally, De La Cruz threw caution to the wind and was the first to attack. De La Cruz swung his sword expertly at Moretti who used his own blade to parry the blow, sending sparks flying as the blades clashed against one another. Immediately I shot in with my own blade to find a weakness, but De La Cruz was too fast and able to bring his sword back around to block the blow.

Moretti, like De La Cruz, was far more powerful than he looked. He was swift and powerful despite his lean build and sickly complexion. I was just doing my best to keep up with the vampires. They fought with such power, but there was also a grace to their movements. It was a stark contrast to the rage and hatred on their faces.

I felt a strange kinship for my father. There was something familiar about Moretti's movements and somehow, I seemed to know what my father was going to do before he did it. It was almost as if our shared blood allowed me some manner of precognition for my father's actions. I racked my brain to determine how I could best use this newfound ability to defeat De La Cruz.

When Moretti swung low, De La Cruz blocked it and swung high at his head, causing him to duck and then swing his blade upwards. De La Cruz moved to the side to escape that blow and brought his sword sweeping down to swipe away Moonsbane. This seemed to be how De La Cruz was fighting, he was mainly focused on parrying and countering Moretti's attacks and treated me like an afterthought. It was understandable, I was only fast enough to attack once for every two from the vampires. I knew I could not keep up the frenetic pace. My muscles were aching from use and the vampires had centuries of practice at this and my few practice sessions with Hunter just didn't compare. I knew once my own abilities gave out the small distraction I provided would be gone and De La Cruz would be able to focus his full attention on Moretti, which would spell the end for both of us.

I stopped attacking for a moment and a look of victory spread across De La Cruz's face. De La Cruz primed himself for a killing blow and a heartbeat before it happened, I saw that my father was going to make a sweeping attack across De La Cruz's midsection. I anticipated that De La Cruz would move back instead of parrying, so I timed my attack to coincide with my father's. I guessed correctly. When De La

Cruz stepped back to dodge the blow and bring his sword down to kill Moretti, I caught him along the back with the end of my blade, slicing through the vampire's shirt and drawing blood.

De La Cruz, caught by surprise, turned violently to lash out at me like a horse swatting away a fly. By doing so, De La Cruz took himself out of the flow of the fight and left himself exposed. Moretti swept his blade back up and around and brought it down swiftly in a stabbing motion straight through the exposed back of Salvatore De La Cruz. The blade sliced cleanly through the upper back of the vampire and came out just below his chest, blood poured from the wound that futilely tried to close around the sharpened edge of the blade.

De La Cruz roared with rage as he twisted and turned to pull the blade free. I lashed out with Moonsbane and sliced the back of the vampire's legs, causing him to fall to his knees. Moretti ripped the blade free unceremoniously, shredding flesh and bone as he did so, before kicking De La Cruz hard in the back, causing the vampire to crash violently to the ground. Moretti hefted the blade high and drove it back down into De La Cruz's back and deep into the concrete floor of the cell. The elder vampire flailed and tried in vain to lift himself up off the ground, but the blade and hilt trapped him in place. Salvatore cursed at us ruthlessly.

"Saturday, your stake." said Moretti, holding out his hand. I handed him the sharpened piece of wood and my father took it without looking at me.

De La Cruz continued to flail and curse and spit, but it was all in vain. Moretti stood behind De La Cruz and placed his hands underneath the other vampire's chin and looked into his eyes.

"It's funny, isn't it, Salvatore." said Moretti "All these years I have been waiting, I had begun to think it had all been in vain, that perhaps I had missed my opportunity. It was your own flesh and blood that urged patience. Perhaps the only person in the world that wanted you dead more than me was your own child. That was always your problem, you ruled with fear, you never understood the subtleties or art of deception. You thought your strength was enough to save you, but now I ask you, is it enough?"

Moretti lifted the stake high into the air and slammed it down into De La Cruz's back, where it pierced the skin and blossomed out through his chest. De La Cruz hissed loudly but did not scream out. Moretti bent down and whispered something into De La Cruz's ear, as the elder vampire began to decay and turn to dust right before their eyes. I did not think I was supposed to have heard what my father had said, but I did. The last words that Salvatore De La Cruz heard before dying were his rival telling him:

"I have won."

Epilogue

Saturday,

    I hope it hasn't come to this and that I may simply discard this letter in the trash once we all return safely from Sanctuary, but in the event that doesn't happen let me try to explain. I am sure things will have come out this evening that might leave you wondering why I wasn't more forthcoming with you. Perhaps you are now questioning if I was the hero or the villain of this story. As to that, I will let history be the judge of my actions, but I want you to know that I did what I thought was best for the city and for you.

    I have seen firsthand the cruelty and savagery of which my father is capable. Your own father and I talked at length about his plans for the city and I recognized that he was the leader that we needed and not De La Cruz, even though he was my family. When Moretti found out that he was going to have a child he began to devise his plan. He was certain that you would be a dhampir and together the three of us could destroy my father before he destroyed the city for his own pride.

    Much has happened in the past 17 years since your father went into hiding, his location known only to me. I was his eyes and ears. He was truly heartbroken to hear that your mother had died - he was so distraught he nearly abandoned his own plan. I had to reassure him you were in good hands, and this was all for the best. I am sure you are having a hard time coming to grips with all of this. I won't ask you to forgive me, all I will ask you to do is give your father a chance. These years secluded away have changed him, I will not deny it. I believe you alone can help him to remember his former virtues.

If you are reading this, I am dead. I can only hope my death in some small way helped to pave the way for a brighter future for our city. The city will need a protector now more than ever, Saturday. To you I leave my office and my resources. Use them to bring justice and protect humanity.

Please tell Hunter I am sorry. Her heart has been hardened, but she, like your father, can still be brought back before it's too late. This city needs you both.

Your friend,
Mallory Moran
Supernatural Sleuth Extraordinaire

P.S - Please keep Violet on the payroll. Admittedly, she isn't great at her job, but I doubt she could find anything else, and I swear she once had a very sweet disposition.

I read the letter over again, wiping away the tears that threatened to drip on the white page. The letter had been waiting on Mallory's desk when I emerged from the Tombs, where my father had been hidden all this time. The office was empty save for me. Anton Moretti had not stuck around for hugs and kisses or catching up, he had muttered something about doing his duty and taking back what was rightfully his and left off into the night. I couldn't even process all of that right now.

This creature hidden down in the Tombs for so long was my father in blood alone. The closest thing I ever had to a father figure was dead and I was sitting in his office. When I reached out to Hunter, she answered on the first ring. I was so glad to hear her voice that the waterworks almost started again.

"Oh my god, Saturday." she said. "Are you okay? What happened?"

"Don't worry about me, De La Cruz is dead. Are you

okay?" I asked.

"I am. I'm fine. Bruised and sore... but Saturday... Mallory..." she couldn't finish.

"I know...Can you meet me somewhere? We have to talk."

"Of course."

Over the following weeks it became clear life among the supernatural community would never be the same. The city was abuzz with the announcement that Anton Moretti had returned. By force he wrested the mantle of leadership of the vampires away from any challengers and vowed to bring the shifters to bear. Long Winter, the former war leader of the shifters took back control after the death of Longfang and it appeared the peace which lasted less than two decades in New York had simply been a brief pause in the thousand years war of the night waged between shifters and vampires. Enchanters and sorcerers, waging their own quieter and more secretive battle for magical supremacy, drew their own lines.

There was no law binding the behaviors of the supers any longer. The mortal population of New York, the majority of whom still believed that vampires and shape shifting monsters were all fairy tales, were more vulnerable than ever. Only when the time came that the humans needed an advocate and protector did they realize they knew where to turn all along.

The Offices of Saturday Shepherd, Supernatural Sleuth Extraordinaire, the high-school kid who walks both worlds.

This is not the end of Saturday Shepherd's story; this is the beginning.

Made in the USA
Middletown, DE
03 August 2024